Queen
of
Hearts

by

Kiniesha Gayle

Copyright 2008 Kiniesha Gayle
ISBN: 978-0-9-795892-0-1
Edited by: Lissa Woodson, Anthony Stepney and Stacey Duvall
Layout: Candace Cottrell, Dann Francis

First printing KG Publishing paperback July 2008

Acknowledgements

All praises to God once more. I have completed another successful project. The road was a difficult one, but you kept me going. There were times went I was ready to give up, bang my head against the wall, and cried but throughout it all God sustained me. Deshauntae, my son I love you, and I'm proud of you. You never cease to amaze me, and challenge me. Everything I do, I do for you. Keep being who you are, and with the help of God, I already see you are heading places.

To my wonderful husband Anthony Stepney thanks for being patient with me. You assisted me so much on this project, without complain and I'm grateful for that. I love you.

All my family and friends that have stood by me, we did it again. Thanks especially to Sherry and Stacy who allowed me to chew off their heads, when things weren't going right or I wanted to vent. You listened and I'm in debt to both of you.

Thanks to Augustus Publishing, Mo Shines, Teress Baldwin, and Candace Cottrell you guys provided so much guidance along the way. I can't say thanks enough.

To the readers, I can't say how much I appreciated you waiting three years for the sequel to drop. It's been a long process, and because of you, along with God, I kept going and never threw the towel in when I was faced with obstacles and challenges.

To the bookstores and vendors, you guys kept me afloat

and help to make *King of Spades* of hit. Thanks, now let's do the same and more for *Queen of Hearts*.

To the haters, in the famous words of TI, "You can hate if you want, but you're wasting your time."

What good is it for a man to gain the whole world, yet forfeit his soul?

Mark 8 Verse 36

Chapter 1

FDR HIGHWAY: NYC

A lifeless chill in the November night swirled around the pier like a vulture fully aware of its prey. Police sirens crept at a distance, growing louder with each passing moment. Searchlights flooded the breaking waters of the East River, sweeping the area decisively left to right. Divers plunged into the frigid and murky depths near the club's pier, breaking through the reckless surface in smooth, practiced lines.

Uniformed and plainclothes officers from NYPD's Homicide Department and the FBI were scattered over the pier's concrete surface, relishing the fact that they, at least, were on dry land. News choppers battled with police helicopters vying for the best vantage point to show this latest grisly piece of news. Each time the NYPD copter circled the water, the air became just that much colder as waves ran from what possibly lay underneath.

Traffic on the FDR Highway stood bumper to bumper. Drivers honked, while some got out of their cars to see what had caused the traffic to become a parking lot. Roads from 71st to 23rd Streets were blocked off as officers diverted the more adventurous drivers to the main streets of New York City. Many motorists voiced their anger as a quick peek at the situation showed absolutely no hope of getting to their destinations anytime soon.

Near the pier, Detective Garfin, a portly, blue-eyed man with thirty years at the 19ᵗʰ Precinct, stepped out of a black Chevy Impala. He adjusted the silver belt over his protruding stomach as it struggled to hold up the black pants, which had definitely seen better days. His once shiny black hair now revealed shades of gray. Scenes like the one unfolding before him had more to do with the process than pure aging alone.

"What've we got here, boys," he asked, crossing the bright yellow tape that separated grim reality from everyday certainty. POLICE LINE—DO NOT CROSS was almost always followed by *dead on arrival.*

Patrick Flynn, a tall sliver of a man, was wearing a police slicker. He stood with green eyes scanning the area as men with slick black body suits continued searching the cold waters for more bad news. "Just like you said, there might be three bodies in the river."

Garfin sighed, reached for a pack of cigarettes, and then rubbed a weathered hand over his scruffy beard. Placing the cigarette to his mouth, he lit it, took a pull, then held it between his fingers. "Why don't these motherfucking drug dealers take this shit to another precinct? The last thing we need is bad publicity in the newspaper for Christ's sake!"

Pulling one last drag on his cigarette, Garfin flicked it to the ground and crushed it under the soles of his once-so-shiny black wingtips. Just like his life and this job, they too, had lost their luster a long time ago.

"Garfin, the divers are bringing the bodies to the surface." Frosty air punctuated Flynn's every word. The man popped his uniform collar before pulling the navy blue police issued coat tighter around his body.

That bit of news was met with a weary glare. "Good, maybe we won't be here *all* night." Garfin pushed past Patrick, carving his way to the officers closest to the end of the pier. Officer Warren, a man with short blonde hair, blew into his cupped hands as he stood just behind another, even taller, detective surveying the scene. "It'll take a lot more than hot, stale breath to thaw out in this freezing weather," Garfin said, before glancing to the left and noticing the crime lab technician who was chuckling at the comment.

"Fuck you," Warren shot back with a grin. "If I was lying next to your wife, then I'd be melting by now."

"Watch it, slick," Detective Garfin said, Lieutenant O'Brien chuckling along with the two men as he stood. "You're not above me putting a foot up your ass, Warren"

"Now *that* place could keep everyone warm," Garfin teased.

"Garfin and O'Brien," Agent Schwartz yelled, sprinting toward the group with a fistful of paperwork.

"This isn't looking too good." He slapped the forms into the waiting hands of Detective Garfin. "The captain's already on the phone complaining that this is the type of attention his precinct *doesn't* need."

Running pudgy fingers through his thinning hair, Garfin went closer to the edge, trying to get a good look at the bodies that had caused all the commotion.

"The DEA is going to get a kick out of this one. It seems like the 19th precinct is having a hard time handling the case." Agent Schwartz taunted.

Garfin had wished upon hope that the call he'd received earlier was just a prank, but the sound of the woman's voice on the other end, the details she gave about how the victims had suffered, and the urgency with which she said that one of them was possibly still alive, spurred him to action. With one call, four cars were on the scene and a swarm of others followed. The first body that turned up meant the rest of the police force followed, along with the FBI and DEA—the latter he could certainly do without.

Contemporary Jazz music drifted across the busy area. Garfin's gaze followed the happy sounds. People dressed in clothes he couldn't afford on three month's salary had been celebrating at the ritzy Water Club just minutes ago, but were now flocked out onto the balcony to see what the excitement was about. Sons and daughters of the richest people in New York society, who were decked out for a memorable evening, now had their opportunity to come closer to real life than their rich parents had hoped. Officers intercepted the staggering and demanding crowd, ushering them back to the confines and safety of the bright white building.

The crime scene had already been complicated with the swarm of media just beyond the tape and the camera crews circling overhead; another headache the precinct didn't need, and one of the main reasons he downed almost half a bottle of Tums every day.

"We got one … with a … weak pulse," one of the divers said, holding on to the handrails of the rickety metal ladder, gasping for breath. The man they fished out of the water was huge; his skin flushed a lifeless grey. Water poured off the victim's clothes, pooling around to the tip of the Garfin's shoes.

"Get an EMT over here now!" Garfin barked, as men in the van with white, red and blue writing on the side sprang to life, carting over equipment and a stretcher. A wool blanket soared through the air, landing on the diver's back as his feet steadied on the concrete. He wrapped it around his broad shoulders as the officers escorted him to a heated van.

News teams rushed forward, only to slam into the blue wall of officers blocking their path as well as their view.

Paramedics worked in feverish unison, trying to save the victim's life. Garfin glanced briefly at the victim stretched out on the ground like a fisherman's catch of the day—a bad one at that, and turned to walk away. A flash of memory made him turn back. The dark wavy hair, the football player sized frame, the normally golden skin now turned pale, and chiseled, distinctively Latin features all seemed that of a man he knew too well.

The second diver made it to dry land, he took a glance at the victim and said, "Damn near got a hernia from pulling his ass out of the water."

Garfin's step picked up as he went back to stand next to Warren and the paramedics. For the past three years, he had tried to bring down the top dogs at Tha Hustle Records but through some fancy footwork by their lawyer, they came up clean every single time. He couldn't wait to get a hold of her.

Finally, one of the paramedics looked up at Garfin. "His pulse is still weak; we've done as much as we can for now. He was lucky the water was cold."

"I don't care if you have to go to Jesus for a miracle." Garfin leaned over so his nose almost touched the mocha-skinned man. "You save his ass." Garfin's steely gaze locked with the younger man's conveying the message that it would be his ass if he didn't comply. "That's Tony Moreno. He's the key to cracking a case I've been working on." Then he gestured to his fellow officers, lowering his voice as he said, "And keep them out of it.

He motioned toward the FBI and DEA. "This one's ours." A light-skinned guy who was inches away, turned and looked at Garfin, Garfin hoped he hadn't heard what was said. The same light-skinned guy, unbeknownst to Garfin, then wrote in his note pad and walked over to a dark-skinned female, comparing notes.

A splash of water made both men's head whip around. A heavy threaded net settled on the space beside them. Two more bodies had emerged from the water. Another team of medics rushed over, checking the watery forms for any signs of life.

Moments later, one medic turned to Garfin and shook his head. The two newcomers hadn't been so lucky, no pulse, no struggle for breath. Dead on arrival.

The two men leaning on the coroner's white van flung open the back doors, pulled out a stretcher, then walked in unison until they reached the first of the bodies. The first was a black woman in her late twenties with long dark hair, a killer curvaceous body, and a fresh wound on her forehead. Placing the lifeless body in the black bag, they slid it into the back and came back for the last one—a young black male with braided hair, still decked out in a white Fendi shirt and black pants. All three were there just like the caller had said. Garfin still wondered who had placed that call.

Minutes later, the vans took off, hauling the bodies to their new home in the morgue.

"Fucking shame," Garfin grumbled, pulling out yet another cigarette. Turning toward Patrick, he pointed to the last coroner's van just before it disappeared along the path the police had cleared leading to the FDR Highway.

"You see how that fucker was dressed?" Garfin's eyes scanned the area once again. He was in a rage at the unfairness of it all, unsettling in his gut. "I can't even afford that shit on a year's pay. With that kind of money, you'd think they'd be smart enough to save their own asses." He lit the cigarette, hoping the nicotine rush might calm his nerves. "No, they think they're almighty and the money can protect them."

Patrick fell silently in step with Garfin as they maneuvered between the straggling remainder from the force.

"I've been on this force thirty years," Garfin said solemnly, a frosted blast of air filtering out with each breath. "And plenty of opportunities came my way to make extra money and I turned down each one." He paused, taking a short puff of the cigarette. "You know how many men working in my unit I personally arrested for being involved with Tha Hustle Records? ...and I'm pretty sure there are more"

Patrick stopped in his tracks. This wasn't news to him, and he was sure it wouldn't be news to the chief, the man he sometimes supplied with information on the inner workings of this particular precinct. Hoping to garner more information, he gave Garfin a non-committal, "No shit?"

"No shit," Garfin replied, weary blue eyes scanning the officers who were gathered near the Water Club and watching as a luxury yacht that was delayed due to the unexpected events bypassed the river's frantic activity and disappeared into the night fog. "Night and day I sat up trying to crack this case, while countless bodies turned up right here in the East River and everywhere else, but there was never anything substantial enough to build a case on. Sometimes, it feels like they had a connection within the department." Tony Moreno and Andre Chin were always one step ahead." Garfin paused, watching the yacht race recklessly over the water then disappear into the fog. "Even their own boys turned up dead," he said, "And a UPS man…who in their right mind kills a UPS man?"

Patrick leaned back on the Impala, which was now parked next to several NYPD cars, crossing his arms over his slender chest.

Garfin took another long drag before pointing to the spot where the boat had raced into the night before docking. "See, these young motherfuckers think their lives are just like that boat, all luxurious and nice. Everything flies by so fast; they practically kill themselves to keep up and to get it all in before they die." He gazed out in the East River for a quick second, warming to his subject. "But what they fail to realize is, just like that boat, their lifestyles can disappear. Then it comes crumbling down."

Tossing the cigarette away, he glanced back at the EMS wagon carrying the only victim they were able to save that night, and shook his head. "Tony motherfucking Moreno," he said with a bitter but revengeful chuckle. "Let's see how you get out of this one."

Chapter 2

NEW YORK HOSPITAL

*B*right rays of sun poured into the hospital room awakening Anthony Luis Moreno from a peaceful sleep. Rubbing his eyes, he slowly lifted to a position where he could summon for a nurse to close the blinds. The smell of eggs, bacon, and hot coffee lingered under his nose and immediately sent a message to his stomach that he was hungry. Reaching for the button which hung from the edge of the silver railing, he pushed the button and lay back waiting to see which one of the gorgeous nurses would answer his call. The stark white walls, semi-comfortable bed, and small flat screen television were far better than the amenities in most hospitals but the embarrassing bedpan and gown that didn't try hard enough to cover his ass were enough to drive any man insane.

As much as Tony hated hospitals, he didn't mind the "special" treatment he received from one nurse in particular. Three days had passed since he'd come out of a three-month coma. He was angry as hell with an appetite for food that was only matched by his hunger for sex.

Tony tried to lift his right hand, aiming for the remote but the handcuffs kept him securely latched to the rail.

"Fuck!" he shouted, yanking at his restraints. How the hell

was he was still under arrest? "Fuck this shit," he yelled at the top of his lungs. "I want my attorney *right now!*"

The door to his hospital room swung open as a nurse with smooth dark skin, short cut hair, and a face and shape similar to Halle Berry walked in. She automatically adjusted the blinds, checked his monitor, and then pulled the blanket back up to his waist, tucking it around him before asking, "Is everything alright Mr. Moreno?" With a voice as sweet as syrup and a smile that actually lit up the joint, not even Tony could stay angry.

"No, everything is not alright, nurse." He glanced up at the badge over her right breast.

Beating him to the punch she quickly added, "Haywood, Nurse Haywood."

He should have been embarrassed that he didn't remember her name, but what he remembered most was the way her hands had caressed his body and the way she washed around his erect penis soothing it every time she touched him, whether it was intentional or unintentional. He was getting stiff just thinking about the bath she gave him yesterday, and the one he would receive later.

"What seems to be the matter?" she asked with only a tinge of concern lingering in her voice. He could tell she was trying not to grin.

Tony gave her an *are-you-serious* look. He raised his right hand and grimaced.

"Oh that," she responded, as if being handcuffed to a hospital bed wasn't all that serious. "Well, the doctor discussed it with the police to see if they would uncuff you," she said while running a hand over his thighs and trying to get him to calm down. Now he knew her touches were intentional. "Unfortunately, Detective Garfin wants you handcuffed while you remain in this hospital and until you're well enough to go to jail."

A sliver of alarm gripped him. "Jail, for what?"

"I'm not sure, I thought they discussed it with you." she responded slowly, taking in the spike on the monitor.

Tony ran his free hand over what used to be his waves, ignoring the fact that Nurse Haywood's hands lingered right on his dick. "No they didn't, they fucking buggin'."

He reached down, stopping Nurse Haywood's movements so he could think straight. "Where the fuck is he? I requested that he bring his ass down here three days ago and this motherfucka still ain't here yet." Tony's voice raised an octave above normal; something that always put the fear of God in his enemies. Well, that along with the follow-up bullet to bring his point home, but that was beside the point at the moment.

Rejected, Nurse Haywood stood and righted his charts, saying, "We called for him sir, and he said he'll be here as soon as he can."

"Call him again."

She only stared at him, seeming a bit disappointed, He realized that maybe he shouldn't have been so quick to stop her little games. Tony tried to turn to his left side and reach for the phone when the door opened, this time, a slender, Hispanic police officer filled the entrance. "What's all the commotion?"

"And what the fuck are you supposed to do, with your toy cop self?" Sarcasm laced Tony's every word. If he hadn't been handcuffed to the bed, Tony would have slapped the man just on general principle. How were they going to send a little willow of a man to keep Tony Moreno in line? What an insult!

"Nigga, you better watch who the fuck you talking to before I put one more bullet in your ass and let you lay asleep for the rest of your life."

"Not if I can get to you first." Tony tried to get up off the bed. The man might have been little but he had some nerve—but men with more balls than what the officer displayed had already met their maker.

"Not under my watch," Nurse Haywood interjected, doing everything in her power to settle a squirming Tony back onto the bed. His monitor had spiked up.

Sitting upright, Tony's voice became deadly, "Tell Garfin to get here now, or else what went down at Tha Hustle Records will be nothing compared to what I'm gonna do next …"

The officer glared at him, moving toward the bed, his body flexed for the challenge.

"Before we take it there," Nurse Haywood said, placing her body between Moreno and the officer, "let me check your blood pressure. Officer Hernandez, would you mind leaving the room, please?"

Officer Hernandez continued to stare as if Nurse Haywood's request did not compute. What did he expect to accomplish with a witness still in the room? When the officer didn't give way, Nurse Haywood placed a hand on her hip, pursing her lips while throwing him an *I mean-right-now*-look. Eventually he got the hint, whipped around to the door and stormed from the room.

She turned to Tony, giving him a harsh look. "A lot of hard talk from a man who doesn't have a lot to work with." she said as she lifted his restrained hand.

"It doesn't take much to handle business," Tony said with a shrug, then reached out and stroked her ample hips with his free hand. He hoped his attitude didn't turn her off. She chuckled then moved out of his reach.

"Cut it out with all the drama. We don't need your pressure skyrocketing today," she warned. "People will think I'm not doing my job." A flirtatious smile flashed across her face.

Chastised, Tony gave her a sheepish grin. "Listen, I just need to know what I'm being charged with. That's all. Is that too much to ask?"

The door opened yet another time and Tony was all set to go off on the toy cop. Instead, his wife, Maribel, and his attorney strolled in as if they didn't have a care in the world.

"Well it took you long enough," Tony fired at them, ending his rendezvous with the nurse.

Unfazed by his client's sarcastic tone, the Caucasian attorney walked over to the small table and wheeled it to Tony's bed. "I had to ensure that I'm on point with everything before getting here."

"Okay, but what's her explanation?" Maribel looked away as if Tony words flew over her head.

Tony had hired Jacob Goetz to protect his interest when he first learned that Porsha was handling the paperwork for Tha Hustle Records.

Chin had refused to give up the empire; he felt he worked too hard to obtain it just to lose it so easily. He wanted to make sure Porsha finished up all the paperwork before he moved on to any other business venture.

"I'm not saying that we should give up anything, Chin. I'm just saying, maybe it's time we pack this shit up. Focus on music, clothing, and your nightclub." Tony tapped the cigarette pack, pulling out a single smoke and putting it between his lips.

"We're already making crazy loot. We have three of the hottest rappers in the industry right now, so why are we still holding on to *el juego*? We should've been out of the drug game months ago. I don't see what's taking Porsha so long."

Personally, Tony didn't trust Porsha, and if the bar ever got wind of what she was doing, they would toss her faster than a baseball to a catcher's mitt. Often times he would question Chin on how long it would take her to finish up paperwork. Chin never had a good enough answer; he would just keep saying soon.

Andre Chin, his former—and now very much dead partner—had grown tired of constantly being under the watchful eye of the FBI and the NYPD. He decided that Porsha Hilton could help turn the empire into a legal and more profitable one. But from the moment Tony laid eyes on Porsha, he didn't trust her. This was for two major reasons: one reason was that she was way too eager to help out. The second reason was because Chin was sleeping with her. Tony's instincts were right on the money. The moment she learned Chin had been unfaithful, the work she had handled was put on hold and certain portions of their operation were compromised. Pussy and business never did mix well, unless pussy *was* the business. If Tony had known that Chin had used his dick instead of his brain, he would've found someplace else to invest his cash.

❂❂❂

"How are you today, honey?" Maribel asked, trying to make up for the days she missed. Leaning in, she kissed her husband's cheek, which wasn't as pale as it once had been. Since the NYPD pulled him out of the water, Tony's once sexy, muscular frame was now almost skin and bones. Maribel, on the other hand, looked stunning wearing a slinky thin strap dress which complemented her graceful figure. She had olive skin and long dark hair with crimson highlights. "I'm fine, honey," he said, turning away from the kiss, still seething at the fact that it took her so long to get to the hospital to see him. He decided he would hold off on questioning her until he finished with Goetz. "Nurse Haywood, could you give us a moment?" The darker woman glared at Maribel, saying, "Nice of you to join us today."

Maribel winced at the insult and gave the woman a half smile.

"And keep that mutt on the leash," Tony said, gesturing to the officer. Haywood laughed before closing the door behind her.

"So what did you find out?" Tony inquired, the moment the nurse was out of sight.

A wide grin split the man's oval face, as if he had won a billion dollar prize. For Tony's sake he sure hoped so. Goetz slowly opened his brief case, "Enough to put those women in prison for the rest of their lives ... and give you some leverage during court proceedings."

Despite the circumstances which, against his will, had now put him on the wrong side of the law, Tony smiled knowing he was one step closer to bringing down his enemies once and for all.

Porsha Hilton and Natalie "BabyGirl" Smith should've made sure Tony Moreno was dead. Real dead.

Maribel Moreno stared intently at her husband, because she too wanted him dead.

Chapter 3

"*T*hat ain't my fucking baby!"

Dragon's voice was grating on BabyGirl's nerves. She'd heard enough of his ranting over the past three hours. What was supposed to have been a romantic weekend was now turning into a nightmare.

"Say what?" BabyGirl leaned against the teakwood furniture, jabbing a finger in his massive chest. "Don't fuck with me! How many times are we going to go over the same shit?" A frustrated BabyGirl threw her hands in the air, and then let out a loud sigh. She went to the window and much to her dismay; the snow was piling up like little white mountains over Broadway and 8th Avenue.

Dragon had been taunting her about the pregnancy ever since they had lunch at Cinque two months ago.

❤❤❤

They were making a toast to a successful future, and being owners of the restaurant and nightclub - Sotto Cinque Restaurant, when BabyGirl began to notice the looks Dragon were giving her. Every now and then he would glance at her stomach and roll his eyes. She made a mental note to address the issue with him later. It became undeniably clear when they toasted, "Queens of Hearts." She watched how cautious he was while toasting. That's when she knew he was jealous.

❤❤❤

Honestly, the whole argument had been wearing her spirit down because she knew the truth. The baby *was* Dragon's as far as she was concerned.

Dragon took a break from rolling a blunt to say, "Well, maybe if you hadn't fucked Chin we wouldn't be having this conversation, now would we?"

Angered beyond words, she placed a trembling hand on her hip. "So it's like that now, huh? Just because I *fucked* him... that makes it *his* baby?"

"Technically, it's a possibility," Dragon replied without giving her as much as a glance. He knew he was skating on thin ice, but really didn't care at that moment.

"For the last fucking time, Daquan Bentley, I fucked Chin *with* a condom, and I've *never* used one with you." Then her anger surfaced at the irony of it all. "Plus, you were the one who wanted me to seduce him in the first place. It was all a part of *your* big plan."

Dragon looked up, dark brown eyes flashing fire. "Yeah, I said *seduce* him, not fuck him."

But there really wasn't any difference... isn't seduction all about fucking? Realistically, Dragon played a role in setting her sights on Chin, explaining the necessity of getting as much as she could from him. She had just done it well...too well!

❤❤❤

While Dragon was incarcerated, he often wrote letters and

called her. During one particular phone call, one she would never forget, he informed her that he had found out some information that had to do with her parents killing. He tipped her off that some guy named Andre had some part in her parents' murder.

❤❤❤

Dragon, oblivious to the pain and anger warring for space within BabyGirl's heart, reached in his pocket for his lighter and then grabbed the ashtray off the table. "All I am saying is, it could be anyone's baby and I don't understand why you won't have an abortion."

BabyGirl glared at him, unable to believe he would say some grimy shit like that. She stood toe-to-toe with him. "Because this is *your* baby and having an abortion would mean I'm not sure who the father is."

"You're also planning on taking in Brianna," he said with a softened tone; the blunt smoke flowing out of his nostrils. "How are you going to manage with your little sister—she didn't even know you existed before they fished her mother out of the East River?" He held on to her hand, trying to get her to make eye contact with him. "Then you'll have the baby, two businesses, *and* me? You're not gonna be able to manage all that."

"*I will* do just fine. I always do. How do you think I survived when your ass left me on my own?"

He released her hand as though it carried some kind of disease and focused on the one thing that seemed to bring him some form of peace—his blunt. "Goddamnit, BabyGirl! Stop being so fucking selfish and get rid of that kid."

"Fuck you! You need to stop being selfish," she shot back, and then she peered at him. "Maybe there's another reason you want me to have this abortion."

Dragon tossed the ashtray and lighter on the bed and walked into to bathroom where he sat on the toilet, hoping to avoid anymore arguments. Despite his efforts to get away, BabyGirl stood at the door waiting. *Damn,* he thought. The woman knew him too well. He gave her an *are-you-serious*-look, before getting up from the toilet, unused, and yanked up his jeans as he walked back to the bedroom. "I'm not trying to hear this bullshit."

He strolled toward the bed, with BabyGirl on his heels, asking, "Is there another reason?"

"Leave me alone!" He climbed into the bed, examined his blunt, and then placed it back in the corner of his mouth.

"Is there?"

BabyGirl didn't wait long for an answer; instead she strolled to the window. The snow was coming down a little harder, building into something that might have them stuck in the hotel for the next few days if they didn't get this over with and get out while the getting was good. The end result of their dispute wouldn't be pretty given the circumstances. Dragon sauntered over to join her at the window, peering at the winter wonderland, probably coming to the same conclusion she had. Outside was colder than a motha, but inside tempers were flaring hotter than a blow torch.

Dragon cast a sidelong glance at BabyGirl before he made his way back to the bed. "I'm not sure if I can trust you."

Heat flushed through her, turning her caramel skin to a bitter bright red. "You're one cold mothafucka," she growled.

"I learn from the best," he winked at her, alluding to the fact that she wasn't a stranger to putting someone out of their misery. His wide grin was the last straw.

Dragon made the mistake of turning his back to her, and was feeling so triumphant about having made his point that he didn't even notice any other movement in the room until an explosion of pain burst from his temple to his chin as her hand connected with his face.

"Bitch, what part of what I said wasn't the truth," a stunned Dragon shot back, rubbing his face and wondering if BabyGirl was carrying a weapon—which was the only thought that kept him from returning the violence. "I once loved a sweet, innocent girl. I go off to jail for a sales and possession and she becomes a stone cold killer." Then he let ego overload his thinking. "Maybe the police can stop sweating Moreno if I point them in the right direction ..."

Before he could brace himself, BabyGirl reared back aiming for a major blow, this time with her fist. Dragon grabbed her hand holding it firmly, applying enough pressure to make her yelp with pain. She tore away from his grasp, ran to the closet, opened her luggage, and seconds later, whipped out her nine millimeter.

Dragon swallowed hard; just as he had feared, despite promises to the contrary, BabyGirl was still packing heat.

Running steady fingers over the silver casing; she said in a tone as deadly as her dark brown eyes, "They may call you the Dragon, but I know exactly how to put the fire out."

The gun, as beautiful as it was deadly, was now pointing in his direction. "Don't you ever threaten me with the cops!"

Although she had made herself a promise not to kill again, it was only a matter of time before Dragon made those words null and void, especially if he was threatening to bring the NYPD down on her.

Power 105.1 FM. brought the sounds of Mary J. Blige and

Method Man performing "You're All I Need" into the room. BabyGirl, lowered the gun slightly, as she allowed her mind to drift off to a time when Dragon, her first love, was all she need-ed to get by. She remembered how he'd rescued her after her parents were brutally murdered, making her feel safe during a time when every scream, shot, and cry for help frightened her.

♥♥♥

Two years ago, on a cold winter day a week before Christ-mas, her parents were murdered.

Her father's business had been going good, not as strong as it had been in the summer, due to his recent arrest, but something that could make ends meet without meeting the end. He had just finished selling off the last kilo of cocaine, and sat at his desk counting out the money. BabyGirl, who ran track at the time, remembered that she had left her sneakers in the upstairs apartment. While retrieving them, she heard keys jiggling in the door and a female voice. The next thing she remembered was hearing guns cocked. She hid in the closet, but when she peeked out, the barrel of a gun rested against the back of her father's head. Her heart beat uncontrollably and fear froze her body.

"Pussy! Where's the drugs and the cheddar?" Two guys demanded

"I don't have shit."

"Yeah, you don't have shit? Search him," said the taller of the two men.

Six hundred dollars was found after searching her father's back pocket. A follow-up bullet to head ended her father's life, his lifeless body laid on the floor.

Her mother became their next target as screams and cries

could be heard before her mother's body thumped to the ground.

The images of that day still replayed in her head just like the license plate of the vehicle the killers were driving. Dragon, who she thought was her angel, came in the nick of time to save her; something she would be ever grateful for.

❖❖❖

Dragon, one of her slain father's henchmen, took care of her while she stayed with him. Now that her parents' killers were dead, she had tried to leave that the past behind.

Now the script had flipped and she was the one with a business and plenty of money. The best part was that all of it was deliciously legal. She wondered if the days when she trusted him, loved him, and stood by him would ever return. She highly doubted it. And it seemed the feeling was definitely mutual.

Dragon strolled back over to the bed. "How the hell you expect me to trust you, when you fucked the hell outta Chin and God knows who else?" Anger emanated from him like steam from a kettle, as he muttered, "All because y'all wanted more than you deserved ..."

That's when it hit her—his anger had nothing to do with the baby growing within her, or even who it may or may not belong to. It had everything to do with the fact that three women, two who were formal rivals, had divided up the spoils of war—the remnants of Chin and Tony's empire and Dragon didn't get a single thing. But hell, he hadn't done the lion's share of the work. The three women had taken all the risks and BabyGirl could have lost everything when Chin tried to kill her the moment he realized she had betrayed him. She hadn't betrayed him, at least not at that point. It was all a part of a ploy to get him to drop his guard and fall in love, making it easier to keep track of his every move so they could take him down.

Tony Moreno had nothing to do with her parents' death, but his close relationship with the person who had, and the fact that Tony did next to nothing to save her life when it would have mattered, made him expendable.

Sandy was the only casualty from BabyGirl's crew—she had been killed because she was stupid and greedy; something BabyGirl, Dimples, and Porsha had not been. Sandy had been a liability from day one, more focused on getting dick than racking up dollars. The trio of women didn't shed too many tears at her death. Actually, it had made life that much easier with one less loose end.

"All I need to get by ..." Mary J. Blige crooned, drowning out the memories; and with it, some of the worries.

BabyGirl sauntered toward the bed, her sheer gown flowing open, showing her ample breasts and matching sheer thong, which rested below her rounded stomach. Dragon, despite his fear, caught a fresh peek and his dick grew rock hard, straining against his boxers before he could get himself under control.

Dragon grabbed his crotch the moment she unzipped him, warming to the idea of burying his dick deep inside BabyGirl's tight pussy. She straddled him, allowing the moisture to pool on his shaft as she prepared to ride him, her way of bringing him under control.

"Like sweet morning dew ..."

"All you do is argue over simple shit," she whispered as his erection disappeared between the soft folds of her hot flesh. "You weren't saying anything when you knew the company's money would be buying us a big house, that BMW you're pushing, or those clothes you're sporting." She ran her fingers down the center of his wife beater. "You didn't have anything to say about my responsibilities then."

"I took one look at you …"

Instead of enjoying the pleasure he knew she could bring, for the second time that night, he let his mouth write a check his ass would have to cash. "You know what BabyGirl… fuck you and your money!" He pushed her away and stood, zipping his pants. "You're acting like I can't eat without you." He threw her an angry glance. "If it wasn't for me, your little bitch ass would still be in a psychiatric ward, broke and homeless. You turned out to be the whore I always thought you'd be."

"And it was plain to see …"

Dragon thought he had put enough distance between them, until he realized what she had in her hand earlier was now coming toward him. The second flash of pain went from jawbone to jawbone as the butt of the gun came down and swiped across his face.

"You were my destiny …"

Seconds later, with no regard for the fact that BabyGirl had multiple bodies to her credit and had become an expert with a weapon; he lunged for the pregnant woman. He began kicking her with all his might, using precision aim to kick her stomach as she screamed and cowered, trying to protect her unborn child.

Instinct kicked in as BabyGirl closed her eyes, raised her hand, and aimed.

The gunshot echoed through the hotel leaving Dragon breathless, but it was equally as deadly as the pool of blood forming between her legs.

"You're all I need to get by …"

Chapter 4

GEORGE WASHINGTON BRIDGE

*P*orsha Hilton's red Ferrari sat in rush hour traffic on the George Washington Bridge. Due to the slow traffic, she placed the stick in second gear. She had just come from an exhausting sexual encounter with Rick Shane, Manhattan's top Assistant District Attorney. He was known for handling a lot of the high profile cases. Although Rick tried his best to please her, he was nothing compared to Chin, and she was getting tired of using a battery operated toy as her only real source of pleasure. She sighed heavily as she thought about the meeting with Encore Records taking place in their office.

When asked what she wanted for all the trouble she had been through with Chin, she had snatched up the record company, knowing that it was the most legitimate of all of Chin's operations. She had seen to that herself. With all the difficulties understanding the majority of the rap lyrics, artist scheduling, and promotion, she was beginning to question if she had made the right choice.

Truth be told, the visit she'd had from Detective Garfin a week ago still had her shaken. Garfin warned her that if she didn't cooperate with his investigation, she would be going down along with everyone who had a part in Tha Hustle Records. Evidently, she hadn't cleaned up the place fast enough to keep it from being under the police's radar. Garfin spoke of some tape that was lingering.

The fact that Tony Moreno was still alive didn't sit well with her either. No one had heard much about him except a few rumors here and there that he had come out of a coma. No telling what he was up to.

BabyGirl and Dimples were more cut out for this business. They were hood chicks that came from the street. They glorify the lifestyle, and grew up around hip-hop, drugs, and violence. Porsha, weary from all the work and commitment it takes to run such a business, was ready to hand the label over to BabyGirl. Not only was she tired, but the business was starting to interfere with Porsha's personal life. There was also too much police activity and it didn't take a psychic to know shit was about to explode.

Unfortunately, convincing BabyGirl to take the company without suspicion being drawn to Porsha was a challenge. If there weren't a few seeds of mistrust sown between them, it could have happened with ease. Now Porsha prayed it would happen before the detective dug his heels too deep.

Porsha considered rolling down the window. Between the mink and the car's heater she had switched off fifteen minutes ago, she was sweating like she just had a good work out. Engine noises from the tractor-trailers and eighteen-wheelers filtered in and she hadn't even cracked the glass yet. Somehow, she always got a headache from such noise. The soothing sounds of Anthony Hamilton's earthy voice echoed in her car. She listened at his attempts to revive a rocky relationship with his woman, "Charlene." As the words penetrated her soul, she wished Chin would have worked on their relationship instead of straying. She sighed, shaking the mental picture of him sleeping with

Chyna and then BabyGirl from her mind. Thirty seconds later, the heat won the battle. She cracked the window, carefully, so she wouldn't inhale the fumes pouring in from the trucks on her side. Although it was freezing outside, the weather didn't bother Porsha. The noise, however, was different.

"I can't wait to get home," she mused. She planned to lay in the Jacuzzi to settle her mind and contemplate her next move, but not before first giving Dragon a piece of her mind. She had booked a studio session for him earlier, but a quick phone call from the engineer informed her that he was a no show, and the female artist laid down her portion of the tracks without him. He better have a good explanation this time.

"I swear this record label shit just ain't for me," she whispered. Porsha didn't have the same hold on the artists that Chin did. She didn't know what he did to keep them in line, and since she didn't have the same power, they were testing her and she was ready to shoot somebody just to show who was boss.

Dragon was always available when it was time to record tracks for his album. But now that his album was released and the remixes were being done, he acted as though he were on top of the world and was invincible. She regretted taking the label instead of the restaurants. Somehow she felt the record label would be worth a lot more as far as profit and notoriety. Just like it had been when Chin was alive.

Thousands of thoughts rushed through her mind, from the first time they met to the moment he begged Porsha to help him get out of the drug game so he could keep his wealth to the first time they made love. "God that man could fuck," she whispered to herself, letting go of the steering wheel just long enough to rub a painful spot right above her breast. She had given him more than she had ever given any other man or ever would again.

She had done everything he ever needed, so how did she get here? Alone, childless, and without a man, Porsha tried convincing herself that she did right by Chin. Meanwhile, Chin's enemies had raked in all the benefits without a guilty conscience. All Porsha ever wanted was to marry Chin, have his children, and succeed in her law practice by becoming partner. Her dreams were all set until another woman entered the picture. Or should she say two women? Damn, that man's dick sure got around.

Porsha tried to focus on the road home, but memories, disappointment, and pure loneliness fueled her thoughts. Suddenly, angry voices coming from a red two-door Honda Accord to her left made Porsha snap away from it all, especially when she heard the words, "Forget you then! You're acting as if this right here," the Hispanic girl said as she pointed to her crotch, "can't get someone else."

"Good luck trying," the man said with a harsh laugh. "With your nasty ass, I'll be surprised if he stayed more than a week."

The girl's hand connected with the man's face, causing their car to veer into Porsha's lane.

Porsha managed to speed past them, rolling the window up as she remembered the time she had to remind Chin about the power of the pussy.

Unfortunately, it was his last lesson.

Chapter 5

Gray, dull walls were caving in on Daquan "Dragon" Bentley. The overpowering scent of stale air gave him several coughing fits before he could regain his composure. The lights were so bright he could barely keep his eyes open. Not that seeing would be any better, but at least he was still alive. A quick chill ran across the back of his neck. Fine bumps like grains of sand piled together and formed on his body in groups. The sweat pants and T-shirt he was wearing clung to his body. First, it had been too hot in the interrogation room, and then it was suddenly frigid. He knew it was a form of torture, so he continued to bare the situation.

As he sat in the hard plastic chair, waiting for what he knew would be the good cop - bad cop routine, he analyzed and thought about the fight with BabyGirl and none of it, the argument or the outcome was rational.

"Damn that bitch!" He slammed his fist on the table. If it weren't for her, he wouldn't be in jail, nor would he be worrying about new charges that might be brought up against him or old ones that could resurface. It was the main reason he had left all the madness alone and focused on his recording career—no crime involved. Well, so he thought in the beginning, but Tha Hustle Records hadn't been as clean as he had hoped. Chin couldn't leave the game fast enough; then BabyGirl came into the mix.

Hell, BabyGirl already served her purpose, so he was struggling to understand why he was holding onto her.

It's not like he loved her anyway. Nor did he give a fuck if she lost the baby. Actually, he hoped she did lose that "little fucker."

Who the hell did she think she was pulling a gun on him?

He built that ho from the ground up and look at the way she thanked him… by treating him like he was her next victim. If he hadn't supplied her with the information needed to take Chin down, she wouldn't have known where to begin. And running a restaurant at her age? He put her on, and now he didn't get any respect from her or her crew.

Dragon plopped down in the chair. "Dumb ass bitch." He sucked his teeth and thought about how he would give anything to finish that blunt. If she found out how much Dragon had played with and preyed on her emotions to get what he wanted, she would've killed him right along with Chin and Danny. She never even thought about how much having the recording studio would mean to him. What the hell did Porsha know about music? That bitch was all bourgeois and conceited; and now she had the balls to give him orders because she held his career in her hands. This time, when he got through with BabyGirl, she would wish she had joined her parents in death.

Seated at the long brown table, Dragon stared at the empty chairs on the opposite side. His left hand was still in handcuffed to the arm of the chair. They already knew that BabyGirl was the one with the gun. What could the police want to talk to him about now?

He knew they were watching his every move from the other side of the reflective mirror across the room. If only they could hear what was going through his mind; that alone could have him behind bars for life.

Dragon's gaze darted around the room, landing on the mirror again. His usually short hair cut was now an afro and begged for a haircut. Sprinkles of hair had formed on his face where smooth skin normally displayed a milk chocolate glow. The first thing he was going to do when he got out was hit Finest Cut.

The doorknob turned slowly. Dragon perked up and pushed aside his anger because he knew it was one of the main weapons police used against victims—anger along with fear. After being yelled at, ordered around, and talked down to while in prison, he knew he had reason to have equal amounts of both.

A man with black hair with patches of gray passed through the door, holding a thick folder in his hand. His protruding stomach swung around the door before the rest of his body. No uniform, but he had an arrogant air that reeked of intricate knowledge of the legal system. But he was certainly no lawyer.

"Good day, Mr. Bentley," the man said with trace of sarcasm in his voice. Walking toward the table, his black shoes tapped on the floor. The shoes were scuffed and had lost their shine. Dragon wouldn't be caught dead in them. Warren's shirt and pants looked like something taken straight out of the dirty clothes hamper. Didn't the police believe in irons anymore? New York City's Finest? Please! More like New York's Sloppiest. Dragon felt he could pull together an outfit on his worst day that would put these fools to shame.

Pulling out the chair, his thin hair bounced as he flopped

down into the seat. The chair creaked in protest. Dragon sneered, eyeing the man cautiously. The man's appearance could fool anyone, but not Dragon. The dark blue suit, white shirt, and tie, signaled an officer, not a lawyer. He could smell cops a mile away; they were all greedy and conniving just like lawyers. And to top it off, the strong scent of Old Spice cologne flowed through the room, signaling that the man had poor taste in cologne.

The man glanced at the window. Dragon wondered what that was all about. Piercing blue eyes now leveled with Dragon's dark brown ones, as though searching for some sort of answer.

Dragon slouched down in the chair, this time extending his legs as though he weren't bothered by being in the 19th precinct on a cold winter night when he should have been back at the Hilton making love to BabyGirl; or at least setting her up for a fall.

Suspicious thoughts of why this particular detective was here flooded his mind. Maybe BabyGirl decided to rat on him, but then again, she only knew a little about him. And she had a lot more to lose. If she did open her mouth a little too wide, Dragon had no problem doing the same.

Fuck living by the street code. If he was going down, every-one was going with him—"especially those three bitches," he thought to himself.

The man tossed the folder on the table as he slid the chair in.

"I'm Detective Garfin…do you want anything to eat or drink?" he asked, leaning back in the chair and crossing his arms over a hefty chest.

Dragon sucked his teeth, then glanced at the two-way glass. He couldn't see movement behind it even if he wanted.

"Want a smoke?"

"Naw," Dragon responded with a slight shake of his head; though he would have killed for a pull off a blunt right. New York's finest should have plenty of that floating around, as much as they lifted for personal use from the in-house stash.

The detective stood, walked to the door and pulled it open. He stretched his fat wrinkled neck out the door. "Officer Warren, bring a pack of cigarettes and some chips in here."

Anger stormed through Dragon. "Do you have a hearing problem or something?" he yelled. "Yo, I just fucking told you I don't want nothing."

The detective growled, slamming his fist on the table, causing the file to shift. "Listen to me, you asshole," he said through clenched teeth, "When I'm through with your black ass, you'll be begging for some help or anything we give you."

"Whatever!" Dragon jerked his head back as he waved the man off. Detective Garfin's stinking coffee and cigarette laced breath, nearly caused Dragon to pass out.

"Don't worry about my breath." Garfin said, letting out a light chuckle. "Worry about the ass and feet you'll be smelling for about the next twenty years, you little motherfucker, when I coast your ass for half the shit in this folder."

Tension spread in the room faster than a curve ball landing in a catcher's mitt.

Dragon saluted the detective, with a quick flick of his middle finger. "Do whatever you gotta do."

"You don't want to fuck with me," Garfin said through his teeth.

Footsteps echoed in the room, causing both heads to turn toward the door.

Officer Warren walked in, tossing the bag of Lays Potato

Chips and a pack of Newports on the table.

Warren walked beside Dragon to take off the handcuffs. "C'mon Garfin, lighten up. How do you expect him to talk to you if you're this hard on him?"

Dragon rubbed his wrist, enjoying the brief respite.

Go easy on him? The good cop had arrived. Dragon wasn't falling for it, and knew Garfin caught on to that fact just as quickly.

"Fuck this dumb ass prick," Garfin said, pointing an index finger at Dragon, and then to Officer Warren as he said, "Don't you have some paperwork to take care of? Let me handle him."

Warren took a minute to sort through an answer. Instead of playing the game, the man backed up, closed the door behind him, and allowed Garfin to continue with his interrogation.

Silence expanded between the remaining men, causing Dragon to lean his head to the right side as he awaited the detective's next move.

Garfin opened the folder and pulled out some pictures. He tossed one across the table, which landed right at the edge, directly in front of Dragon.

"Do you know him?"

Dragon glanced down at the picture before locking gazes with the detective. "What difference is it gonna make *if* I know him?" Of course, they didn't think it would be that easy. Suddenly those Lays looked delicious to him. Though he had spent a year and a half behind bars for a sale and possession charge, the thought of eating peanut butter sandwiches when they placed him in a cell made him reach for the bright yellow, red, and white bag. Compared with jailhouse provisions; chips would win hands down.

"Do you know him?"

Dragon smirked at Garfin, savoring each bite of the greasy chips as though they were offerings from the finest restaurant.

A vein bulged near the detective's throat. Garfin got up and jerked Dragon out of his chair, chips spilling onto the floor as he slammed his body against the wall. "Listen to me, you asshole—"

Warren rushed in the room, reaching for Garfin. "Gimme a few with him!"

Garfin was ready to beat the hell out of Dragon, but conceded as Officer Warren asked. He stepped back and sat down, allowing the officer to move around him. Garfin slumped down in the chair, casting an icy glare at Dragon.

Warren escorted Dragon back to the seat. Dragon snatched his arm away, glowering at the seated detective. So much for doing paperwork.

Warren stared at Dragon. "Don't you wanna go home?"

Dragon ignored him and continued to stare Garfin down.

Warren tried another tactic. "I know you want to smell, lick, and fuck some pussy instead of bending over for dicks all day."

Dragon cut his eyes at the detective and focused his attention back to Officer Warren. "You should know because you probably suck plenty of them trying to get a detective position." Dragon stared at Warren's pale face, then turned his attention to the door.

"Prick," Warren uttered

"Yes dick," Dragon came back,

"Do you know this man?"

Dragon took a look, but held his tongue.

Garfin pulled out yet another picture. "Or this one?"

The gruesome sight of that picture almost caused the few chips he got down to resurface. They were trying to link him to this man's death. Things were worse than he thought …

🂠🂠🂠

March 2004, the leaves were beginning to sprout on the trees. Livingston Correctional Facility's prison yard was crowded, and inmates would meet up with their peeps to discuss whatever. His friend, Sunset, had just been released, so Dragon ended up with a new cellmate. Christopher Cole had a slender-build, light skin, and a low haircut and was in state issued green pants and a white top. They had just finished watching the news about how out of control the drug dealers were in Harlem.

Cole laughed. "Yo, niggas are wildin' son."

"Word!" Dragon added in a nonchalant manner. It was around ten P.M. and everyone in Livingston was getting ready for bed. Lights were about to be out in a few.

Seconds later, the prison automatically became dark, and everything was shut down. Men talking to their cellmates still could be heard throughout the dorm.

"Niggas don't understand; you gotta keep things on the low. Cole spoke while retrieving a plastic bag filled with cocaine, which had been stuffed up his ass since an earlier visit. Dragon caught a glimpse of the activity for a second then turned his head. Cole sprinkled some on his index finger and snorted it up. "I be tryin' to explain that shit to my crew, but they don't wanna listen to the kid. Ever since this new nigga took over, it's like Harlem's been hot." He sniffled, then offered some to Dragon before fluffing his pillow to lie back on the bed.

"Naw, I'm good," Dragon said, pulling himself into an upright position. He wanted a taste in his mind, but Cole was new to him and trust was a factor.

Looking around he uttered, "Who's this new nigga you talkin' bout?"

Cole was hesitant; instead he concentrated on taking another hit. After taking a hit, Cole spoke, "He ain't nobody, just another nigga trying to make a paper."

Dragon took a mental note and decided to revisit the topic later.

Voices from different cellmates echoed in the dorm. Inmates bragged about their past lives and the lives they hoped to have when released. Inmates could be heard crying, arguing with each other, and snoring.

Two weeks after the conversation, Dragon decided to revisit the subject since the comfort level had grown a bit between them. "Who is this nigga running Harlem?"

Looking around, Cole pulled him to the side and began explaining Pit Bull's operation. Cole rambled on about Pit Bull's connections. He went deeper, telling him that Pit Bull and some other dudes murdered a man and his wife back in 2000 and that's how they were able to build their empire. This new found information brought Dragon one step closer to his goal.

Every now and then, Cole would give Dragon new details. One day Cole dropped some information that wasn't supposed to get out, Dragon, foreseeing an opportunity, decided to intensify a beef that already existed between Cole and another inmate named Les. Dragon told Les Cole was trying to kill him. Eventually Dragon's tactics worked. Les fatally stabbed Cole in the shower using a shank that Dragon provided.

Garfin placed another picture in front of Dragon. "What about this one?" he asked as he pointed to the victim.

Dragon swallowed hard, but didn't say a thing. He hoped they didn't try to pin Danny's murder on him...another one of BabyGirl's masterpieces.

"Mr. Bentley, if you don't give us something to work with, we can't begin to talk a deal. And trust me; you're going to want a deal. They *looooove* good looking, tough punks like you in prison." Garfin ridiculed.

Dragon knew Garfin was full of shit because the prosecutor was the only one who could offer deals. Before he had a chance to speak, the door opened and the aroma of coffee wafted into the room. Dunkin' Donuts was Garfin's favorite, and his day couldn't begin nor end without it. A young lady with blonde hair, a wide smile, and trim body brought in a steaming cup filled with the welcomed brew.

Garfin retrieved another picture from the folder, dangling it in Dragon's face for a quick minute.

"Know him?" A smirk came across the detective's thin lips as he gathered his things.

Dragon continued to stare at the picture of BabyGirl's father without saying a word.

"I thought so." Garfin put on his coat and got his file together. "I'll speak with you later. Maybe a few nights in jail will loosen you up—one way ... or another." Garfin had hit a spot.

Dragon closed his eyes, leaned his head back, and let out a long, slow breath. This was the type of drama he was avoiding all along. BabyGirl had better be glad she wasn't anywhere near him right now. Gun or no gun, he'd kill her with his bare hands.

Chapter 6

MANHATTAN CRIMINAL COURT: CENTER STREET

*T*ony cringed as the smell of stinking feet, people who had not bathed for days, and the urine and feces stench from the toilet located at the front of the cell became unbearable. Tony took in the sights, observing how nasty the conditions were. Not a moment of peace in the place. Noises coming from different cells, the guards barking off orders and screams from one inmate to another were getting on Tony's nerves.

The cell was packed with about forty guys practically on top of each other; some lying under the metal benches and others laying in the middle of the cell. Tony adjusted himself on the metal bench and leaned his head on the concrete wall, as he continued to scan his surroundings.

"I hope I get out of this shit soon," Tony muttered.

"Tony? Tony Moreno?" someone to his far right called out. Tony wasn't sure who it was, so he didn't respond. He watched as a man with a tan complexion and a gut that would make the Pillsbury Doughboy proud made his way to Tony's side.

"Tony, it's me, Jose. You don't remember me?" he asked, pointing to his chest.

"Naw." Tony shook his head. He didn't want to associate with anyone.

"Remember when you, me, and King use to kick it in Wash Heights?" Jose asked again "You and King wasn't afraid to run the street all reckless."

"Listen!" Tony said through clenched teeth, giving the man a stern look. "I don't know you, so keep it moving." Tony didn't want that part of his past to ever resurface.

The guy threw up his hands and slowly backed off. As soon as he was far enough away, Tony got up off the bench and walked over to the payphone. Goetz had been taking too long, and Tony was about ready to get up out of where he was. Jail was no place for a businessman. And besides hooking up with Chin, Tony had done everything in his power to make sure he never saw the inside of a place like this. But the more Chin was attacked, the more Tony was pulled into the deadly aspects of Chin's business.

He placed the phone to his ear and was about to place the call when someone yelled out. "Anthony Moreno."

A guard was standing outside the bars, waiting. Tony hung up the phone, walked over to the bars and followed the man down the hall to a small room with only a table and two chairs inside. Jacob Goetz was waiting patiently in the room when Tony arrived.

Tony threw Goetz an aggravated look, as if to say, "It's about time," and hoped his silenced conveyed his aggravation. Goetz took a seat on one side, and Tony—still grim faced—slipped into the opposite chair.

Goetz cleared his throat, placed a briefcase on the desk, opened it, and took out Tony's file. Tony's file was thinner than most, but too thick for someone who desired to walk on the free side of the bars.

"So what I'm looking at?" Tony inquired, while throwing a

quick glance at the stocky correctional officer exiting the door.

"Well, I was getting there, so let's see."

Tony leaned closer and stated, "Give it to me straight."

"You're looking at second degree murder, assault, and money laundering."

"Just what the fuck I need," Tony ran a hand through his hair. "They bugging." Tony pressed his back further in the chair, absorbing what was said and calculating it against his freedom. "I'm not staying in jail. You see this shithole I'm sitting in, Goetz? I need to get out, not tomorrow, not next week—today!"

"I understand, but you're facing serious charges here." Goetz attempted to meet his strong gaze. "That's quite more than I expected."

"Then what the fuck am I paying you for Jacob Goetz? You're my goddamn attorney. For the money you're charging, you should be able to get me off with killing the president. Do I need to hire another attorney? 'Cause the bullshit you spitting to me right now, I ain't feeling that shit."

"No need for you to get another attorney," Goetz countered, loosening his tie. "I'm just informing you on what you're facing."

"Yeah, whatever." Tony dismissed him with a wave of his hand. "Do me a fucking favor and inform me of your plan to get me out of here."

"We're looking at bail anywhere from five hundred thousand to a million dollars."

"What?" Tony push back his chair and rose in a rage. The C.O. watched closely from afar, ready to go in and restrain him if he got out of hand. "I'm fucking innocent here, Goetz; there shouldn't even be a bail." Tony moved over to the wall. He paced back and forth as Goetz, who usually always had something to say, had no words to tell him. Tony knew that Goetz knew his hands were dirtier than a construction worker; however, that didn't matter. The man's job was to get Tony off *guilty or not*. Tony signaled the guard and was then escorted out of the room and back to the cell, but not without throwing a pointed look at Goetz.

What a joke!

♦♦♦

It was while lying on his sick bed in New York Hospital; Tony learned from his attorney that there were tapes installed in the Harlem bases monitoring each and every activity. Right there, Tony learned how much trust Chin had when it came to him. Tony was advised by his attorney to get the tapes because there was incriminating evidence on them. The prosecutor would have a field day.

Tony placed a quick call to Lou informing him to come down to the hospital. Once Lou arrived, Tony learned that Chin didn't even trust him.

"He told me make sure those tapes were on at all times, except for when he was at the base, so every movement could be watched." Lou explained to Tony as he leaned on the vent by the hospital window.

"I'm on those tapes?" Tony inquired while attempting to sit upright in bed. Lou rushed over trying to assist him; however, Tony declined his assistance and proceeded to raise himself. Even in his weakest state, he told himself he would never obtain help from anyone, that's when the enemy or friend would try to attack. Tony learned that from philosophical books.

"Get me those tapes, and make sure all copies are destroyed" he told Lou, with a deadly glint. "If those tapes end up in the wrong hands, it could mean my freedom… and your *life*." Tony placed an emphasized on the word life.

"I got it."

He watched as Lou headed out the door.

That's when he realized things were going to get a lot more hectic in the coming months…and he needed to get out of the game—*fast*.

♡♡♡

A few minutes after being returned to his cell, Tony's jaw dropped when Dragon walked in. He could recognize that man from any angle. Questions flowed through Tony's head as his eyes fixated on Dragon. The guard proceeded to close the cell. Dragon's back was still turned to Tony, but it didn't take long for the man to turn around. His eyes locked on Tony.

Neither of them said a word. The other inmates suddenly became less interested in their conversations and more interested in what may or may not become a problem right before their eyes.

"Moreno, they're getting ready to call your case," a thick, pale-skinned officer yelled from the other side of the bars. Tony tore his gaze from his new cell mate, gauging how much he could say before having to make it to the guard.

Tony brushed slowly past Dragon, staring him down and whispered, "The number's still the same. We have a lot of catching up to do."

About five minutes later, Tony followed behind through a long hallway, hands cuffed behind his back. A steel door swung open and he was led into the courtroom. Tony scanned the room and saw Maribel and his cousin Victor sitting a little too close together on the bench as they looked on. He also saw Detective Garfin sitting with a big grin on his face. "Damn, could this day get any worse?" Goetz greeted Tony with a quick nod.

"Your honor, calling case number twenty nine on the part 12 calendar in the matter of Moreno." Tony got up and headed to the long brown desk.

The judge had a stocky build, with gray hair, and a grim expression on his face. Tony faced the judge as he stood awaiting his fate.

"Your Honor, the defendant along with his deceased partner, was caught on a deli store videotape running from the building where the two victims, Sandi-Ann Richards and Marvin White, were found dead. It is believed that the defendant has direct involvement in the two victims' murders. We also believe that the defendant has some sort of ties with the victims, were a part of the victim's illegal activities, and that other illegal activities transpired within the record company, Tha Hustle Records. At this time, the people are requesting that Mr. Moreno be held without bail based on the charges he is facing which include, second degree murder, assault, and money laundering and the fact that the defendant is a flight risk." The assistant DA, an olive-skinned woman with long, dark hair and a gray suit which hid her shapely body, gave Tony and his lawyer a dismissive gaze.

"What the fuck?" They were trying Tony for Sandy's and Pit Bull's murders. "This is some bullshit," he whispered to Goetz. "I didn't kill them no more than I could have killed those two who ended up in the river with me."

The Assistant DA paused, took a deep breath before flipping the pages of her files. "The defendant also has large sums of money he has acquired within a short span of time and is not able to provide valid proof on how he acquired said amounts of income."

The judge folded his hands and cocked his head, waiting.

The ADA glanced at Tony and Goetz, as though acknowledging it was their turn, but that it wasn't worth the effort.

Goetz, clearing his throat while adjusting his lapel, opened his folder and donned an arrogant expression before saying, "Judge, yes my client was in the building at the time the unfortunate events occurred. However, my client only acted in a manner appropriate to anyone with common sense, which is to flee to safety whenever there are gunshots. My client does know the victims in passing, especially since his cousin lives in the same building; however, my client had nothing to do with their murder, nor does he have any knowledge of any illegal activities the victims were conducting." Goetz paused leaning on the podium. Tony hoped a winning speech was coming because nothing he had heard so far was a winner to him. "Judge, my client is totally innocent of these charges, Tha Hustle Records is a legitimate business, and under no circumstances were illegal activities conducted on their premises. What the DA has brought forth today is all based on circumstantial evidence. My client is a hard working man who has a family... his lovely wife and his cousin are sitting in the audience. The money in question that the ADA is referring to was won by my client through an accident law suit, which my client is more than willing to provide validated proof of." Goetz placed both his hands in his pockets. The ADA turned to the side and looked at Goetz. Goetz now looked at the judge, who was leaning in closer, in the eye. "I'm requesting that my client be released on bail. My client is not a flight risk. He has been residing in the United States for the past twenty years.

Goetz cast a sidelong glance at Tony and gave him a wink.

Tony smiled, he finally felt the man, who appeared nearly incompetent a few moments ago, now seemed as though he were vying for a place on the "Dream Team."

"Mr. Goetz," the judge of Asian descent addressed, "Your client is facing very serious charges."

"Yes, I'm aware of that judge. But if you check the records, it will show that my client has not been in any trouble with the law in ten years."

Garfin, who sat two rows in front Tony's wife and cousin, cleared his throat. Tony shook his head, letting out a sigh as he muttered, "This man better give me bail or else I swear I'm going to create chaos up in here."

"However, since the DA's office has yet to produce anything beyond circumstantial evidence, I'll set bail as long as he secures his bail with collateral and can prove where the money's coming from."

Banging his gravel, the judge spoke, "Bail is set for $500,000 secured bond. Your client will come back to court two days from now to go before the grand jury."

"Yes, Your Honor," Goetz responded.

Tony was led into a holding cell to wait for Maribel to pay his bail.

Chapter 7

PELHAMS: WESTCHESTER, NYC

The loose fitting tee shirt and jeans draped over Baby-Girl's body, allowing her comfort.

"Thanks for bailing me out," BabyGirl said, taking a seat on her friend's sofa.

"Now, Miss Superwoman..." Dimples walked over and sat beside her on the sofa. "...can you tell me why in God's name your pregnant ass tried to charge at that man with a loaded gun?"

Natasha "Dimples" Crawford passed BabyGirl two pain-killers along with a glass of water. "And you lost the baby behind all that bullshit."

BabyGirl let out a loud sigh as she settled in on her best friend's soft cream leather couch. Grief-stricken and depressed after losing her baby, she felt somehow God was punishing her for the murder she did back in Philadelphia when she killed a woman who was only trying to care for her child. A saddened look crossed her face as she realized she was paying for what she had done.

"I'm just tired of his shit, Dimples." She then glanced up into the dark-skinned girl's brown eyes, noticing the seriousness within them. Staring at Dimples, BabyGirl spoke, "Thanks, you been there for me while we were under Pit Bull, and you're here now."

"That's what friends are for," Dimples answered.

Low cut jeans clung for dear life to the curvy hips she'd acquired while working out at the gym. Exercise gave her a better shape than genetics had blessed her with. The white halter-top draped her body and the shimmering glow of MAC powder adorned her body.

"Did you see his face when we celebrated at the restaurant?" BabyGirl whispered. "And the fact that he didn't want to toast when everyone lifted their glasses. He's straight-up jealous.

"Yeah, I saw it, but it wasn't my business to say anything." Dimples responded.

A delicious, spicy smell of garlic floated in the air. One deep inhale and Dimples got up from the sofa to check on the dinner.

Picking up the remote, BabyGirl switched the television from BET to MTV. A white bear skin rug lay on the floor in front of her; BabyGirl stretched out her legs before pressing her feet into its softness.

"Listen, all fun and jokes aside, I'm getting tired of y'all shit," Dimples shouted from the kitchen. "You can't keep arguing like that and expecting me to jump in the middle every time. And you can't keep running to my place each time y'all have a fight. You my girl and all, but you need to find you a man with more going on. As bad as Chin was, I bet he never put you through half the shit Dragon did." Dimples pointed the spoon she was using to stir her dish at BabyGirl. "That's why I'm going to stick it out with Marquis. Now that's a good man."

Pictures of famous African Americans graced the walls of Dimples' home, giving its creamy hue a little life. Marquis Daniels, the latest and the longest lasting from a revolving line of men, truly believed in the power of the black man. BabyGirl could tell not only by the pictures and ornaments, but in how he spoke highly of them in many of his conversations.

A good man? Something about Marquis didn't sit too well with BabyGirl. The way he had come into her friend's life had been a little too convenient and straight-laced. However, she brushed it off until later when she had time to figure it all out. Her own life's drama was enough to keep her busy, as Dimples had just reminded her.

But Dimples had a lot of nerve talking about what Dragon or Chin had put her through. As a friend, Dimples, who knew BabyGirl's main goals in life were to own her company, go to college, and be a part of corporate America, didn't always have her best interest at heart either. She never forgot the time Dimples turned her back, when she needed her the most.

♡♡♡

BabyGirl was upset with Sandy for having the audacity to say that Pit Bull wanted to sleep with her. With no one else to trust she turned to Dimples, her one true friend, or so she thought, in the middle of Sandy's kitchen that hurtful day and asked, "You heard what Sandy said. I have to sleep with him."

She shrugged. "I know, BabyGirl, that's why you just go along. Do what they want." She reached for her hand.

BabyGirl slapped it away. "You've got to be kidding! You're straight with this bullshit, too?"

"Look at it this way—"

Running a single finger across her throat before Dimples

could even finish her sentence, she left the air silent. She didn't want to hear what she had to say.

"I can't believe you, Dimples. I thought you were my friend."

Dimples could afford to be reasonable about the situation. No one was asking her to sleep with anyone.

☑☑☑

No, Dimples had put her through much more.

"Hello! I'm talking to you," Dimples waved her hand in front of BabyGirl's face.

"Sorry, I was just thinking for a minute."

Dimples dropped down onto the sofa beside her. "About Chin?"

BabyGirl gave her a simple shrug.

"Well, Chin's dead and gone, you can't go back in the past, but you can fix the present by getting rid of this clown."

A certain sternness in Dimples' voice made BabyGirl take notice. Placing the glass on the center table, BabyGirl stood and walked over to the window. She gazed outside for a minute. "So what you trying to say, Dimples? That I'm some hood chick that only picks up low life niggas?"

Dimples placed her ruby-red hair behind an ear as she glanced at BabyGirl before making her way to the kitchen to check on the garlic chicken.

Laughter erupted from the television, creating the only distraction in the house. Big Mama's House, the comedy where Martin Lawrence played an undercover cop posing as an old, heavy-set woman was on cable—again. BabyGirl wished somehow she could appreciate the laughter the movie normally could bring. Nothing was funny about the fact that she'd had the unfortunate experience of losing her first child, her first love, and also the man who, for all intents and purposes, could have been her last one.

Dimples took the garlic chicken out of the oven, then placed it on the granite countertop. She inhaled the pleasant aroma once again and smiled at her creation. "I'm not saying you wouldn't have my back. Once, yes. Twice I could see, but when it starts getting to three and four times, then I'd have to start looking at myself and wondering if I was using common sense when it comes to choosing men.."

Dimples turned on her Manolo heels to look BabyGirl straight in the face. "You know what? You need a change." Dimples placed the pots and utensils in the sink, she was a far cry from the roughneck girl that BabyGirl had lived with almost a year ago.

BabyGirl trailed her friend to the dining room. "Since when have you become a housewife?"

Dimples grinned as she placed China, silverware, and crystal goblets on the dining table. "Since I got a man. A *real* man! One who knows not to put his hands on me if he wants to live."

She was saddened by the reminder of both Chin and Dragon stomping her like she was a hard to kill roach, BabyGirl tried to lighten things up. "It's probably the dick and the licking he's putting on that ass that's making you act this way."

"And? At least the nigga's handling his business," Dimples shot back with laughter.

Dimples? A housewife? Never in a million years! Marquis wasn't a magician. It had to be the dick. Taking her seat at the dining room table, BabyGirl took up her fork, and put a piece of chicken in her mouth, savoring the meal. "Dragon's changed, Dimples. He isn't the same as he was when my father was around."

Dimples, who now joined BabyGirl at the table, stopped long enough to peer up at her friend for a moment. "I never wanted to bring this up, but something's been nagging me ever since you told me how he . . . rescued you after your parents were killed." Dimples placed her fork on the side of the plate. "I never did understand how your dad, the stern man you stated he was, would let someone like Dragon, a street nigga, get that close to you. Him kicking it with you was a little too convenient."

"It didn't happen right away. I had a crush on him for a long time, my father didn't know about it."

"How did you meet him?"

"Girl, I remember it like it was yesterday. It was hot in Harlem that day. I think it was the Fourth of July weekend." She sighed, remembering the wonders of that Harlem summer day. "The smell of hot dogs, burgers, and barbecued chicken filled the entire block. Hot 97 was blasting from Ms. Thomas' third floor apartment. Mr. Cee was spinning 'My Radio' by LL Cool J on 'Old School at Noon'," BabyGirl said as she reached for some rice and beans. "I had on a pair of white daisy-duke shorts and a yellow halter-top that was hugging my neck for dear life."

Dimples pulled up a chair and began tasting her handiwork.

"My father was on the block with his fresh white Nikes playing Spades with his friends, a bunch of rowdy old men. My friends Nefa, Keke, and I were sitting on the bench talkin' 'bout who was screwing who, and who wasn't getting any."

Dimples grinned, continuing with her meal.

"Just as Keke was in the middle of telling me that Niecy was caught sucking Jaquan's dick, I saw Dragon walk over to my father and tap his shoulder. Everyone around my father stood, holding their waists where their guns were holstered. Not my dad. He placed his cards on the table, stood to his full six feet, almost towering over Dragon as he eyed him before pulling the younger man to the side."

Dimples stopped chewing her chicken and looked Baby-Girl dead in the eyes.

"I didn't know what was going on or what they were talking about, but everyone stood around watching them. Next thing I saw, my father walked back over to the guys at the Spades table. The men all sat down, watching as Dragon strolled down the street, and they continued playing cards like nothing happened. Dragon wasn't fazed by the guns and didn't show any fear. From then on, I had my eyes on Dragon."

Dimples said nothing. She pulled back her chair and simply rocked her right leg, crossing it over the left one.

""The night my parents were killed he came through for me, and then I knew he was the one for me."

BabyGirl took a sip of juice from the crystal goblet.

"Why did you ask me that question earlier?"

Dimples took in another forkful of food. Moments later, she stopped chewing and looked at BabyGirl. "Have you ever tried to talk to him about his family?"

"Nope," BabyGirl replied, walking back into the kitchen, Dimples following behind on her heels.

"BabyGirl, you mean to tell me you're fucking this man, got pregnant by him, and don't know shit about his family?" She leveled a hard gaze at her friend. "You're smarter than that; or is it that love got you so fucked up that you can't see straight?

Maybe it was catching a kid by that nigga—"

"Who said it was his baby?"

Dimples' fork hit the plate as she peered at BabyGirl. "What? You bitch!" The sinister smile on her face matched BabyGirl's own.

BabyGirl shrugged. "Hey, a girl had to do what she had to do. I wanted Chin's empire and wouldn't stop at nothing until I got it, even if it meant bringing his child into the world to give me rights to it."

"You're colder than I thought," Dimples expressed, eyes widening as she realized her friend was more calculating than she originally thought. She continued eating before coming up with her next question. "Where's Dragon's mother?"

"I think she's dead." BabyGirl said, as she got up from the table and walked over to the kitchen. Leaning on the wall next to the window, she gazed out at the calm sky. "I was so busy trying to find my parents' killer that I didn't have time to go back to that yet."

Dimples arched eyebrows lifted. "You have proof that his mother's dead?"

Confusion stormed through BabyGirl's mind. Why was her friend grilling her? They had survived bullets and near death, and now that Dimples was living a little better than the tiny spot they had once shared with Sandy, things were getting a bit twisted.

Dimples cleared the table, placing the dishes in the sink and turning her back to BabyGirl as she said, "Sometimes it's the ones who seem the most innocent who are the ones that bring you down." She noticed the frown on BabyGirl's face and said, "Take Julius Caesar's story for example.

"Your point is?"

Dimples let out a long, weary sigh before picking up a plate to wash. "My point is, BabyGirl," she paused as though weighing how much to say. "If nothing else, and I mean nothing else, I say to you sinks into your thick skull, please take the next thing I say into consideration." She stopped washing the plate and focused her attention on BabyGirl. "Ask yourself... when your parents were killed and Dragon was supposed to be out hustling for your father, how did he manage to get there so fast? And, if he *loves* you so much, why did he want you to get so close to Chin? Why is he only tripping now that you're pregnant? He wasn't tripping when you had to fuck Chin to get information he needed to build on. Actually, he told you to do whatever it takes, right?"

BabyGirl's mouth went slack as the wheels started turning in her mind. Did Dragon have something to do with her parents' death?

Chapter 8

A car horn blared, causing Porsha to look in her rearview mirror. Ahead, traffic had moved on and she was holding up the people behind her.

Porsha was there for him in every way; cooking, keeping house, fucking and sucking him like a porno star, and even risked her license by helping him and Tony put Tha Hustle Records on the map—clean cash and even cleaner documentation. She had never disappointed Chin and had always been in his corner. Until the day one of her clients informed her he was sleeping with Chyna, her coworker.

As she entered the home she shared with Chin in Staten Island, a glow from the back of the house along with Babyface's smooth voice singing, "A Girl Like You" caught her attention. The chlorine from the pool lingered under her nose as anger built inside her. Porsha's Fendi pumps hit the concrete pavement in a determined gait. Chin always said the shoes made her long legs look elegant. She wondered if he would appreciate that elegance up his ass.

Porsha held her anger in check. The whole setting—the candles, the music, the bubbly, all threw her off at first. But remembering Colin's words made her ask, "What is all of this?" Chin continued to pay her no mind and kissed along her neck and her lips. Porsha needed answers, so she decided to annoy him by constantly talking; she knew it was a turn off for Chin. When Chin couldn't take it anymore he decided to leave and go back to the studio. Porsha saw her perfect opportunity and flipped out on him. During their heated discussion, she informed him that he was probably going back to fuck Chyna. The look that Chin had on his face, told her Colin was not lying.

A few months after, she found out that Chin was messing with BabyGirl, which led to a deadly chain of events.

She couldn't begin to understand why Chin would cheat on her with some little ghetto corporate wanna-be. Especially since Porsha was the one who put her career on the line, as she was sure to lose valuable clients and her position at the law firm if they found out what she had done for Andre Chin and Tony Moreno.

Then to top it off, she knew the woman was carrying Chin's baby—the baby she wanted and begged him to have, only for him to say that it could wait until she had finished with everything needed to make his businesses legit. The life she had dreamed of, the two of them conquering the world, was a thing of the past.

Porsha let out a sorrowful sigh as she rested her head against the leather seat. Loneliness filled her heart, causing tears to form in the corner of her eyes. "I wanted to save you, Chin," Porsha whispered as if Chin were right beside her. "But I promise, I'm going to bring them down one by one... every last one of them. This shit is personal now."

Chapter 9

*B*eing released from jail didn't give Dragon a relieved state of mind since he had laid eyes on Tony Moreno. Thoughts of what Tony could be up to ran through his head, along with the questions about what Tony was being charged with and how it was related to his case. As he shifted on the wooden bench outside of the court awaiting a discussion with his attorney, he contemplated whether or not he should take Tony seriously and call him.

It could be a trap. Dragon didn't actually pull the trigger of the gun that killed the man, but he did play a part in bringing the people behind Tha Hustle Records to their knees. Tony Moreno wasn't likely to forget that fact. Or forgive. As he leaned his head back against the courthouse wall, his mind flashed back to the interrogation room with Garfin.

❂❂❂

During the interrogation, Dragon had found another reason to worry. Smoke from Garfin's cigarette had curled around Dragon's face like a fog. The detective dangled another picture in Dragon's face, nearly pressing it against his nose. "Maybe he'll freshen your memory." A picture of Les stared back at him.

The detective was on to something, but Dragon still wasn't going to talk.

"Here's the deal." Garfin leaned closer. "I want Tony Moreno, and everyone that has their hands in Tha Hustle Records." He moved around and perched his butt on the edge of the table beside Dragon. "I need you to help me," he said, poking Dragon's chest with an index finger.

Dragon shoved the detective's finger off his chest. "I ain't no snitch, and you dumb fuck, how am I suppose to bring Tony to you when I don't where he is?" Dragon got up while using his right leg to shove the chair against the wall. Warren's presence in the room prevented him from throwing the chair at Garfin. "You want them, you're on your own, bro."

Dragon walked toward the door, but it was locked.

Officer Warren stood in the corner of the room, arms folded across his chest as he watched the bickering like a spectator at a Gladiators match.

"Okay, suit yourself." Garfin took a sip of the coffee. "But do you still remember what happened at Livingston Correctional Facility in March 2004?" A smirk formed on his thin lips. "Cole was found dead in the shower." He trudged around the desk, drawing closer to Dragon. "I can easily make the evidence regarding your cell mate resurface, and trust me I got evidence." He smirked again, setting Dragon's nerves on edge. "I can have you in front of a jury looking at years full of wrinkled balls and a sore dick from jerking off." He grinned. "The choice is yours. Don't underestimate me; I got more dirt on you than I'm at liberty to say right now."

Dragon exhaled a gust of air, then shook his head. "I have no idea what you talking about detective."

Garfin came nose to nose with Dragon, "You will when the time is right."

Garfin reached into his pocket, placing his card on the table. "Call me, the offer won't be around for long."

"Whatever," Dragon shot back. "You a weak fuckin' detective, you can't even find the criminals you're looking for on your own... you have to resort to other criminals to assist you. How fuckin' pathetic. They should give the badge to Warren... he'd probably do a better job."

A loud laugh escaped Garfin's lips. "You think I'm pathetic? Then how do you think you look, your life is in the hands of the justice system or Tony Moreno... you're probably shitting bricks right now. I got a whole a lot of dirt on you, Daquan Bentley." Garfin pointed to the folder.

"Fuck you," Dragon yelled, knowing that Garfin got the best of him.

Garfin pulled out the chair he was sitting on earlier, putting his leg up before smiling. "Oh fuck me?" He shook his head. "Look how I'm going to fuck you for being such a smart ass." He took his foot down, and walked over to the door. "Your child's mother...BabyGirl. Is that what she calls herself?" He leaned in close to whisper in Dragon's ear. "Umm...come to think of it, I wonder if she knows about all the people who had something to do with her parents' death?"

"I don't know what you're talking about." Dragon peered up at him.

"Fuck with me and don't give me what I want, you'll know exactly what I'm talking about." Garfin laughed again. "Oh, and about Tony Moreno, you can consider your ass a dead man walking when he gets a hold of you. I think being in a witness protection program would be a good look for you right now. No telling what Tony's capable of." Garfin chuckled as he opened the door and closed it behind him.

Dragon fell back in the chair. "Snitching on BabyGirl or dealing with that Tony..." he muttered, as he rubbed his chin. Football numbers flashed in his mind. He wasn't prepared to do that much time nor was he prepared to go six feet under. He took the card off the table and walked to the door as Warren escorted him out.

"Let's talk, Mr. Bentley," Bistrow's voice snapped him to the present.

"Yeah, let's do that for sure." Dragon got up off the bench and followed his attorney, with a whole lot of problems trailing him.

Chapter 10

"*I* can never let these get out." Tony said, referring to the videotapes. After a quick call earlier, his hitman had told him Lou was taken care of. He was six feet under. Tony couldn't risk him snitching. He placed the tapes in the safe he had inside his bedroom. He didn't want them getting into the wrong hands," Tony spoke as he shut off the television. He had just reviewed the tapes Lou had kept at the base and they were more incriminating than he thought. Ensuring that the tapes were tucked away and the keys safely back under his pillow, he yelled, "Tiffany, have you seen my wife?"

Nurse Haywood, who Tony assumed wasn't far off, strolled in to adjust his pillows. He had requested she take a leave of absence from the hospital and work exclusively for him. She compromised by working for him at night and on her off days. "No," she replied softly. "I think she left the house this time."

Tony nodded, fuming inside as he prepared to give the woman he'd been married to for ten years an earful when she hit the door. Things were getting hectic, by now he was certain everyone knew he was alive, however they weren't able to place their hands on him.

"I'll be back in a little while to check on you," Tiffany said, smiling down at him before her sexy hips disappeared into the hallway.

A few months ago, when he was laid up in the hospital, he remembered how well Nurse Haywood had taken care of him. She was there for financial reasons, but for him it was for stimulation. He knew he didn't really need a nurse; however, he didn't mind admiring her figure every now and then. Maribel was slowly becoming a turn off and Nurse Haywood, with her round perky breasts, nice shape, and gorgeous smile was becoming more desirable day by day. A part of Tony told him that Nurse Haywood knew he liked her a lot but he wanted to wait until the time was right to approach her. He couldn't help but to wonder about her views on dating.

In the comfort of his bedroom, Tony glanced down at his arms, which a few months ago had IVs and were weak and frail. The only two reasons he was still alive were either God had given him a second chance or Satan wanted him to finish what those three bitches had started.

Tony hadn't quite gotten over the fact that his empire was taken over by three conniving females: one slick lawyer, one smart ass, and a hood rat. Every time the thought popped in his head, he prayed time was on his side and he could deal with them one by one.

He sat quietly at the edge of his bed, contemplating his next move. The opened blinds allowed him to look out at the yachts docked in the water at the 79th Street boat basin. He had struggled for days to find the perfect strategy to take down BabyGirl, Porsha, and Dimples and get back every cent they had taken from him. He was close, but needed a grand finale as the finishing touch—a satisfying revenge. He had one thorn in the ass though, Detective Garfin was watching his every move and waiting for him to fuck up so he could get the DA to bring him up on extra charges. Especially since the last ones failed to keep him in jail for now.

"Not over my dead body, much less while I'm alive," Tony whispered to himself. Putting his plan in motion he thought to himself, "This time things will get bloody—as Malcolm X said, '*By any means necessary*'." Tony was no stranger to those methods.

He took a quick glance at the television, then at the clock as a grim reality settled in; his wife was up to something. For the past couples days since he had been home, she had made every excuse in the book to be out. Even if she had to lie and say she would be back in fifteen minutes. Today was no exception, as her fifteen minutes had become forty-seven, and still no sign of her lying ass. Picking up the telephone, he placed two quick calls, one to his cousin Victor, whose job was to keep an eye on Maribel's movements, and the other to Maribel. Tony's efforts to reach them both proved fruitless. Somehow, he couldn't put his fingers on the problem where his cousin was concerned; but where his wife was involved, certainly a problem existed. Their marriage had been shaky before he landed face up on the hospital stretcher, and it was now on the path to disaster. As Tony began to think, he couldn't figure out the biggest mystery of all—why the female saved him that day by calling the police. He quickly erased the thought and went back to Maribel.

If things didn't change soon, and his suspicions proved correct, he and Maribel were headed to the "until death" part of their vows.

Tony reached out, plucking the book *48 Laws of Power* by Robert Greene from the nightstand and flipping it to the section that said, *conceal your intentions*. Tony knew from experience as a businessman, that the rule often comes into play and those three women had taught him that first hand. His partner, Andre Chin, hadn't been lucky enough to live to help him finish them off. He knew Chin would take much pleasure in doing so, whether he had fucked them or not. Too bad it was that fact alone that had brought the man to his knees.

Tony would never make the mistake of allowing pussy to control his mind. That's why Maribel needed to be put in check this very minute and those bitches were going down the moment he pulled a proper team together. Sure he could have one of his boys do the dirty work, but after so many in-house traitors had surfaced and alliances shifting after Chin's death, those three bitches deserved and would receive Tony's personal attention, with a little professional help, of course.

The sweet scent of Escada wafted into the room, interrupting Tony's strategic planning. Maribel strolled over to the bed, grabbed the book out of his hand, and tossed it onto the plush cream carpet; her dark brown eyes shot him a deadly look.

"What the fuck's your problem?" Tony said, glaring right back.

Maribel's red mouth formed into a sexy pout. The shoulder-length deep crimson colored hair blended perfectly with her olive complexion and accented the features of her classically pretty face. Placing her jacket on the wire hanger she said, "You're not fully off your case yet, and here you are reading this damn book to plot. What the fuck's wrong with you?" She turned, placing a single hand on her hips. Tony's dick took immediate inventory of her short, curvy body as his need for her resurfaced.

"You know, I thought I married a financial genius, a man who had millions of dollars in hand, but you threw it all away for a restaurant, record label, and clothing line. All for what? For it to be stolen by three females…," she taunted. "You're weak, Tony. You're weak. Where'd my husband go," she said, Puerto Rican accent punctuating each word as her eyes flashed with anger. "Since you hooked up with Chin and played second fiddle to a man who was a straight dog, your *family* disappeared into the clouds. Even if you don't love me, you could do right by the kids."

"Weak?" Tony got up off the bed to retrieve the book, simmering at the fact that she could even wrap her lips around the word. "Don't…don't you dare go there about the kids. All along I was trying to be a husband, and never, not ever, have you tried to be a wife." He crossed the distance between them in four short strides. "All you do is sit on your ass and complain all fucking day. I come home to a messy house. Getting a home cooked meal is a joke. And our children, who you're so worried about, are eating fast food all day and running around this place like a pack of wild animals." His temper rose to a dangerous level. "You wanna know where your husband went? He was out there handling his business making sure clothes stayed on your back and the children's. Making sure all the bills are paid, so you can stay home and do the homey things since you don't want to work, and keep food in the refrigerator." He leaned in so their noses almost touched. "Now you tell me where my wife went?" His angry stare matched hers. "The wife who was supposed to do her part since I did everything a husband's supposed to do."

At that moment, Nurse Haywood popped in to check Tony's vitals as promised. She glanced at Maribel, then to Tony, and something told her it wasn't a good time, but she had to look out for his health, something he paid handsomely for her to do.

"Tony, you really need to calm down so you don't send your blood pressure up." The petite woman then turned to his wife, "Ma'am, if you can't keep him from stressing out, I'm going to have to ask you to leave until he's able to calm down."

"This is *my fucking* house," Maribel snapped. "And he's *my fucking* husband."

Tiffany's chin rose as she shot back, "Right now he's *my* patient, in *my* care." Tiffany stood her ground as Tony's lips spread into a small, satisfied smile. "I'd like to make sure he stays a patient and doesn't become a corpse. Unless you're *deliberately* trying to kill him?"

Maribel's light skin flushed red with anger. The woman had hit dangerously close to home. Wisely, she kept her mouth shut, wondering exactly what was going on with Tony and this nurse. He had insisted on having her here, although Maribel was dead set against it. The nurse gave Tony one last look over her shoulder, saying in a soft, sexy voice, "If you need anything, I will be here for another thirty minutes."

Tony grinned, watching the woman's petite curvy form disappear. Maribel moved in front of him so he wouldn't be distracted again. Actually, Tiffany was fast becoming more than a distraction. If Maribel didn't get her act together . . .

"Well, maybe if you had stayed home more often…" Maribel said standing at the edge of the bed with a defiant glint in her eyes. "…instead of running around with Chin, then maybe I would've acted like the wife you wanted me to be."

"Let me tell you something," he stood directly in front of her, getting in her face. "I invested my time and money in something that was a sure thing. I worked my ass off at the *Tha Hustle Records* so we can have food in the fridge."

Maribel huffed as Tony lowered his voice to a growl. "That's right, I said, *in the fridge* because it certainly doesn't make it to the table since you refuse to cook."

What could she say to that?

"I work to make sure our daughters' futures are set." Then he went to the closet, flinging the door open. "I work to make sure these fucking Gucci," he tossed a stiletto toward her feet. "Jimmy Choo," another shoe landed next to the first one. "Dolce and Gabbana, and all the other brand name clothes, shoes, and purses can stay in your closet. And you rarely even wear this shit more than once," he snapped, still trying to keep his breathing even. "So don't you dare question me about working late. You should be thankful that I'm not a lazy motha-fucka, but a hard working man. However, your trifling ass don't see that, so now I'm called weak." Shaking his head, he said, "Women, y'all never cease to fucking amaze me."

His intense gaze traveled the length of her slender curves, flowing back up to her full lips, high cheekbones, and deep-set eyes; a dangerous combination of Puerto Rican and Italian beauty. "What happened to the days when we couldn't get enough of each other, huh?"

Maribel backed away, throwing a cautious gaze at the man who lay in the hospital for months as she saw him withering away. She walked over to the flat screen, reaching for the button on top and switched it off. She never could stand a quiet house, but she didn't need a distraction.

Her shoulders drooped as she turned to face him saying softy, "Those days aren't gone, it's just that I'm tired of being stuck with the kids all the time."

"You're not working, so I don't see how taking care of two kids and the house is a problem," he said, matching her tone, his anger dissipating. "We'll get you some help with taking care of the kids, maybe find you a babysitter or something." Finally, his eyes locked on hers. "And if those days aren't gone like you say," he stroked a single hand over her smooth, delicate skin. "Make love to me right now like you used to back in the day, the kids aren't here now."

Maribel froze, avoiding his touch as her gaze lowered to the remote. She picked it up, ignoring the fact that her husband now stood next to her with hands outstretched—trying yet one more time to reach out for the woman he had loved since high school.

"I'm tired right now. I'll take care of you tomorrow." she turned the television back on and began flipping through the channels as though he hadn't challenged her.

"I thought so," he said in a voice as cold as his heart had become. Sitting on the edge of the bed, he grimaced as he noticed the shadow under the door once more. He figured it was his nurse entering to tell him she was leaving. Tony steadied his breathing as she had taught him.

"See, it has nothing to do with that. Your doctor said—"

"Fuck the doctor. I want my wife. He said I'm recovering, I'm not dead. Either you're going to be a wife, or an ex-wife."

Maribel's shoulder length hair fanned out as she whirled to face him. Her jaw dropped at the same moment his erection disappeared.

Tony came to a decision and jumped off the bed. "The choice is yours, but I refuse to play your games anymore. Despite your beefs, as minor as they are, I've been a good man, Maribel"

She inhaled sharply, opening her mouth to speak.

Tony silenced her with the motion of one hand. "Yes, I've made mistakes, but I've always tried to keep what's here at home tight. I never once disrespected you in any way. I want a change around here, and I want it now. Enough is enough."

"A wife or an ex-wife!" She whispered, taking her stare off the floor and putting it squarely on him. "So that's it, huh? You plan on throwing me away for someone else?" She got up off the bed. "Is that nurse of yours doing more than she's paid for?"

"If that was the case, she would be sharing my bed, not you."

Maribel squinted at that admission.

"Having real sex is better than dreaming about it any day. Listen…" Tony held on to her soft shoulders to get her attention. She shrugged him off, walking away until she settled on the satin covered chaise.

Tony took that move to be significant. "I'm not throwing you away for anyone else, but I cannot live like this anymore." Tony reached in the closet, pulled out a Sean John sweat suit, and threw it on. Then he reached for his luggage. "Women always complain that they want a good man, but when one presents himself, it's like most women don't know how to treat us." Tony glared at her as he stuffed a few things in his luggage. "But the ones that kick y'all ass get respect. Where that sort of logic comes from, I don't know." Tony took a deep breath before pulling the zipper. "All I'm saying is that I'm moving out to give you space to think about what you want to do." He jerked the zipper, pushing clothes into a second suitcase. "I don't want a half ass answer either. I want to know whether you're ready to make the necessary changes to be my wife, or if I should go ahead and start filing the divorce papers."

Maribel stared at him and didn't say a word.

"All it takes is food on the table, a clean house, my kids tak-

en care of, and my needs taken care of. I don't ask for much."
Tony lips curved into a sad, bitter smile as he shrugged. "Like
I said, the choice is yours." He could remember a time when
there wasn't a day that would go by without them indulging
in all the freaky sex in the world. He also couldn't forget the
romantic nights they'd spent feeding each other dinner before
cuddling.

"So that's it, huh?" she said, a hint of surprise in her tone as
she ran her French manicured fingers through her highlighted
mane of hair. "You're just gonna desert me and the kids?"

"I am not—" he stopped, realizing that he had no reason
to feel guilty. Technically, for a man who had taken her bullshit,
paid the bills without asking her for a dollar, and jumped whenever she or the kids wanted him to, he was totally within his
rights.

"Like I said, you'll have enough time to *think*!" He picked
the bags up off the floor, feeling a surge of relief as he headed
for the door.

Maribel's eyes widened when she glanced down at his
hands. Tears welled up in her eyes just before she lunged at
him, holding onto his sweatshirt; a sweatshirt that now hung on
his once-football sized frame

"You can't go!" She was now holding his sweatshirt in a
tight grip. "I promise I'll be the best wife. I'll cook, clean, do
whatever, but you can't leave. Who's gonna help me with the
kids, huh?" She wiped the tears from her face.

Her tears had always moved him. The pouted lips along
with the sniffs and sorry-ass face made her more like a spoiled
child, always getting her way—until now. For a minute he
wanted to give in, but he knew better. She would never change.
This wasn't the first time he'd put his foot down, but this was

the first time he truly meant it. Tony knew game when he saw it. Maribel was good for running straight game. This woman had "drama queen" stamped on her forehead. What about the nights he'd longed for her and had to settle for second best? What about the decision he'd made to take that insurance settlement and invest it in Tha Hustle so they would never knock on poverty's door again? Yes, he had made a mistake by allowing Chin to have so much control and allowing the man to follow his dick instead of his heart, but wouldn't make that mistake again. Tony Moreno deserved better.

"I'm sorry, baby, but I have to go." He pushed her hands off him, and walked to the door, feeling a little rush of blood go straight to his head. He closed his eyes and took a deep breath, steadying his heart and mind. Opening the bedroom door, he called, "Tiffany,"

"Yes, Mr. Moreno" Tiffany came to the door with her jacket already on.

"Help me to the Audi with my bags please. I'm leaving."

"Is everything okay?" she inquired softly, almost lovingly.

"It will be once I leave here," Tony responded picking the bags up off the ground.

Tiffany disappeared for a few moments as Tony grabbed the last of his things.

The nurse walked back in and glanced up at him with a smile, before inquiring, "Ready?"

Tony glanced down at the shapely woman, grinning though his heart had become heavy with pain. "Thank you." Then he turned to his wife, the source of that pain. "I'll call you."

Maribel took one look at the nurse and muttered, "Fucking bitch" before lunging at Tiffany. "You're not getting my fucking house you whore." Her fist connected with Tiffany's cheek, knocking her to the ground.

With a good kick to the stomach, Tiffany pushed Maribel off her. Tiffany now had a fistful of Maribel's hair in her hands.

"Enough," Tony barked, pulling Maribel away from his nurse.

Tiffany got up to her feet, straightened her uniform, fixed her hair and said. "Are you ready?"

"You gonna be one sorry ass bitch when I'm through with you," Maribel threatened.

"No, Mrs. Moreno, you're the sorry ass bitch because you can't recognize a good man when you see one."

Tony grinned at the woman's statement. He took one last glance at his wife with a tear forming in the corner of his eye. The thought of hurting her hurt him too. But after being given a second chance, and having been screwed by three other conniving females, he knew from here on out, sympathy would be the last thing he would feel for anyone. She'd either become a true wife or just another ex like the rest who came before.

"One woman in check—three more to go," Tony whispered.

Tiffany opened the door, allowing the silence of the hallway to grace their presence.

He glanced at the gorgeous woman holding onto his arm, wondering how Tiffany would react if she found out about the deadly side of him.

Chapter 11

THA HUSTLE RECORDS: NYC

*P*orsha sat perched in her office chair as she picked up the phone to dial BabyGirl's number. She had thought long and hard about giving up the record company. She decided it would be the only way for her to ease her guilt. Tha Hustle Records had always been Chin's heart and soul. When she sat in the office, thoughts of her part in the murders that night lingered. The office still reeked of death and she would never forget the look on Chin's face the moment he realized that BabyGirl had made Porsha a part of her scheme.

She had strolled into the office while Chin was having his morning coffee. He was surprised to see BabyGirl unannounced, but was more surprised when Porsha pulled up beside her. A puzzled look froze his face like yesterday's horrible blizzard; however, she never entertained his look. Deep down in her heart, she wanted to give him a second chance, but coming after experiencing such betrayal, saving him from being killed was out of the question.

"I should have listened to my heart." She placed the phone at her ear, listening to the tone. Porsha sensed disaster coming down the line, and with Tony being alive, no one knew what to expect. No one had heard from him or knew of his whereabouts; nor had he stepped forward to reclaim his portion of the empire. Turning the record company over to BabyGirl and Dimples would be best. She didn't have the heart to carry on with it. And she knew from experience, Tony Moreno's silence could be deadly.

Porsha dialed the number and waited for a response.

"Hello," BabyGirl's calm voice purred from the other end.

"It's Porsha."

BabyGirl hesitated before asking simply, "What's up?"

"I would like us to meet briefly in my office tomorrow." Porsha spun her chair around to look out onto the street. Chin always loved a clear view of the world below. A view Porsha now enjoyed when she was stressed and needed to take her mind off the trouble brewing in "paradise."

"Pertaining to?" She heard the attitude lingering in Baby-Girl's voice.

Carefully choosing her words, she knew her next statement had to be clear and convincing, something she learned while in law school.

"Making business more profitable and a wonderful opportunity for you and Dimples to make extra money." Money was Dimples' weakness and success was BabyGirl's. By putting it that way, Porsha had covered both.

"Okay," BabyGirl replied softly, as though she were still uncertain. Despite the things that connected them, there was still a lot of bad blood between them.

"So let's meet up at the office tomorrow at one so we can go and have lunch."

"No problem, we'll be there."

"Sounds good," Porsha responded as if she had no concerns at all. As soon as the two women signed on the dotted line, she would be home free. Erasing all traces of her having anything to do with the company was paramount.

Slowly placing back the receiver, she clasped her hands and leaned back in the chair as the ultimate plan for revenge formed in her head. She flipped through her Rolodex and plucked out a single card before dialing again.

"Captain Mahoney," the voice answered on the other end.

"This is Porsha Hilton. I need to know the status on our little deal."

"I'm working on it, it's not like things used to be when I was helping you and Chin." She could hear the annoyance in his voice. Frankly, she didn't care because she was paying him thousands of dollars for the tapes.

"Don't fuck with me, Mahoney," Porsha warned.

"I'm trying… that's all I can do, and if I were you I would get it together because Garfin is on his way there."

Porsha sucked her teeth and hung up her phone. As she placed her face in the palm of her hands she muttered, "I need those tapes from the building."

Unbeknownst to Porsha, she was not the only person Mahoney was working with.

Chapter 12

THA HUSTLE RECORDS: NYC

*S*oft drops of snow fell on the windshield of the Range Rover. The windshield wiper worked profusely to clear the glass as Dimples and BabyGirl sat awaiting Porsha. A FedEx truck pulled up beside them totally blocking them in. BabyGirl watched the deliveryman as he spoke through a headpiece. *He is sexy,* she thought.

"What the hell!" Dimples said, pressing the button to release the lock on the door. Dimples' red Kenneth Cole Leather Jacket accentuated her curvy shape, but certainly wasn't warm enough for the freezing temperatures. BabyGirl watched as Dimples walked around to the driver's side of the truck to give him a piece of her mind. To her disappointment the driver wasn't in there, but had already headed into the building.

"Such an inconsiderate bastard," she yelled as got she back into the car and slammed the door.

BabyGirl laughed at her friend's apparent frustration.

Turning to face her friend, Dimples asked, "Would you mind telling me what's so fucking funny?"

"The other day you were acting so calm when Dragon and I got into it, and now you're pissed off about something that's real petty."

"Whatever, bitch!" she hissed. "You weren't so calm when Child Protective Services denied you custody of Brianna because of your ongoing domestic dispute with Dragon."

A serious look crossed BabyGirl's face, "That is a different story."

"And I'm pretty sure you won't be so calm when you're standing in front of the judge two weeks from now."

BabyGirl turned her head to face the building.

"I thought so," Dimples taunted.

As the cars and pedestrians carefully maneuvered their way through traffic, the snow was beginning to fall heavier. Waiting was beginning to try their patience. It was five minutes after one and Porsha was still nowhere in sight. Dimples dug through her pocketbook for her cell.

"This heifer's behavior when it comes to time is beginning to get on my last nerve."

BabyGirl nodded in agreement while noticing the FedEx guy walking toward his truck. She made it her personal business to step out of the car and approach him before Dimples did.

"Excuse me," she called to the driver who by now had stepped into the back of truck and was rumbling through the packages while talking through his ear piece.

Her presence startled him; he looked at her and continued on with his conversation.

"Excuse me," she yelled this time stepping up in his truck without permission.

"Can I help you?" The Fed Ex guy now turned his attention to her and asked with a nasty attitude. "And why are you standing in my truck?"

"Well, if your inconsiderate ass wasn't blocking us, I

wouldn't be in your truck speaking to you right now."

"Let me call you back," she heard him telling the person on the line.

He stared her up and down before pointing to the street sign. "I'm pretty sure you can read what the sign says right there. However, in case you can't, let me do the honors. '*No Standing, except Commercial Vehicles loading and unloading. 3 hour time limit.*' I know you understand that. And judging by the looks of things," he gestured to the Rover, "that's not a commercial vehicle."

"I don't give a fuck what it says, the issue is you're blocking us in right now, and we'd like to get out."

"You know there is a thing called manners." He pressed the issue, while continuing with his work. "It can take you a lot farther."

His feistiness was turning her on.

"Well, maybe you need to teach me some?" she added, her tone softer than before.

"Okay, I will. We'll start first with me asking politely, *Please* get out of my truck."

She enjoyed his sassiness, it reminded her of herself. She actually liked the challenge and would've kept it up if time permitted. Especially since the man was fine. Light skin with hazel eyes, muscular build, deep dimples, and low cut hair —all of that combined with his attitude made him even sexier.

She wanted him after giving him a thorough look, and decided to go in for the kill. Shit, why not? The dumb fuck she had at home was acting up anyway.

"Okay, I'll leave...once you give me your number so we can continue our conversation."

The guy stopped and turned to face her. "Are you flirting with me?"

"Well, it depends on how it looks from your perspective."

"Well, from my perspective…" he placed the package on the seat and gazed in her eyes. "…you're flirting with me."

She gave him a sexy grin which, from her experience, most men couldn't resist. "I don't think it's a crime."

"No, it's not."

She took a gander at the building. Porsha still hadn't come out. Instead, she saw a portly white man with graying hair, he seemed vaguely familiar, but she couldn't place him at the moment he exited the building. She turned back to her intended prey.

"Well, are you going to give me the number or what? I don't have all day."

"Fair exchange ain't robbery," the guy added.

"I must agree. Fair exchange is never robbery. But it also depends on the exchange …"

"I apologize for coming at you like that," Fire, the truck driver said from the FedEx truck.

"Accepted," she yelled back.

"Well, well, if it ain't the love connection." Dimples dipped in as BabyGirl made her way back over to the car. "Here I am cursing at his inconsiderate ass and you're just as inconsiderate as he is."

Porsha, who now decided to join them, was standing behind Dimples peeking her head around to get a look at the guy. BabyGirl caught the flash of jealousy in Porsha's eyes.

Chapter 13

I-95: NYC

An early morning ride on the I-95 was just the thing Dragon needed to clear his head and figure out his next move. On any normal day, Dragon's BMW would leave tire marks on the concrete as he pushed it above 90 miles per hour. But for some reason, with all the drama that had been unfolding, rushing to get home was the last thing on his mind. Despite the recent blow up with BabyGirl, he wanted to go back home. He was tired of being bounced from place to place, and he honestly felt his so-called friends were getting tired of him staying with them. The unstableness in his life reminded him of when he was young and was going from home to home. He had just finished partying up a storm with a few of his celebrity friends at Club 40-40. His own comfortable bed was calling him. Dragon fidgeted with the buttons on the radio until deciding to leave it on KISS 98.7 FM, needing something to keep him awake until he made it to the home he shared with Baby-Girl. He didn't know what to expect. He had not been home since the incident, nor had he called her to apologize about the baby.

As the disc jockey's voice faded, the song "Far Away" by Kindred played through his speakers. He was so caught up in the couple's message of chucking it all and getting away, he didn't realize he was now singing along with the catchy tune. Something about the song captivated him. How he wished to be far away from New York, the drama surrounding Tha Hustle Records, and Tony Moreno. No telling what he was up to. Dragon also wasn't sure whether or not he was on the top of BabyGirl's death list. All the drama that life had dealt him recently had him crumbling on the inside, and for the first time in his life, he believed a thug could cry.

He continued driving at the speed limit while cars zoomed past him on the left and right sides. Some were even rude enough to cut in front of him, but he didn't give the normal middle finger response. The scenery playing out before his eyes was similar to his life—as fast as people came into his life they were out of it in the blink of an eye. As soon as Dragon thought he was on solid ground, someone knocked him over pushing him into quicksand.

As he continued to cruise, he explored one of the biggest fears he had. One of the pictures Garfin had in the file was of his stepmother and his siblings. How in the world had Garfin figured Dragon had anything to do with their deaths? His father was to blame for them. Dragon blamed Jason Bentley for the unfortunate turn of events that led to his mother's addiction and the demise of the family.

Dragon's life was never slated to be perfect, especially once his father had abandoned him. How he had ended up a mirror image of his father—a dragon in every monstrous sense of the word—Dragon could only guess.

An argument between his parents angered his father to the

point the man had packed his bags. Then to cause Anita, his mother, more pain, his father said, "Daquan, pack your bags, I'm taking you to Disney World." As his father walked through the door that night, he told Dragon, "I'll be back for you."

Like a young, impressionable fool, Daquan had followed his father's instructions; filling his little brown case with clothes. He knew would make his father see how much of a big boy he was.

Nights passed and days came and went and still no sign of his dad. For two weeks straight, a ten-year-old Daquan refused to leave the window or take off his clothes. He had fallen asleep in them night after night.

He wished upon hope that his father would burst through the door, making good on his promise—as he had before. His mother cried every night, as she tried to get Daquan away from the window and into bed, or to take a meal. He would rush home from school every day in hopes that his father would be waiting. Eventually, Daquan came to grips with reality. Sadness and anger settled in his little heart.

Anita found her own way of dealing with his father's leaving—first by drinking, then by acquiring some new shady-looking friends, and eventually turning to crack. Weeks after his father left, his mother could barely function, and when she did, it was nowhere in the realm of what she had once been. There were days he'd find his mother on her knees giving head to some man or woman, each time making Dragon angrier at his father for not returning. Then her actions put both of them in danger.

Sometimes if it was too cold, strange people would come into their house and stay for days at a time, using his mother in one way or another. Once there was a thick, brown-skinned man with a husky voice laying on the only piece of furniture left, since his mother had sold everything else. Daquan watched his mother as she lay curled up on the floor and the man stood over her yelling, "Bitch, is that what you call sucking dick?"

The man struck his mother with his fists. Daquan ran to his mother's aid only to be lifted and slammed into a corner by the man's beefy hand.

"This is grown folks business! Stay the hell out of this."

The man gave Daquan a cold stare, sending chills up his young body. Tears streamed down Anita's face; matching the ones her son was trying to hold in. So Daquan sat there, watching as his mother got the shit kicked out of her and plotting what he could do to protect himself from that point on.

There were nights when Dragon would go to bed without dinner; sometimes water was all that was available. With his mother's descent into drugs, he had found another way to survive. Anthony Smith had made him one of his workers and the money gave Dragon the ability to save up and make the trek to find his father. He obtained the information on his father's whereabouts through a family member.

As he got off the Amtrak near Maryland's airport, he hopped a cab, which took him on a ride through the decent areas of Baltimore. Dragon passed areas with enormous homes set in gated communities, totally different from the little apartment his mother had in Harlem. This is the life he wanted and couldn't wait to have.

"You've reached your stop," the driver spoke

He trailed up the path with his suitcase in tow, rang the bell, and waited.

A beautiful Hispanic woman answered, holding a young baby in her arm.

"Can I help you?"

"I'm here to see my father, Jason Bentley."

The lady looked him up and down, eyes narrowing at his torn up shirt and wrinkled and tattered corduroy pants, before yelling, "Jay, who's this boy at my door talking about you're his father? You better straighten out this shit, Papi; we don't have room for any of your little bastards."

Daquan wanted to curse the woman out, but remembered that if he was going to live in the place, he'd have to get along with the woman—whoever she was.

Jason Bentley, who was six foot-two and had a dark complexion, came to the door. He too asked, "Can I help you?"

That question pierced Daquan's heart, but he manned up and still replied, "It's me daddy—Daquan."

The coldness in his father's gaze matched his voice as he looked down at the suitcase clutched in his son's hand and asked, "What do you want?"

"Mom's too strung out to take care of me. Child Protection is going to take me away if I don't find somewhere to go. I want to come live with you."

Jason Bentley shook his head, grimacing as he ran a shaky hand through his low cut curly hair. "That's not my problem anymore. I have a new family. We can't take you in."

Daquan's heart sank. This was the second time his father could have made a difference, instead, he didn't care. Daquan turned to walk back down the path, not knowing how he was going to get back to the city now that the cab was gone.

"Since you came all the way from New York …"

Daquan froze, wondering what would come next.

"I'll allow you to stay here for a week."

What difference would a week make? Daquan would still

be in the same situation.

"I'll give you some money and I swear to God, I'd better not hear from you again." He got close to the child's face, "Understood?"

Daquan stared deep into the face of the man he had once adored. A man he didn't recognize anymore. "Yeah, I understand."

A week would be more than enough time to exact a fitting revenge. His father would pay for mistreating his mother. He would make him pay for all the times he stood by the window, for allowing his mother to turn to drugs, and for making his life a mess.

Within the week, Daquan was able to take in the luxury and lavishness of his father's new life, seething at the fact that his siblings were given the most expensive clothing, shoes, and toys, all while Daquan grew up enduring dirty clothing, pet mice, and strange people coming in and out his home. His father would hold them, cuddle them, comfort them, and play with them, but would barely say two words to Daquan.

His stepmother was barely civil to him, and sometimes was so ungodly cruel that Daquan went to bed crying—especially when the woman tuned her lips to talk about his addict of a mother or the fact that Daquan was nothing and she couldn't wait for him to leave.

His stepmother rambled through his things one day when he went out for a walk and found a gun sewn into the bottom of his suitcase. She gave it to Jason and they argued until she said, "To hell with a week. That little bastard needs to go now!"

His father came in, placed the gun back in the suitcase, and told Daquan, "Tomorrow you leave," and walked out.

Later that night, his father left an envelope on the dresser next to the bed and didn't even bother to say goodbye before leaving for work. That was the thing that made Daquan snap. Once again, the man was walking out of his life without so much as a goodbye. How simple the word was—two syllables. Was his new family that important?

Daquan slipped on a pair of gloves, reached into his suitcase, walked into the living room, aimed the gun he had purchased to protect his mother and himself from her customers, and shot that Hispanic bitch in the heart. He followed with a shot each to his baby sister's heads and his brother's heart. The house went dead silent.

The cab pulled away from the curb and dropped him at the bus station. Before Daquan stepped onto the Greyhound, he made one last call to his father and said, "Now it's your turn to feel pain."

The last he heard, Jason Bentley was doing triple life sentences in prison.

Daquan returned to Harlem to find that his mother's condition had worsened. The only reason Daquan had a roof over his head was because Shondra, his mother's friend, felt sorry for the two of them and took them in. Eventually, having the extra people in her home became a burden and a source for Shondra's pain and discontent. Her boyfriend beat her because he wanted the freeloaders out of her house, though he was a freeloader himself.

Two weeks before winter recess, Daquan—now named Dragon—was walking down Malcolm X Boulevard with his friends, happier than he had ever been since his mother had quit smoking crack. She was even attending weekly meetings. As he got closer to home, he saw the circle of people gathered in front of Shondra's house as if there was some sort of church function or something going on. At first Dragon didn't pay it much mind, but then Shondra burst through the door, running, crying, and yelling, "I'm so sorry. I'm so sorry."

Puzzled about the woman's ranting, Dragon asked, "What's wrong?"

"Your mother...I'm so sorry—" She reached out to hug him, but he moved back. The worst thought came to his mind, but he didn't want to believe it was true.

"Tell me what happened."

"Your mother was on her way to Anthony's base and she turned up dead."

Those were the last words he heard for a few minutes as his mind went numb.

Walking past the distraught woman, Dragon went into the house and got Shondra's man gun.

With one destination in mind, he wasn't as careful as he should have been making the journey to the nearest drug den. Drivers honked their horns, tires screeched, but nothing made him stop. The temperature had to be close to fifteen degrees, however, the cold beating on his skin and the frost in the air didn't matter. His body wouldn't allow him to feel anything but anger.

St. Nicholas Street wasn't as crowded as usual. Speed, the local drug dealer, was preparing to leave. Dragon broke into a run so he wouldn't miss the man.

"Hey! Hey!" he said, pulling up to the tall, brown-skinned man.

"Have you seen my mother?"

Speed stopped dead in his tracks before giving Dragon a quick glance, then opening the door to his Acura.

"Yeah, earlier. I think she was following Mike into that

brown building over there." He explained that Mike was pissed because she had smoked the entire stash of crack he had her store in her apartment, even though he told her it didn't belong to him.

Mike was one motherfucker Dragon couldn't stand.

Speed didn't entertain the conversation for much longer. Cold weather didn't make people very talkative.

"Go check it out," Speed urged, knocking the snow off his boots before getting into his car and pulling off.

Mike and his friends were in the hallway sitting on the steps eating Chinese food and drinking Coronas. Mike's lips curled into a sneer.

"What the fuck you want, you bitch-ass nigga?" he growled.

"Where's my mother?" Dragon replied with a cold blank stare.

"Well, if it ain't the little brave heart strolling up thinking he can be all stern and shit like that." He shivered sarcastically. "I'm supposed to be *scared*?"

Then Mike moved his box of Chinese food out of the way as he stood. Dragon took in the position of Mike's cronies before asking again, "Where is my mother?"

He wanted to see if the man would have the guts to speak the truth to his face.

"Well, if you really want to know, your mammy's taking a nap…a very long nap." Then Mike sealed his statement with a sinister laugh as if it were some type of joke.

Dragon didn't blink or think. He emptied two bullets into Mike, then swung to his left hitting another man, flooring him the moment he opened his mouth.

The last man standing managed to say, "I didn't have nothing to do with it." He inched backward. "Mike helped in killing her and so did Anthony Smith. I didn't—"

Dragon shot his punk ass, too.

Swerving into another lane and barely avoiding an accident brought him back to the fact that he should have been concentrating on the road. Street hustling had never been his thing, especially because he hated how drugs destroyed his mother. He wanted to be a lawyer or a doctor, but the streets turned him on to a grim reality that life wasn't easy. But there were other ways to survive.

Rapping was his dream, but supporting himself and his mother's habit meant selling nickel and dime bags, and who better to sell it for than the man who smoked his mother, Anthony Smith, BabyGirl's father.

Chapter 14

Becco Italian Restaurant: NYC

*A*ll three ladies were greeted at the door by Pedro, their host, who led them to a reserved table adorned with a white linen table cloth, white china, and fancy silverware. He flashed out their napkins, placing them on their laps. The atmosphere was warm and inviting, dark colors created an intimate feeling which was the reason the place was one of the favorite Italian restaurants for lovers.

"Nice choice, Porsha," Dimples complimented while looking over the menu.

"I come from a family with money, so I'm familiar with the finest restaurants New York has to offer." She glanced at both of the women, noticing the look of disgust written all over BabyGirl's face, but held her composure.

Dimples inquired, "So what's the urgency? Why did we need to meet?"

"Well ladies," Porsha took a sip of water before continuing on. "I've been doing a lot of thinking."

"And?" both ladies replied.

The slender young Italian waiter stood by Dimples, asking, "What will you have today?"

"Yes can we have Buffalo Mozzarella and Crostini for appetizers? I would like to order a T-bone steak with mashed potatoes, lettuce and tomatoes. I'll also have a glass of Moet and Chardon."

Turning to BabyGirl he rolled off, "Sig.na il vostro ordine per favore."

"Excuse me?" BabyGirl responded with a lift of her eyebrow.

"That's Italian for, Miss, your order please," Porsha translated with a haughty tone.

"What about simple English?" BabyGirl mumbled.

Porsha glanced at her thinking, "*What the hell did Chin see in this ghetto ass bitch anyway?*"

"Well, in that case," BabyGirl said, pointing to a spot on the menu. "I'll have the Pan Fried Snapper Fillet with Marsh Samphire and Green Olive Tapenade."

"Anything to drink?" his blue eyes stared at BabyGirl.

"Yes, a glass of red wine."

Dimples ordered a King George Whiting Fillet in Beer Butter and thin chips along with Moet and Chardon. As the waiter left the table to fill their order, the tension began to thicken.

"I've been thinking a lot." Porsha emphasized, with a mild flourish. "About signing over the record company to you and I take the Restaurant and we can all have a piece in the nightclub."

"Why such a sudden change?" Dimples asked with suspicion in her voice and a wary expression.

"Fuck hip-hop, it's a waste of my time. I don't even listen to that shit anyway."

BabyGirl took a sip of her water and stared at Porsha. "Are you sure it's just hip-hop or is it because Tony is alive and you're worried about what he might do?"

Damn, the woman was smarter than she looked.

"Not at all," Porsha countered smoothly. "Hip-hop is just not me. Give me the neo-soul, R&B, or songs with some meaning...not a whole bunch of gibberish."

"Well, maybe you're right. I mean, Chin would want someone with knowledge and love for the music to run the company if he was alive," Dimples taunted.

"Don't you dare bring Chin into this," Porsha growled, glaring at Dimples.

"Someone's a little touchy," Dimples teased.

"You know what? I don't have to take this nonsense!" Porsha stood to leave.

"Sit your ass down," BabyGirl snapped. "Finish telling us about making this move. You're acting as if Chin's a motherfucking prized possession."

"Well, he must have been because you were fucking him too," Porsha shot back.

Water came shooting out of Dimples' mouth and her hand flew up to catch the rest.

"Bitch, please! Your man was fucking me and loving every minute of it, so *I* was the prized possession." BabyGirl's lips curled to a sneer.

"*And* he got me pregnant."

Porsha gasped.

"Yes, I was carrying his baby." BabyGirl leaned toward Porsha. "Shows how much respect he had for you."

Porsha took her glass of Moet and threw in BabyGirl's face.

BabyGirl shot out her fist and punched Porsha in the left side of her face. Porsha, a little dazed, responded with a left uppercut of her own. BabyGirl grabbed a fistful of hair and smashed her fist into Porsha's face.

People in the restaurant stopped eating and all eyes were focusing on the ladies going at each other.

The manager and waiters came rushing forward.

Dimples jumped in the middle shouting, "Ladies! Stop! Get it together!" She pulled BabyGirl off Porsha, who tried to get in once last punch.

"Miss Hilton, is everything all right?" The manager asked in a stiff tone.

"Yes, Maggie, everything's fine," Porsha straightened out her shirt. "I'm sorry. Could we resume lunch please?"

"Sure, but I will ask you ladies to refrain from fighting. If it happens again I will have to have you escorted out of the restaurant …"

The waiter, who remained nearby waiting for a signal to serve their food or to take it back in the kitchen, approached the table cautiously.

The auburn-haired manager nodded and the waiter proceeded to place the plates in front of each person, pour Porsha more Moet and Chardon, and ask, "Is everyone okay?"

"Yes," they chorused tightly.

No more words were exchanged between Porsha and BabyGirl. Dimples however, decided to inquire, "When can we sign the paperwork?"

"ASAP," Porsha spoke then cut a piece of her T-bone steak.

She quickly brought her eyes up from her plate, meeting BabyGirl's gaze head-on and taking in the deadly glint in her eyes. Porsha then looked in Dimples' direction just as she glanced at her watch, then pulled her cell out of her bag.

"Excuse me ladies, I have to make a quick phone call."

Pulling out her chair she added, "Please act civilized while I'm gone."

Porsha gave her a fake smile. BabyGirl didn't bother to answer.

Who the hell was so important that she had to call them in the middle of an important meeting?

Chapter 15

96ᵀᴴ STREET: MANHATTAN, NYC

"The suspicions you had all along are now confirmed," Captain Mahoney spoke over the phone. "Your wife is cheating with your cousin and we have proof of such."

No words left Tony's lips as he sat on the bed taking in everything. The only sound that could be heard was the faint sounds of the television in the background. Nurse Haywood was scheduled to show up any minute and he wanted to wrap up the conversation before she arrived.

"I want all the tapes and pictures you have." Tony placed a cigar at the corner of his mouth and pulled his body further up on the bed. He blew out a few puffs of smoke with his eyes fixated on the television. His cousin and his wife had both crossed a line they weren't supposed to and they would both be dealt with accordingly.

"I just want to inform you that this will be the last bit of information I will be able to give you; things are getting a little hectic and I don't –."

"Whatever." Tony cut him off and closed the cell phone, before flinging it on the side table. Getting up off the bed, he proceeded to rub lotion over the remainder of his body. Nurse Haywood flashed in his mind. Tony appreciated how she took care of him, so he planned to surprise her with a gift.

With the combination of Maribel cheating, him not being around his children, and almost dying, Tony felt like he was being punished for sins committed in the past, especially for the incident with King. He figured that had to be the reason the world around him was crumbling. He had lost his family, everything he had worked so hard to build, and almost his life. And to think, he once had to school Chin on how to keep his females in check.

A sigh escaped his lips as he rubbed lotion on his hands and arms, working his way up over the scroll which contained the synopsis of his life. The tattoo engraved on his hand, reminded him of the hardships he had been through and encouraged him not to give up.

He was just about finished when the green towel hanging around his waist slipped. Getting a grip on it before it completely fell, he wrapped it tighter. His hands slightly bumped his dick and the thought of him of being without a woman for a while brought a rise to his manhood. Nurse Haywood was in for a treat.

"Ah..." he sighed, glancing on the dresser where the gift box was perched. The Audemars Piguet Facettes ladies watch cost him a lot, but he didn't regret it. The dark, sexy nurse was worth every dime. The way she cared whether he lived, and lived well, even when his own wife turned her back, made Tony ponder why he had married Maribel in the first place. Tony paused for a minute, wondering if he was slowly becoming like Chin—whipped. BabyGirl had been a deadly miscalculation on both their parts.

♡♡♡

When Chin first got a glance of BabyGirl; he wanted her

so bad he was willing to shell out $3,000 for her without even knowing a name. He remembered teasing Chin, talking about the fact that he was pussy locked. Chin was so busy defending himself, all Pit Bull, and Tony could do was laugh. Now Tony was doing the same thing.

❤❤❤

"What are you smiling about?" Nurse Haywood stood at the door with her arms folded.

Tony spun around totally forgetting he had given Nurse Haywood a key. The towel around his waist fell to the floor again, this time exposing a growing erection. Tiffany took a quick glance as Tony grimaced.

"No need to be embarrassed," she walked closer to him, placing her hands on his manhood, gently stroking it. "I washed it plenty of times when you were in a coma." A child-like giggle escaped her lips.

Tony wanted to say something but Tiffany didn't give him a chance. She walked out of the room, leaving the scent of her Chanel perfume and a full-blown erection behind.

Tony walked over to the door, peeking around the corner catching another good glimpse at her rounded ass. Questions floated through his mind: Did she have a clue how much he was feeling her?

He dressed in a simple pair of boxers and white T-shirt, topping it off with a silk lounging robe in case something popped off. He ran a brush through his waves and sprayed on some cologne before taking one last look in the mirror.

Making his way to the living room, the sound of Marc Anthony crooning "You Sang to Me," filled the area. She looked up at him, asking, "Aren't you going to finish getting dressed?"

"Eventually," he lied smoothly. "But I couldn't help but come out and see how beautiful you are."

"Whatever." She pushed his shoulder and giggled. He loved that sound.

"Go get dressed," she ordered.

Tony didn't move.

"Why are you staring at me like that?"

"You're beautiful," Tony said softly, trailing a hand through her hair.

"Thank you," she answered with a blush, crossing one leg over the other and forcing her skirt to ride up, giving him more of a view.

Tony leaned in closer, planted an unexpected kiss on her lips, and then pulled away. An uncomfortable silence expanded between them.

"What was that for?" she inquired.

"I have no idea, I'm sorry."

"Go put some clothes on."

Returning to the bedroom, he came back out seconds later with his hands behind his back, still dressed the same.

Tiffany laughed. "Tony, go get dressed!"

"I bought you something," he handed her the gift box.

She stood, allowing him to place it in her hands. "You didn't have to." She shook her head and gave it back—unopened. "You know I can't accept a gift from you Tony, I'm just doing my job." She glanced down after the word job, as if she was embarrassed about something.

Gently turning her face toward him, he stared in her eyes before saying, "Will you please accept my gift?"

Slowly, almost reluctantly, she extended her hands, took the gift from his massive hands and opened it. Her jaw went slack.

Inside laid an 18-carat white gold Audemars Piguet watch. She scanned it, noticing the pink baguette sapphires and white mother of pearl dial.

"This must have cost you a fortune." She reached out to Tony, embracing him.

She felt so good in his arms; he kissed her lips once more, then stopped to gaze in her eyes to gauge her response.

Triffany pulled away. "I think it's time for me to go." She reached for her belongings.

Her eyes told him she wanted him, but maybe her mind said something else. Tony stood behind her, kissing her on her neck this time. She didn't stop him. Instead, a slight moan escaped her lips. He slowly reached around her body, caressing her perky breasts.

"Ummm…" she held on to the back of the sofa.

Tony lifted her shirt, continued to kiss down the center of her back all the way to the top part of her round ass and paused, "Do you want me to stop?"

"If I wanted you to stop," she whispered. "I would've done that a long time ago."

With his question answered, he spun her around and raised her hand above her head, while still kissing her soft lips. He pulled her white shirt up, taking it off and exposing the Victoria's Secret bra which covered her perfectly shaped breasts. Moving from her lips, he kissed her neck, and then between her breasts, carefully working his way toward her waist. He leaned in closer so she could feel his erection pressing against her body.

Using her right hand, she reached down and stroked his manhood. Tony pulled down her bra, cupping one of her breasts in his massive hand as he leaned in and used his tongue on the other. She shivered with pleasure, tilting her head back and wrapping her slender legs around Tony's back as she pulled him down on the sofa.

"No, get back up," he demanded.

She gave him a puzzled look; however, she didn't question him. He removed her jeans and anticipated entering her soft center and working her into a frenzy. He hadn't been turned on like this in a while and he planned on taking his time to savor every minute of it. Her pants were off, and the thong was lost in her perfectly shaped ass. Tony slowly kissed each of her ass cheeks before following with soft bites. He slowly tickled her clit at the same time.

Her moans grew louder and her vagina was soaking wet, which made Tony even hornier. He continued to kiss her back, thighs, and ass, as her body pressed further in the sofa. The angle she was bended over in allowed Tony to see everything perfectly. His tongue salivated like the dogs that were tested in Pavlov's theory. Unable to control himself, he kneeled on the floor behind her spread cheeks, and positioned his head so his tongue could lick her pussy.

"Oh...God," she now moaned.

Moving his tongue in and out of her opening, she gyrated on his mouth. Tony slowly moved his tongue from her sweet opening, and began sucking on her clit.

"Don't stop," she begged in between moans. Juices flowed from her inside like the Nile River.

Her clit was slowly swelling in his mouth and he didn't hesitate to suck a little harder.

"You like how it tastes?"

Tony knew it tasted good, but couldn't answer with a mouthful of pussy. Rising up off the floor, they switched position and she was now on top of his face—riding. Tiffany caressed her breasts and stroked Tony's dick while he licked her.

"I...I...I'm cumming," she cried. Her body shivered as she grabbed Tony's head and pressed it further in.

"Oh...oh, baby," she purred, riding him faster and harder as her juice poured all over Tony's face. He caught every drip without missing a beat.

She smiled as she slid off Tony's face and headed straight for his thick dick. She licked her lips in anticipation while her slender fingers caressed his balls. Tony gripped the back of the sofa, as a pair of sexy lips gripped his shaft. She moved her head up and down slowly, while using her tongue to tease the tip of Tony's dick every now and then. Tony's legs stiffened and his toes curled as the intensity of the sucking caused him to shake as if he were having a seizure.

"Baby, that feels so good," The words rolled off Tony's lips.

On the verge of cumming, Tony eased her off his dick, cupped her in his hands, and placed her on his dick. She bounced up and down as if she were a basketball dribbling down a court. Her pussy held a tight grip on his dick, as he moved in and out of her love box. Their lovemaking continued for another half hour before Tony climaxed. Lying on her shivering, moist body; he kissed every inch of her face. He was feeling her before, but Tony was slowly falling for her.

The bright, full moon shone through the window, as she lay comfortable in Tony's arms. Lighting a cigar, Tony laid back and smiled as he thought about the next move he was going to make.

It's time to shake things up, he thought.

Chapter 16

NYACK: NYC

"The nerve of that bitch," BabyGirl growled, while rubbing the left side of her head. A knot from the fight earlier in the restaurant was slowly forming at the corner of her head. She wanted to hurry home and place some ice on it to prevent it from getting any bigger.

She would have to get rid of Porsha sooner or later; today confirmed that she was still jealous where Chin was concerned. It was only a matter of time before Porsha tried to kill her or turn her over to the police.

The more she tried to distance herself from having to use deadly force to cover her tracks, the more opportunities arose that made her want to do exactly that. It wasn't the first time BabyGirl had to deal with someone working against her, and she was pretty sure it wouldn't be the last.

Using her right leg to tap the brake of her brand new Mercedes, she put on her right turn indicator, checked her side mirror, and switched lanes. Her Benz now cruised across the lighted Tapanzee Bridge. The sight of the water, the boats docked, and the houses that stood on the hill reminded her that having them had always been her American dream. Now that she had achieved it, she had no intention on having anyone ruin it, especially not a smart ass lawyer who was dumb enough to get involved with a man who was way out of her league.

Tony was another one on her agenda, but she figured if she could get rid of Porsha first, she wouldn't have to worry about the police tapping her door quite as soon. Tony wouldn't mention her to the police. He would settle the score on his own terms.

Her cell vibrated and she took a quick glance at the unfamiliar number. She hesitated to answer it at first, but curiosity kicked in and she soon flipped it open.

"Hello."

"Hey, sexy," the unfamiliar masculine voice responded on the other end.

BabyGirl answered with an uncertain, "Hi."

"You forgot about me already?"

"I guess," she said in a dry tone, racking her brain trying to figure out who it might be.

"It's your secret admirer," he crooned, his voice both seductive and sexy.

"Oh really?" Sarcasm laced her voice.

"Yes."

"Listen, love," she snapped. "If it was any other time, I'd be up for it. But right now I'm tired, hungry, and irritated, so if you don't identify yourself in a few, I'll familiarize your ass with the dial tone faster than lightening."

"Oh, someone's had a bad day," he teased.

"Look—"

"It's Fire, the Fed Ex guy whose truck you had the balls to step into."

"Are you just now getting my message?" she inquired.

"No, I actually meant to call you back, but I was busy catching up with something."

"Um-Hmm," she replied pursing her lips.

"You mad at me, love?" he asked.

"Not at all."

"Kinda forgot about you since you took so long to call,"

"Wow," he replied.

"How are you anyway?" She asked in a tiresome tone.

"I'm fine. You have so many boyfriends that you can't remember who's calling?" he inquired.

"Probably less than the number of girls you have blowing up your phone," she tossed back.

He chuckled in the background before saying, "You got jokes, huh?"

Holding a firm grip on the steering wheel, she made a left turn. She was now only two blocks from her home.

"So what are you getting into tonight?" Fire inquired.

"On my way home to relax."

"Been working hard all day, huh?"

"You know it."

She could hear water running in the background. The road became darker as she continued on her way. "They need to put street lights on these freakin' streets," she mumbled.

"Who are you talking to?" Fire asked.

Had she said that out loud? "Myself."

"Someone needs some mental health counseling," he suggested, which brought on more laughter.

"Whatever, they just need to put lights on these damn streets."

A few houses from her driveway, she noticed a shadow lurking near her front door.

"Fire, I think someone's trying to break into my house." She pressed the brake and pulled over. The shadow moved again, and she saw a tiny orange light moving randomly.

"Where are you?"

"By my house, duh!"

"Quit with the sarcasm! Drive past your home and call the police."

"Okay."

BabyGirl wasn't a punk, but she wasn't stupid either. Fire's advice was good.

"What's your address? I'm going to call the police too."

She hesitated. Not willing to give a stranger her address, she said, "I'll call you back."

"Don't hang—"

"Fire, let me call you back." She hung up, cutting off his next statement.

She inched up, checking out the car near the curb in front of her house. The license plate displayed the word, "*Dragon*."

She pulled her car in an empty space, walked up the driveway, and sure enough, Dragon was sitting on her front step.

She turned back up the path. "I'm calling the police right now,"

"Wait," he got up off the steps and darted toward her, grabbing her arm.

"Don't you fucking touch me, Daquan. What the hell are you doing here?"

"I want to talk to you."

"Yeah, you can do that while I'm calling the police." She began pressing the digits.

She felt the only reason he was sitting outside instead of snatching up all his junk inside was because she had changed the locks.

"Just put the cell phone down," he pleaded.

"Talk!" she shot at him.

"I've been doing a lot of thinking, BabyGirl, and I want to make it right between us." She tapped her feet on the ground with the cell still in hand. "I'm so sorry for the way I've treated you. You're a good woman and you deserve a good man." He came close, placing his hand on her shoulders. "I want to be that man."

She could smell bullshit a mile away and he was stinking up her driveway. She was ready to give him a tongue lashing when she suddenly remembered that Porsha needed to be dealt with. Dragon was the perfect candidate.

She didn't bother to respond to the 911 operator, instead, she hung up the cell phone, placed her keys in the door, and went inside.

She walked, placed her keys on the hook, and rubbed her temples.

"Are you a'ight?" he asked, following behind her.

She made sure to carefully choose her words before answering him.

"No, this bump on my head is starting to hurt me."

"How did you get that?" He spun her around to take a look at the bump. Just what she wanted as she was luring him in.

"Porsha! That bitch made me knock my head on the table."

"Why?"

"We had a fight."

"Over?" he asked, following her into the living room.

BabyGirl knew Dragon wasn't really interested in what she and Porsha fought about, he was just playing the game, trying to get back into her graces.

"You," she said simply, pushing his ego.

"Really?" His eyebrow shot up. BabyGirl held back a smirk.

She slipped onto the recliner, placed her legs up, and laid back.

"Yes, I told her that she's doing the rappers an injustice by not promoting their albums right, especially yours. I even told her she should give up the company or make you president since you know the business."

Dragon could barely conceal his elation. He got up from the sofa, pacing. "My album should've been further up the charts than where it is now. My shit is hot! And what's the fuckin' problem? Why she don't want to hand over the label? The vicious glint in his eyes had returned. Greed always worked. "What did she say?"

BabyGirl leaned forward in the recliner. "I don't know, but she had the nerve to say she didn't even like Hip-Hop or Rap, and fuck it because she didn't listen to that shit."

"I've got to go see her ass tomorrow because this bitch is bugging now. Music is my life. How the hell am I supposed to survive?—to feed myself?" Then he shot a quick look at her, adding, "...and my girl?"

BabyGirl rolled her eyes heavenward. When the fuck had he cared about her? And she didn't miss the fact that it took him a few moments to add her to his list.

She watched him pace back and forth.

"I don't trust her, Dragon," BabyGirl said, making her way to the kitchen. *Let him chew on that,* she thought. He was so vulnerable when it came to his career.

He followed her, leaning on the wall. "What makes you say that?"

"I think she's talking to the police." BabyGirl walked over

toward the kitchen to retrieve some ice. "She is just too edgy right now and is too quick to cover her tracks."

"So what you gonna do?" he asked.

"I don't have a clue." She placed the ice pack against her head. "I'm ready to just give it all up. It's not worth it."

Dragon crossed the room, placing his hands on her upper arms. "You've never given up before." Then he held her. "Plus, you've got me. If it comes to us having to deal with Porsha, you know I've got your back."

Just the words she wanted to hear. She lowered her lashes, allowing the softness of her voice to cover her glee. "I don't want you to get in more trouble than you already have, Dragon."

"I know." He kissed her forehead. "Yeah, but check this … if we don't do something we'll both be doing time."

She nodded, allowing him to embrace her, but not giving him an opportunity to do more. "I just need to rest. Tomorrow we can talk." She kissed him on the lips, knowing it signaled forgiveness and the fact that they had sealed the deal.

It was about time she was able to get something done without getting her hands dirty.

If Dragon believed she would ever forgive him for putting his hands on her and causing her to lose her child, he had another thing coming. Dragon *should* have learned a lot from what happened with Chin. The night he had left her for dead had sealed his fate.

"I'm about to blow your fucking brains out." The words pierced through her body as Chin held a nine millimeter against her forehead.

At first a giggle escaped her lip, before saying. "Nigga, you better stop playing and remove that shit from my head."

"Stop playing. Boy, get the fuck up off of me before I kick you in the nuts."

But the smile quickly left her face as she realized how serious he was."

Chin had found out she was involved with the robberies transpiring at the base. Prior to the incident, she attempted to come clean, but it was always the wrong time. That night, Chin beat her so badly that she swore if she ever recovered, she was going to kill him. It was the first and last time Chin would ever cross her.

Dragon was pushing it.

Chapter 17

THA HUSTLE RECORDS: NYC

The silence at Tha Hustle Records greeted him like a host in a restaurant. It was seven in the morning and Dragon hoped he could get to the office early to speak with Porsha without any distractions. Since she hadn't arrived yet, or so he thought, he saw it as the perfect opportunity to do a little snooping. As he made his way through the office, he noticed the changes Porsha had made. The walls that were once adorned with music plaques and pictures of Chin and Tony receiving awards or posing with various celebrities had been replaced with African Artwork. The place that was supposed to churn out hit records now didn't even crack the top ten. The long sofa that sat in the lobby, where Dragon and plenty of other artists who were waiting to get signed or to speak with either Tony or Chin, was replaced with two chairs, a brown small desk, and a table covered with women's magazines.

"What the fuck!?" he rifled through different African American magazines ranging from Sister to Sister, Essence, and O, which was Oprah's magazine. What happened to the F.E.D.S, Don Diva, and Dub, he thought, as he threw down the magazines, knocking some on the floor in the process.

"BabyGirl was right," he whispered. "This chick ain't feeling Hip-Hop." Dragon continued down the corridor, pausing at each picture that hung on the wall, carefully examining them. Right before he got to Nicole's desk, he remembered the beautiful woman who once sat behind it. He also remembered his part in Chin's secretary death.

Dragon continued down the hall of Tha Hustle Records. He wasn't much of a reader unless the words contained his lyrics. However, Claude McKay's poem "Harlem Shadow," which hung on the wall, stood out. It grabbed his attention because he was from Harlem. He read the poem in its entirety, but his gaze kept going back to the line, "Of poverty, dishonor, and disgrace." He reflected on each of the words. Poverty was something he knew firsthand. Dishonor? The way he'd destroyed his father's life spoke to that. Dishonor also caused him to get kicked out of Anthony Smith's camp. Dragon had disobeyed one of the five rules of the streets and BabyGirl's father never let him forget it.

❤❤❤

Sitting at the base, Dragon was a little out of it, forgetting that customers were about to come, he was having a conversation with his new found friend. Anthony Smith walked in; catching Dragon snorting coke right after an attempted robbery occurred on the base. Anthony beat Dragon in front of his crew. Between blows, Dragon saw the look of disgust they gave him. Then they dragged him to the street, leaving him for dead. *"Never get high on your own supply…"* was not only a line in one of the Notorious B.I.G.'s songs, but it is a true to life street rule – and he had violated it. Dragon recovered and formed a plan to get rid of Anthony Smith. The plan went perfectly.

❤❤❤

Dragon walked on until he stood in front of Porsha's office.

To his surprise, the door was open and she sat behind the desk looking over some paperwork.

He tapped on the door and walked in.

Porsha scribbled something on a piece of paper, looked briefly, and then grimaced when she noticed him. She continued working.

"Porsha, I'd like to speak with you."

"What breeze blew you in here?" she growled.

Dragon waited for her to say more, but she continued to work.

"Excuse me?"

"You heard the question," she said meeting his stare with an angry one of her own. She leaned back in the chair and clasped her hands. "You haven't shown up for any of your studio sessions, nor have you done any of the promo spots we had lined up, so why are you here now?"

"Cut the bullshit, Porsha," Dragon snapped back, as he walked closer to her desk. "It's not like you give a damn about the artists anyway. You're pretending and that's why I have a problem."

Dragon dropped down into the chair nearest the door.

"Give me a good reason why I should give a damn about your album? You don't give a damn, so why should I put my effort into anything when you don't even care?"

Dragon leaned forward in the chair. "First of all, you and I both know you don't like Hip-Hop. You're only in it for the money. And you only got into it in the first place because you were trying to impress Chin."

He let that sink in for a moment before adding, "Chin's not here now, so why are you still frontin', holding on to the label as if it means something to you?"

"Who the hell are you to walk up in my office questioning me and my relationship with Chin? Let me remind you, in case you forgot, that I am CEO of this company so I can hold on to it as long as I want, and do whatever I want."

"What you're doing is a fucking joke. The other artists are already complaining and some are trying to get deals with other companies. People are gonna blow it because you're messing up their cash flow. I suggest you cut me in on the label, since it's obvious you can't run it."

Porsha's bitter laughter filled the room. "Are you serious? Why would I give the company to an incompetent bastard like you?"

"What? You know what, let's see if you will be talking all that when Tony walks up in here and takes his shit back." Dragon replied.

"Don't you dare..." she pointed her index finger at him. "come in here and mention that man's name."

"Bitch, you better relax," Dragon got up from the chair, hand poised to strike.

She didn't move but her eyes dared him to let the blow fall. "Go ahead you pussy! Do what you do best."

"You bugging." Dragon said, lowering his hand and shaking his head.

"Let's get this straight. You're in my mothafucking office; therefore, you need to watch your tone and your weak ass approach. I'm not your girl, and I'm more connected than your little hoodrat girlfriend. So if you don't relax yourself up in here, I can have you wiped out faster than you think."

"Are you threatening me?" Dragon moved around the desk so they were eye to eye.

"Nigga, you'd better back the fuck up." She pulled out a

gun, pointing it at him. "Bottom line is—I don't have to play your cat and mouse games. If you want to talk about something constructive—like getting to the studio on time, like not blowing your promo tour —then fine; until then, get your damn shit together before you approach me in an unprofessional manner. Other than that, I suggest you raise your black ass out of my office because you've pissed me off. And I don't make threats, Mr. Bentley... I make promises."

Dragon stared at her and then inched away. He would definitely deal with Porsha later. The worst thing she could have ever done was point a gun at him without pulling the trigger.

Chapter 17

THA HUSTLE RECORDS: NYC

"Who the hell does he think he is walking up in my office demanding shit," Porsha fumed as she placed her gun back in her desk. Dragon was working her nerves. The moment those two hood rats signed on the dotted line, he would be their problem. Good riddance. She took a good look at the paper to insure that she had covered her ass completely.

Taking a sip of the Starbucks coffee her secretary had brought in after the commotion with Dragon, she got up and made her way to the window. Leaning on the glass, she scanned the streets of New York, and then focused on a pair of young lovers who were kissing and hugging.

Tears rolled down her face as she remembered Chin and longed for his touch, his kiss, his sarcastic jokes, and his smart ass mouth. How dare Dragon test her. Chin was her heart. So what if she didn't like Hip-Hop. She'd done whatever she had to do to keep the company afloat.

She sighed heavily, weariness settling in her soul. Lord she was lonely, so very lonely. The next man in her life, if there was one, would have to measure up to what Chin had done for her.

The intercom buzzed, interrupting her trip down memory lane. She walked back to her desk, glancing at the clock and mumbling, "About time," as she punched the intercom.

"Ms. Hilton?" Nicole's sultry voice on the other said with a slight edge that Porsha didn't miss.

"Yes, Nicole."

"There's a lady out here who would like to speak with you, but she refuses to give her name."

Porsha pulled out her chair. She resumed her place at the desk, wondering what kind of games BabyGirl was playing. "Well, tell her if she refuses to give her name, she needs to come back when she can."

Nicole tried relaying the message, but the female voice cut her off and demanded, "Hand me the phone."

"Hello!"

"Can I help you?"

"Well, first of all, let me introduce myself again, since you appear to have forgotten the voice," the woman started. "I'm Mrs. Moreno."

Porsha's heart slammed against her chest. She sat still contemplating her next move. "I guess Tony wasn't man enough to come up here, so he sent you."

Opening the top right hand drawer, Porsha put her hand on her gun for the second time that morning.

"No, he didn't send me. He doesn't know I'm here. I have some information I think will interest you."

Thinking for a moment, she finally said, "Come in."

The Maribel she met before had looked more like a desperate housewife—one of Tony's major complaints, if Chin told it correctly. The woman before her was gorgeous. The Ralph Lauren jeans and Liz Claiborne blouse hugged her frame. Her sleek look was finished with low cut Kenneth

Cole boots.

Porsha watched as Maribel glanced around the office. Maribel's eyes landed on the desk and trailed over to Porsha's hand, which was resting on a gun. Undaunted, Maribel pulled up a chair and said, "That's how I know we'll make the perfect team." She opened her purse and pulled out a gun of her own.

Porsha peered at the woman as she put the nine millimeter which she had taken out of the drawer and placed on the desk next to Maribel's.

"Great minds think alike."

Maribel sat back, waiting for Porsha to make the next move.

"What brought you here?"

Maribel sighed, shaking her head. "Why so feisty?"

"Quit the fucking games and get to the point," Porsha snapped.

She needed a drink and the mini-bar wasn't that far away, but she couldn't take her hand off the gun until Maribel was out of her office. Chin had taught her that much.

"Someone was real sloppy. Tony's still alive."

Maribel waited for Porsha's reaction. There was none. Her experience as an attorney taught her not to show emotions easily. Especially fear.

"And …?"

"It doesn't take a genius to figure out you're running the company that belongs to him. So it's only a matter of time before he strolls up in here and comes for you."

Maribel parted her lips to say something else, but the intercom buzzed. This time it was BabyGirl and Dimples out front and ready to do business. She could have had the woman ushered out the side entrance, but ruled against it. Tony wasn't just her problem; those two hood rats should be in on this, too.

"Send them in."

As she waited for BabyGirl and Dimples to enter, she turned to Maribel and asked, "Can I get you something to drink?"

"No thanks."

The door opened, and the two women entered, glanced at the stranger, and then looked in Porsha's direction.

"BabyGirl, Dimples, this is Mrs. Moreno. Tony Moreno's wife."

Porsha grinned, waiting for the fall out.

"And why is she here?" Dimples inquired, opening her bag as if she is searching for something. "We own the empire. Make sure you relay that to your husband. And if he ever tries anything," she moved closer to the Latina, "It'll be war."

Maribel gave her a little yawn. "Is that so?"

"Ask him about our track record and he'll be the first to tell you."

"Well it appears as if your *track record* isn't all that. He's still alive, ain't he?"

BabyGirl stepped up. "What do you want? As she said, the label and the restaurant are off limits, the money is ours. He threw the dice with Chin and lost. Are you prepared to die along with him?"

"Whoa! Nobody said anything about dying." Maribel stood, waving the women away. "No one said anything about dying. All I'm saying is that I know a way we can bring Tony down for good."

BabyGirl peered at her. "Why are you so willing to bring

down your own husband?" Her eyes narrowed in on Maribel. "You have it all good. So what's in it for you?"

The Latina paused as though weighing what to say next. "Tony left me for that pitiful nurse of his. He needs to be taught a lesson."

Dimples threw a look at BabyGirl, then Porsha before saying, "I'll give you credit, Maribel, for coming to us of all people to set him up ... you're one vindictive bitch."

"Not a smart move, killing your sole provider, but it shows guts."

Gathering her things, Maribel scribbled her number on a piece of paper. "Whenever you ladies are ready to do business, call me."

"What is it you have for us?" Porsha asked.

"The same thing you've been talking to the Captain at the 19th precinct about."

Porsha stood in shock and wondered how Maribel knew she'd been talking to the Captain. BabyGirl and Dimples snapped their neck in her direction.

"I don't know what you're talking about."

Walking back over to the desk, Maribel leaned in and whispered, "You're beloved Captain can't help you with those tapes, you know why? Because he is working with my husband, who now has the tapes, so if you want those tapes, contact me at your earliest convenience. You will be surprised how much you can do with the tapes."

Porsha took one more look at the paper that contained Maribel's number and tucked it away.

"You talking to the police, Porsha?" Dimples asked.

"Not *that* kind of talking." Porsha walked over to the bar to pour a drink.

"So what kind of talking is it?" BabyGirl asked.

Porsha sighed and said, "I want to get the tapes that contain all the robberies, so they can be destroyed." She hoped what she said to hold them was enough.

"That's it?" Dimples asked in a suspicious tone.

"Yes."

BabyGirl's phone rang, interrupting their conference.

"Hey, luv. I'm almost done …. You're still here? …. Why don't you hang out in the truck for a few minutes and I will meet you there?" Right as she was about to end the call, an unknown number beeped in. She took one look and ended the call.

Porsha was irritated by the fact that BabyGirl was talking to the new guy. She looked at her self-proclaimed enemies and spoke. "So are we going to call her to obtain the tapes?"

"Hell yea," Dimples chimed in as she leaned against the window. "We need to see what the tapes contain, so we can cover our asses if we need to."

Porsha looked in BabyGirl's direction, awaiting her take on things. She switched off her cell, saying, "I say we approach it with caution. It's no secret we need the tapes, but at what cost, and how are we sure there are not more tapes out there. I don't think she is stupid enough to only make one copy. Maribel cannot be totally trusted. We need to weigh the pros and cons, but I say we get rid of Tony on our own and deal with Maribel right after."

"But she has kids!" Porsha rationalized.

"I have no plans on doing life behind bars—or dying. So either it's her, you, or me."

Analyzing the situation, Porsha saw the old BabyGirl creeping out little by little. If BabyGirl could kill Maribel in cold blood, how could she be sure that she wasn't on the deadly woman's list, too?

Chapter 18

THA HUSTLE RECORDS: NYC

The red Audi owned by Tony Moreno, sat outside Tha Hustle Records. Tony tried to convince himself that he had not seen Maribel enter the building. Earlier, when he had pulled up to his home on his way to see his children, he noticed Maribel scrambling out of the house, jumping into her BMW, and jetting off. Tony, with confirmed suspicions of her cheating with Victor, decided to follow her. To his surprise, the trail led him to the front of his old office. Tony decided to confront his wife once she exited, but then he saw Dragon walking out of the building. *What the fuck?*

The look on the other man's face couldn't be considered anything less than deadly. The only time Dragon's face was all screwed up like that was when he was angry enough to kill. Tony wanted to seize the opportunity; he wondered who had pissed him off. Dragon was cold and heartless if the right buttons were pushed; Tony had worked long enough with him to know the many sides of him. As much as Dragon was a genius with his music, he was a cold, heartless human being.

♡♡♡

Chin had drawn Tony's attention to a song that Dragon had written called, "Blood on My Hands." Chin felt the lyrics were so violent and strong that it would turn off women. That same day, Chin brought it to Tony who felt the same, but Tony looked at it from a different point of view. The lyrics sounded like they came from a man with psychological issues. In the song he was admitting to doing some things, however, one wouldn't be able to tell whether or not the song was based on true events. The song sounded like a cry for help. Tony was right on the money, Dragon had a deep troubled past.

♥♥♥

Many times after that experience, Tony shared his concerns about Dragon with Chin, only for Chin to sweep it under the rug. Eventually, Tony set up appointments for Dragon to speak to a psychiatrist since it was in the label's best interest to have an artist who was sane. Unfortunately, Dragon never followed through. Tony was angry then, but now realized since Dragon hadn't changed all that much, it could work in his favor.

Dragon was about to cross the street when Tony pulled up, cutting him off. He rolled down the window, ordering the man to, "Get in!"

Dragon froze, trying not to show any fear, but Tony sensed it.

"That's how you greet an old friend, with silence?"

Dragon nodded, but kept on walking. Tony drove beside him. "We need to talk business, man."

"We can talk out here."

A light chuckle escaped Tony's lips. "Damn, I scare you that much?"

"Naw, I just have a lot of shit on my mind and someplace to be. Sitting down to talk is not an option right now."

Tony knew he was bullshitting. "When I'm done, we'll be

seeing eye to eye."

Dragon looked around a couple of times before finally getting into the car.

Tony flicked the switch to let up the window, but Dragon said, "I'm hot, leave it down."

Tony held in a laugh, but respected the man's wish as he drove off.

"What's up, man?" Tony gave the man a reassuring grin. "Weren't you supposed to call me when you got out?

Dragon squirmed a little in his seat, showing a little discomfort. *Yes, this should be quite interesting,* Tony thought.

"I've been doing a lot of running around, so I haven't had the chance." Dragon replied, glancing at Tony and then quickly staring out the window. "But I was going to."

Tony nodded, though once again smelling bullshit he tailored his words so he could keep Dragon calm. "Listen man, there's no beef between us. Just like Chin, you were a son to me, so as far as I see it, you were pushed in a corner and did what you had to do." He let the man stew on that for a moment. "Now those three females…they have a lot to worry about."

Dragon still seemed uncertain, and rightly so. Tony had no intentions of letting Dragon totally off the hook, but figured toying with the man's emotions and getting what little he could from him would be to his advantage. Tony flicked the switch so the doors and windows would only unlock from the driver's panel.

"I hear you," Dragon stated, while still maintaining his composure.

"How's the album coming along?" Tony inquired as he made a right onto Broadway, knowing damn well he didn't give a shit about Dragon's album. Tony had put up all the capital and the three women were collecting all the benefits.

"To tell you the truth, I don't even know. Porsha's moving shady, man. How's a fucking woman gonna control how a label should be run leaves me clueless…a woman who don't even like Hip-Hop, at that."

Tony bellowed with laughter.

"What's so funny?"

"You." Tony glanced at him for a moment. "You helped put that woman in there." He laughed again.

"This is my mothafuckin' career and you taking this shit lightly?" Dragon fumed clutching the door handle. "Let me the fuck out."

Tony jerked the wheel and pulled the car over to the curb, but didn't unlock the door. Tony turned to Dragon. "Let me tell you something, nigga. You let pussy control your mind and convince you to take down the empire. Just like Chin let pussy control him. I'm sick of cleaning up y'all's shit. We were doing right by you, but your ass became greedy, then let some female or females fool you into believing if you helped them you'd get a cut."

Dragon swallowed hard and tried the door again—it didn't budge.

"Look at you now." Tony glanced at the man's clothing, jewels, and then his face. "Living in BabyGirl's house, soaking up her money, and being dictated to by another woman—a woman who's now your boss." Tony shook his head. "Fucking despicable for a man, in my country you'd be considered a 'puta'… those bitches ain't cutting you in on shit! You'd better wake the fuck up and be a fucking man or else you will continue being the worthless punk you've become."

With that said, Tony unlocked the door and added, "Get

your sorry ass out of my car and call me when you're ready to allow the real Dragon in you to breathe fire."

Chapter 19

19TH PRECINCT: NEW YORK

BabyGirl's head spun as she thought of a way she could get on Tony's tail. A few nights ago, Dragon informed her that he had bumped into Tony, and the man was after her. Dragon didn't go into details. She took a sip of her mocha frappuccino then placed the cup back into the cup holder as she watched plain clothed and uniformed officers walking in and out of the station. Why would Tony tell Dragon he was after her, and let Dragon off the hook so easily, there was more to the story than Dragon was letting on. Either the man was working with Tony, or Tony was using Dragon as a pawn—she figured it was the latter. She needed to figure out what Tony was up to—and fast.

A week had passed since meeting Maribel at Tha Hustle Records. Maybe she could use her as a pawn also; then she could keep on Tony's tail.

Placing a phone call to Maribel became a top priority, but not until she handled the meeting she had with Garfin today. Somehow he decided to first call her the day Maribel visited. Talk about mere coincidence. At first she ignored his calls. Then Garfin showed her how serious he was. Police had walked into her nightclub and shut it down for no apparent reason. Then the club and restaurant started to receive bad reviews in *The*

New York Times, Daily News, Post, and some of the local papers. Even the health inspector visited the restaurant more than he should.

Garfin was really out to prove a point, but she still didn't give in. Business was starting to suffer, so the last time he called she finally answered. He asked her how much longer she wanted to play with him and threatened to shut her down for good. She was smart enough to know how dirty cops could get.

Placing the oval shaped Dior glasses on her face, she entered the 19th precinct. The last time she was there was after the fight with Dragon.

Making her way up to the big brown circular front desk, she said to the officer behind the desk, "I'm here to see Detective Garfin." Two detectives, one in a black suit and the other in a navy blue suit, walked past her as they clowned about a recent arrest.

"Such a fucking scumbag," the detective in a black suit grumbled while his partner chuckled.

Everything was a fucking joke to the police. But when they were the ones under the microscope, she would bet they weren't laughing.

The officer behind the desk slowly looked up, asking in a loud voice, "You're here to see what detective, ma'am?"

BabyGirl wanted to reach behind the desk and smack the shit out of him for yelling out her business. People had turned to look in her direction. BabyGirl held her composure, walked over to the desk and said through clench teeth, "I'm here to see Detective Garfin." She hoped the look she gave the officer conveyed the message that she wasn't in the mood for his issues.

"Have a seat in the waiting area."

Taking a few steps back, she made her way over to the

wooden benches. The benches faced the entrance where officers were bringing in a man who was so high he could barely stand, even with help.

She wanted to find out what Garfin wanted and to determine whether or not he was a threat. If she had to take him down—she had no problem with that. It wasn't like she hadn't done it before.

Forty-five minutes passed and there was no sign of Garfin. The shifts had changed and a female officer was now behind the front desk. Impatience grew on BabyGirl like mold on a tree. Her Jimmy Choo heels were now tapping the floor. The officer looked at her several times, glancing down at BabyGirl's shoes before looking into her face.

"Ma'am who are you here to see?" the officer asked with irritation in her voice.

What the hell is this bitch getting irritated about? Crossing her right leg over the left so the officer could see her shoes, she said, "Like I told the other officer—twice, I'm here to see Detective Garfin. He already called him. We had an appointment for four, but since he seems so damn busy, I'll catch him some other time. " Her patience had grown thin and she didn't care about privacy anymore.

As the officer was about to dial, BabyGirl saw a protruding stomach coming through the door. Garfin didn't say hello, call her name, or even ask who she was, instead, he told her only to follow him. How long had he been observing her? Suspicions flooded her head.

The interrogation room was dimly lit and contained just two chairs and a table. Garfin dropped two files and his appointment book on the table.

She pulled out her chair and took a seat, waiting for Garfin to do the same.

"I didn't say for you to sit."

BabyGirl looked at him for a moment and then hit the door.

"Where the hell do you think you're going?"

"First you made me wait almost an hour, and then you're going to be disrespectful, too. I don't need this bullshit."

He frowned, before pulling out a chair for her.

Food and drinks were offered, but she declined saying, "I'm here to get down to business, since you've made it your business to try to ruin my life."

"Get down to business, huh? I like your style." He smiled before pulling out a cigarette.

"Do you mind?" he lifted it slightly.

"Not at all," she said with a shrug. "Do what you have to do, it's your life not mine."

She watched as he lit the cigarette.

"So, how has life been treating you?" he asked leaning back and allowing a cloud of smoke to escape his thin lips.

She stared in his eyes, before responding, "The same way it's been treating you."

Garfin chuckled. "Give me a fucking break, Ms. Smith. Putting the cigarette in the tray he said, "I'm not wearing Fendi and Dior. So it's obvious you're doing better than I am."

Clearing her throat, BabyGirl responded, "Where are we going with this, detective? I mean, what do my clothes and what I'm able to afford have to do with today? Frankly, you're wasting my time."

"Wasting your time," he said with a laugh that set Baby-Girl's nerves on edge. "Are you serious? Since when does a woman who has nothing to do but run a restaurant and try to kill her boyfriend have anything but time?"

"That was self-defense. The bruises I sustained, that the ones your officers have pictures of, and the hospital records are enough to support my case." She looked for a reaction, but he didn't respond. "And are we here to talk business or hate on my lifestyle, since you can't seem to afford to live that way?"

Garfin remained silent, puffing away as an intense staring match transpired between the two.

"There have been a lot of illegal activities going on at Tha Hustle Records.

"Your point?"

"Your name's been coming up a lot. People are saying you're the ringleader."

"Oh really!" she said, giving him a wide grin. "Well, it's nice to know people enjoy calling my name. However, I don't know what you're talking about."

"Cut the bullshit." He slammed his fist so hard on the table that he accidentally knocked the coffee over. As he scrambled to get the files out of the way, one of the documents fell by her feet. She glanced down. *Meeting with Daquan Bentley and Assistant D.A. Shane scheduled/ 11:00a.m*

Garfin snatched it up glaring at her as she gave him an even wider grin. He shoved the paper back into the folder.

Dragon hadn't mentioned anything about meeting with the DA's office. That could only mean one thing—Dragon was cutting a deal and serving up players. She finally met Garfin's gaze. She knew he was waiting for her to say something about what she had seen, but she chose to remain quiet.

"No, you cut the bullshit, Detective Garfin, and get to the real reason why you brought me down here. You know I wasn't the owner and I didn't have anything to do with Tha Hustle

Records back then. I just recently became the CEO, so you need to talk to all the prior owners.

"And who would they be?"

"You're a smart detective, you found out my cell phone number, so I'm pretty sure you'll be able to figure out who was behind the company."

"I'm trying to save you a lot of grief and help you out, Ms. Smith," Garfin replied. "You need to cooperate."

"Yeah right, you're trying to help me. You're trying to save your damn self. Didn't the news say something about officers from this precinct being involved with some dirty dealings with Tha Hustle? Didn't you get all you needed from them?"

Garfin's face flushed red with anger.

"Now either you are going to tell me the real reason I'm here or I'll be leaving."

"You're not going anywhere until we clarify some things." Regaining his composure, he went on, "Old crimes do have ways of resurfacing."

"Oh yeah?" She stood. "Watch me leave. You don't have an arrest warrant and if you did, I'd be in jail not in this room. Which means your case is weak, detective."

She took up her bag and headed for the door.

"Don't push me to get that warrant in order to get to the bottom of things."

She gripped the door knob.

"Hold on," Garfin blurted out. He then got up from the chair and walked closer to her, placing his hand on the door to keep it closed.

"What!"

"You think your slate is clean, huh?" He leaned in so close she could smell coffee on his breath. "Let me just tell you this—

sometimes even the perfect murder is sloppy and people often leave clues that forensics can pull up."

"Once more, detective," she said calmly. "I have no clue what you're talking about."

He gave her a sly small grin. "Well, let me refresh your mind. The fatal shooting in Philadelphia; another fatal shooting with a UPS guy, two undercover officers—dead, three bodies from the east river, and you in the hospital with an unexplained bullet wound."

BabyGirl struggled, trying not to show any emotion when she was really scared as shit.

"See, the difference between me and other detectives is that I have all the patience in the world." He pushed an index finger in her chest and added, "The moment I get you right where I want you, you're fucked. So trust me, the next time we meet, you'll be in handcuffs."

"Oh, officer," she said in a breathy, seductive voice, "I didn't know you liked your women that way. Can't seem to get it up unless a woman is helpless?" She gave his chest a pat. "I can totally understand. They told me you were desperate. No wonder you're trying to ruin my business. Powerful men with weak dicks will do whatever they have to in order to get a woman in bed."

He flushed with anger, hoping that the officers looking in on this interrogation weren't laughing at him and hadn't taken any of her allegations to heart.

"Next time you want to talk with me, call my lawyer first." Then she grinned. "By the way, she's into handcuffs too. But then again, you already know that, right?"

She walked past him, out of the building, and got into her Benz. Only then did she accept the fact that she was in a whole lot more shit than she thought.

Chapter 20

Snitches get stitches. Was the phrase that Dragon often told his customers when they were buying drugs from him. He wanted to make them aware that it's not cool to snitch, and if they ever did, especially on him, they would end up in the hospital, or worse, a body bag. As the phrase rolled around in his head, Dragon took one last look in the mirror, ran his hands over his low cut hair and chuckled before acknowledging that he had become the very thing he had warned his customers against.

With Garfin rippling his world on one side and Tony hemming him in on the other, his back was against the wall. The police didn't frighten him as much as Tony Moreno did. Though Tony told him he didn't have any beef with him, Dragon wasn't stupid. Whether Dragon wanted to admit it or not, it was only a matter of time before the Tony would finish him off, too. He had worked with Tony a long time and knew the man was a genius who knew how to be calm when he was about to go to war. Witness protection was sounding pretty damn good.

He learned through his lawyer that Tony Moreno was going to trial in two weeks. Unfortunately, Dragon was facing trial in two days unless he had something good for the D.A. Based on a recent conference, the case against Dragon wasn't looking too good. According to his lawyer, the D.A.'s office had strong evidence against him. Not to mention he had no idea what Les, the inmate who killed Cole, would say. To top it all off, Garfin was on his case like Matlock. There wasn't a day that went by without Garfin taunting him about wanting to see him fry. The police pulled Dragon over for one bullshit reason or another nearly every day. He had more tickets for his tinted windows, Breathalyzer tests, and minor traffic violations in the past three weeks, than he had in the year and a half he'd owned the BMW. Garfin said it was only the beginning if he didn't co-operate with the district attorney. Garfin had showed him how grimy he could be and Dragon didn't want to see what else the man was capable of.

Dragon thought long and hard about the choices he had to make. Snitching wasn't what he wanted to do, but going down with Tha Hustle Records and doing football numbers was not an option either.

He adjusted his collar, grabbed the car keys off the table, and took one last look in the mirror. The reflection in the mirror was of a man who was confused, tortured, and whose life was going down the drain. He had hoped to have a family by the age of twenty-five, but the way things were going with BabyGirl and his sudden change of feelings for her, he knew that wasn't going to happen. He feared ending up like his father, suffering in prison. Dragon shook himself out of that state and stated,

"Here goes."

The FEDS, DEA, and the D.A. had promised that if Dragon provided information that brought down Tony, BabyGirl, and Porsha, he would be put in a witness protection program. New York was too hot for him right now.

Jumping into his BMW—one of the many gifts from Baby-Girl, he took a smooth ride into Manhattan. He could almost swear that a patrol car was following. Twice he tried to lose it, but it stayed right on his tail. He picked up the phone to call his lawyer, before deciding against it. He might get a ticket for talking on his cell phone without an ear piece since it was illegal in New York.

BabyGirl was going to prison behind all this. The girl was pure evil now, and had even tried to kill him. But the one thing he had to admit was that she had never gone to the police about him, no matter how much the evidence was stacked against her. A small part of him felt responsible for the way she turned out.

Dragon flashed back to the conversation he had with Tony when the man called him pussy whipped. He knew that really did cost Chin his life and Dragon was not about to let some female cost him his.

"Fuck it. I gotta think about me."

The BMW slowly made its way down Lafayette Street before turning into a parking garage. Ten minutes later, he was heading toward the Supreme Court, where his attorney awaited.

"You ready?" Mark Bistrow, his attorney inquired.

"I guess; if you're sure there's no other way."

Bistrow placed his briefcase on the ground, taking a quick look around. "We could go to trial, but things aren't looking too good for you right now. You're actually facing some serious charges here."

"Man, I'm paying you all that money. Why the hell can't you get me off? They can't connect me to half that shit."

"Get you off?" Bistrow stood closer and with a hushed but

firm tone, looked Dragon in the eyes and continued, "How am I supposed to do that when the charges are this serious? I told you from day one, I'm a straight up attorney and if I can get you off, I'll do my damnedest, but you're asking for a fucking miracle. Take the fucking deal!"

Bistrow reached in his pocket, pulled out a pack of cigarettes, and offered one to Dragon, who declined. What he needed was a blunt; that would somehow clear his mind.

"Listen, they're not really after you, they want Natalie Smith, Natasha Crawford, Tony Moreno, and Porsha Hilton."

Dragon sighed.

"Listen, you're in a fucked up situation. I'm trying to work here with you. I'm not going to take your money and tell you I can get you off when the shit's looking almost impossible right now."

Dragon looked over as a correctional bus transporting prisoners passed by. Dragon didn't want to end up like any of those men.

"Now before we go in there, I need to know what you want to do. Because if I walk in there and tell Shane you're not going to cooperate, we're going straight to trial and all deals—and offers of protection—are off."

Dragon sucked his teeth and sighed. "So basically, I don't have any choice."

"Oh, you have choices; I just can't promise you a good outcome.

Bistrow took one last pull of the cigarette before stomping it out on the pavement.

"Okay, let's do this then."

They were up against one of New York's toughest Assistant D.A.'s, Rick Shane. Shane was a detective who later made the transition into the Prosecutor's office. During his time as a detective, his record was outstanding. As an ADA, his conviction record far superseded his arrest record. Bistrow and Dragon walked into the courtroom where they were supposed to meet Shane. Five minutes later, Shane stepped out, and Dragon acknowledged the man with a nod. Shane was dark-skinned, wore a black pin-striped Armani suit, black shirt, white tie, white cufflinks, and gators on his feet. The attorneys shook hands before Shane extended his hand to Dragon saying, "Thanks for coming in."

Dragon just looked at him.

Following Shane toward the elevator, Dragon's thoughts raced a thousand miles per hour. After reaching the fifth floor, they walked through a set of glass doors and entered a conference room where another ADA—a female of Hispanic descent—was present.

"This is Daquan Bentley and his attorney, Mark Bistrow. This is Melinda Santiago, ADA."

Shane placed Dragon's file on the table before saying, "So, Mr. Bentley, you're here to provide information that will be vital to our case against—"

"Yeah, whatever," Dragon replied.

Bistrow gave Dragon a warning look.

Shane threw a glance at Santiago before saying, "Let me know if you're ready."

"Let's get this over with."

"My kind of man," Shane said with a smile. "The man wants to get down to business, people. I say we should accommodate him." He nodded to Santiago who pressed the button on the recorder.

Dragon stared at the recorder and the room fell silent.

His heart was beating like a jockey trying to bring his horse across the finish line.

"So tell me what took place during your time at Tha Hustle Records."

Dragon told them how Chin and Tony had bases set up, where the drug transactions transpired, and how Tony would often put an ass whopping on people before murdering them.

An hour later, he was telling the story about the fateful day the murders took place at Tha Hustle Records. Shane asked, "Did you have any idea what was going to happen that night?"

Dragon blinked inquisitively and looked at Shane.

"Because earlier you stated that you told the engineer and …what was the woman's name?"

"Temptation."

"Right, Temptation. You told her to go into the next room."

"In a way, but I ain't know it was gonna go down like that though."

"What *did* you know?"

"I thought we were just going to shake them up a bit, rob the place, and leave. Never in a million years would I have thought she'd kill them. It's like since she became friends with Dimples, she's turned into this monster."

"Who are you talking about?"

"BabyGirl."

"You mean Natalie Smith?"

"Yeah, that's her name."

"How was she involved with this?"

Dragon then told about BabyGirl's involvement in the robberies and murders of the police officers, he also told how Porsha and Dimples assisted.

"To be honest, BabyGirl was the mastermind behind the whole thing. Then she threatened me, so I had to do what she said."

"And why's that?"

"Well for one, she controlled my career and I was starving, I need to feed myself somehow. Then she said she could somehow pin those murders all on me or if that didn't work, she would simply just kill me"

"She said dead rappers sell more records anyway. I knew I had to play my part to save my own ass.

"She made it so none of us could snitch on anyone else."

Chapter 21

"I'm getting tired of this fucking shit already." She threw the PDA across the room. This was the sixth time, she had called Shane and his phone went to voicemail.

Porsha wrapped her slender body in the white fluffy sheet and glanced at the 8inch dildo that lay beside her. Lord knows she'd had enough of the battery operated toy and she wanted a real man to knock the inside of her walls around. Sounds from the flat screen television could be heard. A series of Sex in the City played on the television. At times, Porsha felt like the characters and wondered if she would give up on finding Mr. Right and just continue to fuck for the rest of her life. A cool breeze came in from the window, causing Porsha to draw the blanket. Slowly spreading her chocolate thighs, Porsha used French manicured fingers to massage her clit, while the other hand caressed her dark breasts. She could feel herself swelling as she became aroused by the touching. Slight moans escaped her lips as the sensation captivated her body.

A short ringing from the cell indicated that someone had sent Porsha a text. Her fingers came to a halt between her legs and she used the hand that was caressing her breasts earlier to reach for the phone, flipping it open, she discovered that Shane had sent her a text.

Can't talk now, I will call you in a few. I'm with my wife and kids.

"Whatever," she hissed, and placed the phone back on the nightstand. For some reason, masturbation was not giving her the same pleasure and she missed having someone to come home to. Chin was a lot of headache at times, but she would have given anything to have that ache instead of being some-one's mistress.

❤❤❤

As Chin looked up at her from the floor in his office, pain filled his slanted eyes. The love Porsha had for him washed away all of the pain he had caused. She wanted to save him, but couldn't. As ruthless as BabyGirl was, Porsha knew saving him would only make her next on the vengeful woman's list. It was either Chin or Porsha and she wasn't sure Chin would save her if the shoe was on the other foot. But did he get what he really deserved? He didn't deserve to die. Not like that; and certainly not by the hand of a woman who had no rights to him in the first place.

❤❤❤

In the midst of pleasing herself, the cell went off again. Shane had decided to call. Wiping off her hands on the navy blue Nautica towel, she answered.

"Hello!" Her attitude was obvious.

"Well, someone has an attitude," Shane replied.

Porsha rolled her eyes, then let out a loud sigh. She was tired of his shit, and she wanted it to be known.

"What's your problem?" he inquired.

"I was in the middle of something."

"Like?"

"Caressing my entire body since someone has been neglecting to do so."

"Porsha, you know I have a wife and children, so my time is limited."

"You know the requirements of the mistress," she shot back. Applause came from the television playing in the background, as if even the television was in agreement with her.

"Anyway," Shane changed the topic. "Your boy Dragon is singing like a sailor."

"Huh?"

She wanted to make sure she heard what Shane said correctly.

"Who?" she sat up, her back resting against the headboard.

"Dragon came down to my office, and sold out the entire Tha Hustle Records staff, he told us, in detail, how every robbery went down, who committed what murders, and how the money was laundered."

"What!" Porsha got up off the bed and paced the green carpet. She stopped in her tracks, "Shane, that tape cannot get out."

"Sorry Porsha, but another ADA was in the room. The tape has to be brought into evidence, there was a witness lurking."

Porsha leaned on her dresser, her eyes trailed up to the wall that held her law degree. She wanted to argue, but wasn't sure if the phone was tapped. Secondly, she knew if he could pull some strings he would, but politics was in play because this was a high-profile case. The precinct had been coming under fire since it was learned that some of the police officers from the

19th precinct aided Tha Hustle Records. The media had blasted the whole department for it.

"Thanks," she was grateful for the bits of information he was able to supply.

"So what do I get for delivering this message?"

Porsha's chain of thought was messed up and she could no longer think.

"Shane, I will call you later."

"So I get no…"

She didn't wait for him to respond before hanging up her telephone.

Running through her telephone, she searched for Baby-Girl's number. Portia had never done prison time before and had no intentions on doing any time in the future.

So you're a snitch huh, Dragon? I guess you never heard the term, snitches get stitches. You won't be that lucky, instead, you will be bodied.

Rage filled her entire body. "Who the fuck does he thinks he is? Literally, who the fuck does this nigga thinks he is?" she blurted out. "First his ass walked up in my office, demanding that he get a piece of the empire, now he's snitching. He's dead."

"Hello," A sleepy BabyGirl answered.

"We need to meet!" Porsha took a shirt and tight-fitting sweatpants out of her drawer and threw them on while she talked. Her round butt sat perfectly in the snug pants. Porsha glanced at herself in the mirror.

"I hope you're talking tomorrow because I'm sleeping."

"Right now…we are going talk."

"Listen," she could hear BabyGirl adjusting in the background. "Call me back when you realize you can't ask people to meet you at three in the morning."

"Okay, fine by me, but when the police come knocking your door down and place you in handcuffs for all the shit that went down at Tha Hustle Records, don't blame me."

"What the hell are you talking about?" Porsha realized she had finally gotten BabyGirl's attention. *Good, her ass needs to get up anyway.*

"Porsha, what are you talking about?"

"Dragon's a snitch. Now meet me at the diner located at 42nd Street."

"What!"

Porsha hung up her phone without any further words.

Chapter 22

NIGHTCLUB: NYC

"My wife is off limits, and he knows that." Tony cringed inside as he sat on the bar stool. Although his plan was about to unfold, Tony wanted to deal with Victor on the spot.

"This is a hot club," Victor yelled over the loud music which blasted from the speakers.

Tony turned to him and smiled before lifting his glass of Hennessey. Barmaids in short shorts and tight shirts walked around and served drinks on trays. Victor became excited each time one passed by.

"I wanna bring all these freaks home," he leaned in to whisper to Tony.

Tony said nothing, he just nodded in agreement. He wondered what category Victor placed his wife in. The performers danced on a square stage located in the middle of the bar. Every now and then, Tony glanced at the black door to the far right of the bar; this was where his grand finale for the night was expected to emerge.

Strobe lights hung from the high black ceiling and flashed in different directions, giving the club a freaky ambiance. A blonde stripper was on stage sliding down a pole. A quick glance at Victor assured Tony that Victor loved the action on stage. Every now and then he even yelled out something freaky and threw a couple dollars at the stage.

This better go well, Tony thought to himself as images of his wife strip dancing for Victor flashed in his head. Tony became angry at the mere thought. He had paid the club owner enough money to make sure everything went as planned; one of the stipulations was for every camera to be off. He didn't want to be traced back to the scene.

"Anything else to drink?" one of the barmaids inquired, her chocolate brown hair really brought out her baby-like features.

"I will drink you," a drunken Victor spoke. The woman smiled, "On second thought, a cup of Henny will do." The women turned to Tony and asked the same question, Tony declined and then she walked away without giving Victor's comment a second thought.

The stripper who was on stage earlier brought her big butt over and knelt in front of Victor, she allowed her caramel ass to jiggle in his face. It was his birthday, so Tony figured Victor was going all out. She moved closer so her ass was pressed against Victor's face. He moved his head from side to side in her ass while he slapped her cheeks. Soft moans escaped her lips as she rubbed her large breasts.

Five minutes later, Victor's face emerged from her ass and he motioned to Tony to get some. Tony declined.

"Naw, it's your birthday do your thing."

Tony sat observing his surroundings. He watched as men received lap dances from different women and some headed to the VIP room. Tony was more convinced than ever that pussy could really captivate someone's mind. He knew he was guilty of the same.

◪◪◪

His finger worked in and out of the blonde stripper who was sitting on his lap. Tony could tell she liked it by the juice that was flowing on his hand. The musky smell of sex lingered in the air.

"Turn around and let me spank that ass," Tony suggested.

Without hesitation, she did a quick spin and whipped her golden ass toward Tony.

His large hand pulled back and—*whack*—the sound crackled as it landed, drawing the stares of men nearby.

"I like that, Daddy," she said, grinning. "Do it again."

"Naw, Ma, I need somebody fresh over here," he told her, placing a couple of bills in her thong. She walked away, putting a switch in her hips for his sake.

"Slow down, Tony." He remembered Chin saying, "You're spending it all in one place."

"It's a'ight, man. I've got it like that."

Reaching into his pocket, Chin took Tony's wallet, pulled out a few bills, and handed them to him. "That's your limit, man. Chin refused to let him throw his money away on women he was not taking home.

◪◪◪

Tony smiled. He was thankful for Chin because he was pretty sure he was acting as much a fool as Victor was now.

He focused his attention back to Victor, who had his head buried in a stripper's pussy. He licked as if he was down to the last drop of an icy pop. The thunderous music that was beating in their ear drums earlier, was slowly dying down.

The next act was about to come on stage. The lights became dimmer and the door which Tony was watching earlier, now opened. Three women walked toward the stage area.

"This is your surprise, man," Tony nudged Victor in the side.

"God damn," Victor bit on his hands. "You the best, cuz, that's all I have to say."

Victor was ordered to the stage a minute later, where he was placed in a brown wooden chair. The first stripper, who was in a red patent leather short suit, tied Victor's hands behind his back, and placed a ball in his mouth, then she tied cloth around his mouth to hold the ball in place.

The curvy stripper that was dressed in a French maid outfit stood in front of Victor, she took a whip and flashed it, sending a whizzing sound throughout the club. She bent over a bit, exposing her ass. The club went into an uproar as a third stripper came and began to feel on her ass. Leaning over Victor, the other stripper ran a popsicle along his neck. Never missing a drop, she ensured all of it was licked up. Victor's head swung from side to side, the boy was acting like Tarzan in a jungle.

Ten minutes into the act, a dense fog came up, blocking out everything. Silence graced the club because no one could see what was going on. By the time the mist cleared, Victor was off the stage and all that was left was a new pair of women fucking one another. Victor, the three strippers, and Tony disappeared through the door the strippers had emerged from earlier. The door led to the basement.

When they reached the basement, the ball and cloth were removed from Victor's mouth. He began arguing and threatening the women as they laid him, still bound, onto a clear plastic tarp.

"Yea, you thought this shit would be over. I told you my cousin would be here to fix all of y'all." Victor tried to get up to lunge at the women, but was knocked right back down.

Laughter escaped from the women's lips.

The faint sound of the hip-hop music blasting in the bar could still be heard in the basement. Tony could tell Victor was excited to see him, until he realized Tony was just standing there. A weird expression came over Victor's face, as he observed Tony strapping on latex gloves.

"What's going on, man?" Victor inquired with nervousness laced in his voice.

"You have a sexual addiction that needs to be cured."

"Man, I don't know what you're talking about. I love sex just like any other men."

"Yea, a little too much," Tony pulled the gloves further on his hands, making a slapping sound. "Is that why you fucked my wife? You couldn't resist her?"

"I don't know what you talking about," Victor tried to sound convincing.

Inching closer, Tony spoke, "So now you're taking me for an idiot…not only have you fucked my wife, but you're lying to me."

Victor began to scream, but to his dismay, no one could hear because the loud music drowned out the all the noise coming from the dark room which only contained old stage equipment and boiler pipes.

"What's this?" Tony pulled out pictures of Maribel and Victor walking out of various restaurants hand in hand.

"I don't know."

Tony punched him.

"Explain this to me then." Tony held up a picture of Victor sucking Maribel's tongue."

"She was going through a lot with you leaving,"

"Yea," Tony responded cutting him off, "So you took it up on yourself to cuddle her?"

Victor stared at Tony.

"Answer me," he kicked Victor straight in the nose, breaking it.

"Ahhh…" the man screamed.

"Shut up and stop acting like a bitch. Now answer me."

"Nothing like that,"

"So what is this?" Tony dangled another picture of Victor with his head buried between Maribel's thighs.

No words except for, *sorry,* left Victor lips.

"Sorry, that's all you can say?" Tony stepped on the man's nuts, Victor winced in pain.

Blood was now draining from his nose and flowing straight to his lips.

"You were my right hand man," Tony leaned over him as the women removed Victor's pants.

Tony walked over to the corner.

"What are you doing?" Victor attempted to lean up to look, then he tried to move so they couldn't take his pants off.

"Shut the fuck up," one of the women said, her voice was masculine.

Walking back over, Tony placed Vaseline on a twelve inch dildo.

"Turn his ass over," Tony commanded.

"Tony, come on man, I'm sorry, we're family don't do

this to me."

"Family, huh?"

One of the transsexuals tried to spread Victor's butt cheeks, but he clenched on them so they couldn't be opened.

"You weren't thinking about family when you were fucking my wife."

"Gentleman, or ladies, which ever you prefer," Tony spoke, "Do me the honors and place your foot on his head."

A twelve-inch heel came smashing down on Victor's head. He flinched as pain tore through his body.

Once the transsexual opened up his ass cheek, Tony shoved the dildo right in.

"Ahhh..." Victor screamed.

"Is this how you shoved it in my wife, Victor?"

"Fuck you," Victor spoke. "Just kill me and be done," he pleaded.

"No, I'm gonna let you have it, killing is too easy."

Tony shoved the dildo further up Victor's ass. Blood and shit began to pool on the dildo.

"You nasty ass," Tony spoke. The women began to hold their noses as a stench began to emerge from Victor's ass. "I wonder if Maribel would love you right now."

Tony continued to work Victor's ass without mercy as he continued to scream. Fifteen minutes later, he removed the dildo and walked up to Victor mouth.

"Suck it." Tony demanded "You like sucking."

Victor, with the little strength he had left, spat on Tony.

Prying open Victor's mouth with pliers, Tony plunged the dildo covered with shit and blood down Victor's throat.

"Taste how nasty you are, you fucking bitch." Tony and the transsexuals laughed. "Bitch ass, suck this dick. You better practice because you have three more to suck on."

The trannies had their dicks out, waiting for Tony to finish.

"I'm finished, boys, deal with him. Make sure, his body is burned, and remove his teeth, but give me the tongue. I need that, since someone I know loves it so much."

"No problem." the chubby transsexual responded.

Making his way back up the steps, Tony turned and looked, "So much for family, huh?"

"Hell has no fury…" Tony spoke. "This is just the beginning. The streets have not seen anything yet."

Tony shut the black metal door behind him, closing out the sound of his cousin's cries.

Chapter 23

NYACK: NY

"Hello?" she whispered into the phone, carefully trying not to wake Dragon. Silence lingered on the phone.

"Porsha?" she spoke, again looking around to see if Dragon heard anything. He was still sound asleep and hadn't moved from the position he was laying in. Removing the phone from her ear, she strolled across the plush brown carpet to place the phone back on its cradle.

"This heifer… how dare she call me this early in the morning, only to hang up the phone in my ear? It appears as if Chin didn't teach her enough manners, so I will have to," BabyGirl mumbled under her breath.

Pausing for a brief second, she stared at Dragon's slender frame; the room was dark, but all sorts of lights were going on in her head. The most prevalent was to shoot him dead right where he was sleeping.

"Naw, that would be too easy," she rationalized. "Maybe I should stab him in his sleep." She continued to look at him and spoke as if someone else was in the room and they were weighing out the choices they had.

Flashing back to a song her father always sang, she smiled to herself as the words came clearly in her head. "Six millions ways to die…choose one." Her smile widened knowing she would have fun choosing one out of the six million ways to kill him if everything she heard about him turned out to be true.

Sauntering across the carpet, she removed her clothing from the walk in closet and made her way to the kitchen. She needed to place another call, but she couldn't inside the bedroom. Once downstairs, she walked past the island in the center of her kitchen. Shiny stainless cookware hung from the ceiling, which would show one their reflection if they looked in it. She didn't stop to admire her pots, something she would have done on a regular day. Instead, she moved to the granite counter that held the Panasonic gray cordless phone. Her petite hands pressed the digits, in a few seconds, Dimples was on the opposite end.

The white clock above the microwave read 3:45 A.M. With Dimples line still ringing in her ear, she prayed the woman would pick up. Being caught by Dragon with her clothing on and on the phone at that hour of the morning was something she didn't feel like explaining. One of the instructions from Porsha was to ensure Dimples came along.

"Whoever this is, this better be good, you calling my goddamn house at this time in the morning." Attitude saturated in Dimples' voice.

"Dimples," she whispered. She looked toward the kitchen entrance to make sure Dragon wasn't up. "Get up. We need to talk."

"Ah...you funny, call me back in the morning," responded Dimples in an aggravated tone.

BabyGirl figured Dimples was about to hang up on her.

"You better not hang up on me, now wake the fuck up and listen," she shot back through clenched teeth.

"Now you done crossed the mothafucking line! You're calling my home this late and cursing at me on top of it? This better be good, bitch, this better be good."

"Some shit went down," BabyGirl spoke while tiptoeing up to the kitchen entrance to peek into the living room to see if Dragon had entered.

"Well, you should have flushed it down the toilet, that's where *shit* belongs."

"Would you quit acting up, bitch, and listen to me?"

"I'm fuckin' tired."

Deciding that she would use the same line Porsha did on her; BabyGirl rested the cordless phone on her shoulder, taking a quick pause before saying "Okay, fine. However, when the police start pounding your door, don't say I didn't warn you."

"Police!?" Dimples shouted. BabyGirl laughed as she remembered how that same word had sounded when she visited her in the hospital after being shot on one of Pit Bull's assignments.

"Please tell me what the fuck you are talking about," Concern laced her voice.

"Now you wanna listen?"

"Quit the fucking games and spit it out."

"Listen, I can't go into details right now, all I can say is that Dragon is snitching."

"Get the fuck out of here,"

"Hold on, let me see if my line is clear,"

Switching over, she checked to ensure a dial tone was on the other line. Hearing the dial tone relieved her stressed nerves a bit.

"Is he on his way to the morgue?"

"Huh?"

"Did you call the coroner to pick up his body after you put a cap in his ass?"

"No, I didn't" she whispered.

"Why are you whispering?"

"Because he is in the bedroom and I'm just calling you to tell you where to meet me."

"Shit, he's gonna be dead soon anyway, no need in whispering."

"Just take down the address and meet us at the diner and don't be late."

"I won't, but you better kill that nigga, cause if you don't —I will."

"Okay." BabyGirl cut the lengthy conversation short.

She was in such a hurry she ended up picking up Dragon's car keys instead of hers.

♡♡♡

The forty-five minute ride from Rockland County to Manhattan had her thinking a million and one thoughts. Seconds away from the diner, she waited for the light to change from red to green. The streets of Manhattan were still busy. Sure enough, it was the city that never sleeps. The light changed and she found the perfect parking spot in front of the diner. Porsha, who was already there, had her head lowered and was sipping hot tea.

"I wish the shit would just burn her fucking throat."

She hadn't forgotten the fight she had with Porsha in the restaurant. Opening the glass door, BabyGirl stepped inside and joined her at the table.

"So what's so important that you had to call me out of my bed this early in the morning?"

No sooner than she asked the question, the doors to the diner opened once more and in walked Dimples.

"This better be fucking good. 5:15 A.M. and I'm walk-ing inside this damn diner." The woman bitterly spoke while passing an elderly couple who was having coffee. They stared at her in disgust. She shot back a nasty look before the couple returned to minding their own business.

"Relax, and stop drawing attention to us," Porsha shunned Dimples. BabyGirl could tell exactly what Dimples was think-ing by the disgusted look on her face. *This heifer thinks she's is better than us.*

"So what's so important?" BabyGirl inquired.

"*Your* man…" Porsha pointed in BabyGirl's direction, "Is a fucking snitch."

"First of all, you need to calm the fuck down. Secondly, don't point your fingers at me because I'll cut your fuckin' hands off if you do it again."

Dimples looked around before saying, "Calm down."

"Calm down? How the hell do you expect me to be calm, Dimples?" Porsha whispered in an angry but hushed manner. "All the murders we committed at Tha Hustle Records are coming back to haunt us. Just like that saying 'the sins of the past are coming back to haunt the success of the future.' I knew that motherfucka could not be trusted."

"You knew what you were getting into when you got down with us," BabyGirl shot back. "Now when you handle criminal cases, do you panic like this, or do you plan a strategy?" Baby-Girl questioned.

Everyone finally calmed down; they all knew BabyGirl had a point.

"Would you like to order anything?" the waitress dressed in black and white asked. A pad and blue pen sat in her hand.

"Yea, gimme a glass of orange juice and a toasted plain bagel." Dimples ordered.

"Just a hot chocolate," BabyGirl added.

"Anything else for you, ma'am?" she asked, turning to Porsha.

"Another tea will do fine.

They waited as she scribbled down their order and as soon as she was out of ear shot, they went back to their discussion.

"All I know is Dragon is a dead man walking."

BabyGirl stared at Dimples, her demeanor letting on to the fact that the woman had already convicted Dragon before even hearing the evidence.

"So you just jump to conclusions before hearing the evidence?" She questioned Dimples.

"I'm saying…"

"You ain't saying shit." She rolled her eyes at her friend. This is not the first time Dimples chose another side. Pit Bull was another good example.

♡♡♡

She had just moved in with Sandy after the death of her parents and Dragon was sent to jail. Pit Bull wanted them to work for him; both girls were ready and willing until Pit Bull decided to flip the script and demanded that BabyGirl sleep with him. BabyGirl tried to stand her ground, but got minimal support from Dimples when she had turned to her to side with her. Instead, her friend surprised her by telling her to go along with the plan. *Who the hell did she think she was, it was not like anyone was asking her to sleep with them.* That was the day she knew Dimples would sell her out to save her own coat tail.

♡♡♡

While driving to the diner, BabyGirl had found the card with D.A. Shane's information in Dragon's car; however, she wouldn't dare speak about it. She let Porsha do all the talking, but had already decided to deal with Dragon on her own terms.

"Well anyway, I was home taking care of something, when my telephone rang..." Porsha started.

"What were you taking care of at three in the morning?" Dimples asked with a sinister grin across her face.

"None of your business," she shot back.

"Sounds like someone needs some sexual healing," Dimples laughed.

"Anyway,"

Porsha was about to start her next sentence when the waitress came up to the table with their orders. Taking a quick peep out the window, Porsha noticed that it had begun drizzling, "Great!" she thought to herself.

"Shane called me," she stated, picking up on their interrupted conversation.

"Shane?" BabyGirl repeated.

"Yes, why? Do you know him?"

"Nope, just wanted to make sure I got the name right."

Porsha had confirmed what BabyGirl suspected after she found the card in the car...Dragon *was* snitching.

"He called to give me the heads up that Dragon was snitching and we might be facing jail time. "

"What did he tell you Dragon said?" Dimples inquired. "And what kind of relationship do you and this man have that he would be calling you, especially when he's supposed to be the one to bring you down?"

"Does all that matter?" Irritation flowed in her words.

"Just wondering, that's all."

Dimples asked the right question, BabyGirl thought. Something told BabyGirl that Porsha was only giving them bits and pieces of what she knew.

"Well, what did he say?" BabyGirl asked.

"He didn't say too much because we were on the phone, however, he stated that he had everything on tape and will have to use it unless somehow the tape gets destroyed and Dragon winds up dead."

"So not only do we have to worry about Lou's video, we have another tape to worry about also? Great, just fucking great." BabyGirl sighed, slouching back in her chair. "Did you call Maribel about the tapes?"

Her hot chocolate smelled rich and creamy, however, the news she'd just heard wouldn't allow her to enjoy such a delight.

"Yea, but she is playing games. It's gonna be hard for us to get the tape, so I say we kill him." Dimples added in without any emotion.

The atmosphere became quiet and all eyes were on Baby-Girl. They watched and waited for BabyGirl's reaction.

"I know you're not expecting *me* to kill him?"

"Why not," Dimples asked in a sarcastic tone. "You damn sure killed Chin when you found out he killed your parents, and that nigga was fucking you just like Dragon is now and was probably taking care of you better than Dragon ever will."

Porsha adjusted in her chair. One look at her face and one could see that jealousy was lingering in her eyes.

"Fuck it, snitches get stitches right?"

"No, more! It'll be a bullet in this case," Dimples corrected.

"I knew you would see the light," Porsha added in.

"So who's gonna kill him."

"BabyGirl?" Dimples asked.

"Bitch, you know damn well I can't kill him. I live with the nigga; I would be the first person they suspect."

Everyone paused again. BabyGirl took a sip of her hot chocolate as her eyes moved from Dimples to Porsha.

Clearing her throat Porsha spoke, "Fuck it, I'll handle the shit myself."

Perfect, BabyGirl thought to herself with a sinister grin.

Chapter 24

The queen-sized bed was large enough to fit three people, however something was missing, and Dragon realized that as soon as he swung his hand to the right side of the bed. BabyGirl was not there. Raising his dark body, which almost matched the darkness in the room, he looked to make sure his eyes weren't playing tricks on him. The cable box which stood on the mounted glass shelf read 5:00 a.m. Maybe she went to the bathroom, he assured himself. He took a quick peek at the master bathroom, which was located in their bedroom, there was no light on.

"BabyGirl,"

There was no response; the house sounded as empty as the day they purchased it. Dragon's 5'8" frame rose off the bed. Wearing only a wife beater and boxers, he strolled through the house. Opening another bedroom door, he called out once more,

"BabyGirl?"

"Where the fuck is this chick?"

He walked into the living room, almost bumping into the big crystal sculpture that stood in the center of the room. Still there was no sign of her. An early morning growl came from his stomach. He was starving, so he walked into the kitchen. Dragon switched on the lights and walked over to the double-door, stainless steel refrigerator to retrieve the milk so he could make himself some cereal. Moving toward the pantry, he opened the door to check for his favorite cereal. While making the cereal, he picked up the cordless to check the caller ID. He noticed Porsha had called at 3:45 A.M. and the last number BabyGirl called was Dimples.

"What is she up to?" he wondered while pulling out the bar stool to sit at the island and eat his cereal.

Wanting to know her whereabouts, he dialed her cell. The phone went straight to voicemail so his efforts were proven futile. He dialed once more, but once again the voicemail picked up.

"Yo, where the fuck you at? It's fucking five in the morning and your damn phone is off, are you with some nigga?" He questioned the voicemail as if it could answer back.

Hanging up the phone, he sucked his teeth and continued to eat his cereal. He was consumed with anger. Walking into the foyer with the bowl in his hand, his eyes just happened glimpse at the key rack. His keys were missing.

"Oh! She thinks she's slick, huh... taking my keys along with hers so I wouldn't be able to go after her. A'ight, let's see how she explains her way out of this one."

Dragon walked back into the living room which was just steps away. He placed his bowl on the shiny tiled floor and sat on the black leather sectional, pulling the recliner out. The sofa faced the entrance, and he wanted her to be surprised when she walked in.

"Surprise, bitch!" he thought. "Naw...surprise bitch with my gun pointing at her would be better." He smiled at his ingenious plan, then raced over to where he kept his gun, took it out, and went back to the sofa. He was in a killer mood, so picking up the remote, he pressed the button and turned on the stereo, Fifty Cent's "Many Men" came blaring through the surround system. Dragon nodded to the infectious beat while singing along with the catchy lines. "

Many men wish death upon me, blood in my eye..."

Opening the ash tray area in his sectional, he took out the little blunt he had left, and lit it up. Not too long after, impatience kicked in so he got up and walked over to the front window, pulling back the blinds and peeking out. There was no sign of her or his BMW.

Retreating from the window back to the sofa, he continued to smoke.

"This chick right here really thinks it's a game. She bugging, but a'ight, she gonna see who is bugging when she walks up in this bitch."

Keys jiggled in the door forty six minutes later. The house was still in total darkness, waiting for her to switch on the lights. He listened as the door closed behind her curvy body. He knew she was tiptoeing because he barely heard her feet hit the floor. Dragon didn't even give her a chance to go to the bedroom before he flipped on the lamp and had the nine millimeter pointed at her. She jumped, surprised to see the light and gun flashing in her face.

"Where the fuck have you been?"

"Oh, I wasn't expecting to see you up," she responded in a calm manner, placing the keys back on the rack.

"And I wasn't expecting you to be gone," sarcasm filled his every word. The gun was still aimed at her.

"Well, I had something to take care,"

"So whatever you had to take care of couldn't wait until the morning?" He watched as she removed her shoes.

BabyGirl paused for a brief moment then stared at him, "No, Daquan,"

Oh she got guts with her answers too, a'ight I see where this is going. He thought to himself.

"My leaving has a lot to do with you."

"Excuse me?" he replied. Puzzled, he got up from the sofa and lowered the gun.

"You heard me," she said, "The whole situation has to do with you, and I would like to get your side of the story."

"What story?" He looked confused.

Sitting down on a chair to the far right, she answered, "Dragon, how long we have known each other? We've been through mad shit and you would really do *this* to *me*?"

"Do what?" he asked.

"I loved you, Dragon, yes, we have our ups and downs, but I can't believe—"

"Believe what, BabyGirl? You need to tell me because right now, nothing you are saying to me makes sense."

He wondered what the hell she was talking about. He walked over to her, pulled her off the chair, led her to the sofa, and allowed her to rest her head on his shoulder.

"Why would you snitch to the police, Daquan?"

"What?" Dragon jerked back; her head flew off his shoulder.

"Snitch? Girl please, you know that ain't my style."

His inside was racked with nervousness, he didn't know how much she knew or what she had found out, but he had all intentions on finding out.

For the first time, he felt the Witness Protection Program

may not be a bad idea, he was about to catch a bullet sooner than he thought.

A tear streamed down her face, "Haven't I been through enough already? I know I'm not the most perfect person in the world, and I might have done a lot of messed up things, but I never turned my back on you. Society made me what I am, Dragon, you should be able to relate to that based on what you told me about your past." She cried out. "If you felt the pressure was getting to be too much on you, then you should have talked to me and we could have figured out how to work this out."

"BabyGirl..." he knelt in front of her and held her hands. She was right, as bad as things were, he knew she never would have turned him in.

"I never snitched." He couldn't bring himself to tell her the truth. *Maybe I did the wrong thing,* he thought. Then reality kicked in, *fuck it, it's every man for himself.*

"What is this then?" she held up the business card that had Shane's name on it. She sniffled then sat in the chair.

"C'mon BabyGirl, you going by that? You already know how these prosecutors will try to cut deals with you to get you to snitch, but that's not me." He was becoming more furious by the moment, but tried to hide his anger as best he could. "Call the damn man if you need to find out yourself if I called him."

She stared in his eyes for a good five minutes, "I don't have to... he already called Porsha and told her word for word everything you said. And *that,* luv, made you a mothafucking snitch."

She stood from the chair with grace, and walked toward the steps leading upstairs. When she got to the last step she turned around and uttered, "Fix this shit, or you might as well pick out your casket because the morgue don't allow a body to sit on ice too long."

"Did you just threaten me?"

Turning she said, "Oh no, baby, that's a promise." Her words were colder than ice.

"How am I supposed to do that when I didn't even tell his ass anything?"

"Later for that shit, you and I both know you did. I'm not going to jail behind your coward ass."

Taking another step, she demanded, "Fix it."

He watched as she made her way up to the bedroom, until only a silhouette of her frame could be seen.

Dragon knew he had no choice, in her mind he was already dead. The biggest challenge was who would get to whom first. And he did not intend to die.

Chapter 25

WASHINGTON HEIGHTS: NYC

"How could they do this to my son, Antonio?" Esther, Victor's mother wailed in a heavy Spanish accent. "My son is burned beyond recognition."

"I don't know, but I promise I will find Victor's killer and deal with them accordingly." Tony assured the thick, dark-skinned Hispanic lady.

Maribel sat on a brown wooden chair in the corner of the room crying her heart out. You would have thought Victor was her husband. Tony continued to watch her as he held Esther Medina in his arms. If the people he'd hired followed through correctly, then Victor's tongue should be sitting on ice waiting for the next trick Tony had up his sleeve.

News Twelve, which was being shown on the 27-inch television, flashed the grisly murder once more. A strong draft blew through the open window causing the thin white curtain to flow back and forth. Maribel, who was wailing louder, made Tony want to slap the shit out of her, but he needed to make sure no one found out he had a hand in Victor's killing.

A vibration coming from his hip caused him to jump, but it was his cell phone going off. Easing himself out of Esther's hold, he walked to the window so he could get a clearer reception. Reception in Washington Heights could be horrible at times.

"Hello?" he answered as Maribel's eyes focused on his lips. Being the nosey person she was, she wanted to know who he was talking to. Tony leaned over the windowsill and peered out the window.

"Okay, I will be there in a few."

Closing the flip phone, he walked over to Victor's mother, who was sitting on the burgundy sofa. Victor's sister had been cooking beef stew and yellow rice in the kitchen. She offered Tony some, but he declined because he had other important matters to take care of.

"You're leaving?" Maribel questioned. One could hear the disgust in her voice. *Who invited her here anyway?* Tony thought.

"Yea, I have some things I have to take care of."

As he kissed Esther on the cheek, he heard Maribel say, "What's wrong with you? We are having a family crisis and all you can think about is leaving? You're such a cold-hearted bastard."

"Stop!" He turned his head slightly to the right while using his index finger to silence her. "Don't you dare tell me what I am and what I'm not without examining yourself."

"Whatever Tony, I can't wait to get a divorce and take the children away from a monster like you."

Tony snapped. Without thinking, he darted across the wooden floor, grabbed Maribel by the neck, and jacked her up against the wall.

"Hay dios mio!" Esther raced off the sofa toward them. Victor's sister followed with a spoon still in her hand.

"What have I told you about threatening me with my kids, huh?" he barked as he jerked her neck around. Every now and then her head hit the wall.

"Antonio…" Esther pleaded, "Please let her go."

Tony wasn't a woman beater, but Maribel was pushing it. Releasing his grip, he opened the door, and walked out. Tony realized at any moment, he could kill her with his bare hands.

♥♥♥

Pulling up to Tha Hustle Records, the images of what had happened earlier flashed in his head. He wanted to apologize to Maribel, but refused to; she'd been out of control lately and he felt she needed to be taught a lesson. Going to see these three females didn't give Tony much to work with either, he was still pissed off as hell. Focusing his eyes on the main entrance, he could tell the place hadn't changed at all. The entry door was still glass with gold strips. People went in and out, some in regular outfits, others in business attire. Once he shut of the engine, it wasn't long before someone banged on the car.

"What the fuck!" he snapped.

"Don't' be banging on my shit," he warned Dimples.

"Whatever, nigga, just hurry your ass up so they don't suspect I'm gone." she shot back.

Dimples looked around to make sure her surroundings were clear. Wanting to make sure she covered all areas, she glanced up to Tha Hustle's window; no one was looking out.

Dimples entered the building first, Tony followed five minutes after. Riding in the elevator reminded him of the old days when he and Chin would ride to their office. The elevator still announced the floors…nothing had changed. He stood smiling to himself until the elevator doors opened. That's when Tony felt like someone had stolen the life from his body. The office resembled an African Art museum as opposed to a record company. The plaques and awards that he and Chin had worked so hard to earn no longer adorned the walls.

What the hell, he thought to himself. *I definitely have a lot of remodeling to do once I get back my empire. I'll bet none of the artist's are being promoted like they should if Porsha is so hung up in African art.*

The door to what used to be Chin's office was slightly ajar and Tony looked inside inquisitively. Major changes had been done inside the office. The money green sofa and carpet were no longer there. Instead, the sofa was replaced with white chairs, the carpet was now grey, and Chin's cherry wood desk had been replaced with a grey one. The blinds were grey and white.

"Well, finally we meet again." Tony announced as he marched into the office.

Everyone gasped. Seeing Tony was like seeing a ghost.

"The last I heard, you were supposed to be dead." Porsha spoke.

"Somebody didn't do a good job." He sat in one of the white chairs.

"Remind me to keep these when I take over," he smiled.

"Never in your wildest dreams," Dimples chimed in.

"No, in your worst nightmare, bitch."

BabyGirl reached for her gun, but it was empty.

"Missing something?" Tony asked, motioning to the gun. "Could one of you bitches pour me a glass of Henny?"

No one moved.

"Fine, I will do it myself."

He retreated to the bar which still stood in the same

place.

"I'm here to claim my empire." Tony stirred the brown liquor and ice with this finger.

The women glanced at each other, then burst out in laughter,

"Negative, you ain't getting shit," BabyGirl responded.

"Baby, I get what I want...by any means necessary." He spoke in a calm but arrogant manner before taking a sip of the liquor.

"And we kill for what we want," Porsha added.

"Nice." Tony responded sarcastically before taking his seat. The bright sun rays were shining in, so Dimples moved to adjust the blinds.

"The paperwork is final," Porsha informed.

"Says who? You and I both know what the original paperwork said. The empire goes to the person listed on the will or a family member, if both owners are dead. I'm still alive." Tony placed the glass on the table and opened his hands, his palms faced up.

Porsha acted like a timid mouse.

It didn't take a genius to figure out that their backs were against the wall, but it was obvious they were still up for a fight. So was Tony, he liked a little challenge and the excitement that went along with it. A strategy formed in his head. *Divide and conquer.*

Glancing in Porsha's direction, he noticed her words showed bravery; however, she wasn't really built for this type of thing. He sensed she was going to crack at any moment, so he decided to play on her weaknesses.

"Porsha," Tony started. "You are fucking despicable for a woman."

"Excuse me?" Porsha's head snapped back, she was ready to give Tony a tongue lashing.

"You heard me," he picked up the glass and took a sip from it. "How can you do business with a woman who slept with your man, and then later on killed him? Not only did she drag you into it, but she proved the strength she possesses."

Reaching in his pocket, he pulled out a cigar, lit it, took a pull, and released a cloud of smoke.

"There is no smoking in my office."

"Oh, you mean my office,' he smiled and took another pull.

"For a big time attorney, I expected more from you, at least in the name of Chin. I'm starting to think Chyna was more loyal to him than you were." "Fuck you, Tony, Chyna was a whore."

"And you weren't?" Looking her up and down, he continued.

"A high priced one too."

"How do I know you were there for Chin?" she replied.

"I'm sitting here claiming the empire." He leaned in, "The question is, were you there for Chin or his money? I mean, you did help kill him."

"Get out!"

"Can't handle a little truth?" he said with a menacing grin on his face.

Grabbing the ash tray she had on her desk, he knocked the ashes off his cigar and continued, "So much for no smoking in *your* office."

Porsha rolled her eyes.

"I know you cannot possibly think BabyGirl is your friend. If I were you, I would keep my eyes on her. She might be plotting to kill you."

"Whatever, nigga, if I wanted to kill Porsha I would have killed her a long time ago, so get the fuck outta here with that." BabyGirl was all up in his face. Tony could tell steam was coming out of her like a kettle.

Success... he hit the target and had started to boil the water.

"You right, but you and I both know you're smarter than that. Actually you're smarter than both of them and you are probably plotting to kill Porsha right now."

Porsha took a quick look at BabyGirl, her eyes searching for truth in what he was saying. BabyGirl gave Tony an evil stare.

"Like you're not planning to kill us," BabyGirl, who was now sitting in one of the white chairs, said.

"Of course...that's no secret. But unlike you; I don't do it in secrecy."

Tony had successfully planted seeds of doubt in Porsha's head.

Tension ripped through the room like a tornado making a quick sweep.

"You're weak, Porsha Hilton. With a brain like yours, hood chicks are not supposed to be leading you; you're supposed to be leading them. Tell me something, Porsha, do you think you can honestly trust BabyGirl?"

Tony didn't wait for a response as he moved on to his next victim—Dimples.

"And who are you? The follower bitch?"

"Nigga, back the fuck up," she yelled as she attempted to lunge at Tony.

Tony didn't care if she had been assisting him before; she

was just as despicable as the rest. If only her team knew she was the one who saved him that fateful night... Ever since Chin first laid eyes on BabyGirl at Big Tymers Nightclub, Tony has been communicating with her. She was the one who helped point him in Sandy's direction with the robberies.

"I dare you, Dimples. Remember, you have a lot at stake. You know who you remind me of? Pit Bull. That's exactly right. You have the potential to carry out shit, but are so busy plotting and scheming that you can't even put the idea together and make it work. I admire your courage though; a person like you would do well on my team." He taunted. "You need to do one thing, be the bitch you claim to be, stand on your own and stop running behind this bitch," he said pointing to BabyGirl. "*Then* you will make it."

Chuckling to himself, the scene unfolding in front of him reminded him of "The Sopranos," a hit show on HBO.

"BabyGirl, BabyGirl," he placed the cigar back in his mouth. "To reiterate, you are the smartest, but you lack leadership skills. You can't even keep your man in check."

"As if you can keep your fucking wife in check...if I were you, I would keep a close eye on her."

She hit a nerve. Tony wondered what she knew, but he didn't let it show, he remained calm and continued to speak.

"Ladies..."

He got up from the chair, and walked toward the window. He took a look out the glass window, the same one that had always offered Chin some sort of peace.

Chapter 26

THA HUSTLE RECORDS: NYC

"Let the blood bath begin, because I'm not giving up shit. I worked too hard to get this empire, and I'm not letting it go that easily." BabyGirl knew she had started a deadly chain of events. She was ready for whatever. "My father's money helped start this since Chin decided to take him earlier than God planned to."

Moving from the window, he walked over to her. "I don't give a fuck what Chin did to build this empire, I'm telling you I have money invested in this shit and I'm not bowing out until I get what's mine. If you want to start a war, suit yourself, but it's time for me to collect what you stole. The great Tony Moreno is not scared of a little bloodshed."

"And neither am I," she walked toward him. "What you think? You walk up in here and try to reclaim your empire and we should jump? It doesn't work like that."

"It works how I want it to work; it's my way or no way at all. Besides, I still have the law to back me. Maybe you should let Porsha, *the great lawyer*, inform you on that, since her specialty has been adjusting contracts lately."

"I tell you what I admire, your perseverance. And since I see your negotiation skills and your luck with women are not so great, we can just sit down, cut you a check and you can go about your business,"

"Cut me a check? You must not hear me; I have money invested in this company."

"Well frankly, I don't care. Now you can either consider this offer or prepare to die."

"I like your style," Tony smiled referring to BabyGirl. "I can already see how this is going to turn out in the end. It's going to be either me or you. Unfortunately I can't say your gun skills are as good as the game you talk."

BabyGirl chuckled while Porsha and Dimples stood at bay.

"Believe me when I tell you, it won't be Porsha putting a cap in your ass next time; it will be me. I assure you, all my victims stay dead. You can check my references, Chin and Danny from Harlem, they will tell you what happens when a man tries to step to me. Oh I forgot..." A sinister grin crossed her face, "They're dead."

She pointed her fingers at him in the form of a gun, and winked. Porsha got up and walked to the bar. She poured herself a glass of Grey Goose.

"Pour me a glass too," Dimples spoke.

"I hope you do realize that this is no longer business for me, this is personal." Tony took out another cigar and lit it.

"Oh, it's been personal for a while now. Ever since you allowed Chin to beat me near death, you became like him. Business," she paused, "was just the extra icing on the cake," BabyGirl sat on Porsha's desk. She could tell Tony was fuming with rage.

"I helped saved you. I should have let him kill you; maybe I wouldn't have had my empire stolen from me then." Tony informed. "You're fucking with my patience," Tony said with an aggravated tone in his voice. Tony then took out his gun, which had a silencer, and fired a shot in BabyGirl's direction. Everyone in the room jumped or ducked for cover as the bullet missed her head and pierced the wall. "Next time, it will be your head. So y'all better stop playing games with me and give me back my shit." Tony threatened as he opened the door and slammed it behind him.

Raising her head back up, BabyGirl attempted to retrieve her gun, but remembered the clip was empty. Porsha and Dimples were still lying on the floor cowering.

Such a bunch of punk bitches.

Eventually they both got up off the floor and tried to regain their composure.

"So what do we do now?" Dimples inquired.

"We need to figure out a plan on how to take out Tony," Porsha spoke.

"Any ideas?" Dimples questioned.

BabyGirl became quiet, as if she was in deep thought. Any wrong moves could cost her life, so she had to come up with the right scheme.

"That man is a dead man, that's all I know." She picked up her bag and headed for the door.

Chapter 27

CRIMINAL COURT: NYC

*W*ith his head hung down, Dragon paced the tile floor back and forth. He was fucked; he didn't know what Shane had told Porsha. He struggled as to whether or not he should say something to his attorney. He decided not to, he'd done enough damage and didn't know who to trust. Releasing his dark hands from the hold he had them in behind his back, he looked at his Jacob watch, 4:30 P.M., and he was still waiting for the judge to call his case. It was a Friday evening, and frankly, Dragon had better things to do. Every minute or so, he couldn't help but to wonder what the three females had up their sleeves. BabyGirl's words, '*Fix it*', haunted him like an unsettled spirit. He wanted to sit and rest, but he couldn't because his thoughts were all over the place.

"What time should we be seeing the judge?" he asked his attorney.

"Soon, when Shane gets here we should start."

He finally took a seat beside Bistrow and asked, "I'm not going in front of the grand jury am I?"

His attorney didn't give him a response. A brown-skinned court officer was closing the gold doors to another courtroom.

"Damn, I know I am not getting out here for now," Dragon

sighed; he wished the judge would hurry and call his case so he could know his fate. His body became even more restless as his heart pumped a thousand beats per minute, anxiousness was kicking in.

"Did you hear me?" Dragon's voice rose a bit above the normal level.

Bistrow, who was dressed in a dark blue suit with a burgundy shirt and tie, was searching in his bag for something and was startled by the man's tone of voice.

"No, you signed the papers waiving prosecution by a grand jury. Therefore, the judge will be the one to sentence you."

Dragon was starting to feel a little uneasy; after having been through the process as many times as he had, he didn't trust the justice system. Somehow they always found a way to screw him and he didn't expect any different today.

"I will see you on Monday." A thick Hispanic court clerk who was passing by yelled to a fellow co-worker.

"You know, of all the times I have defended you, I've never seen you like this. Nervous?" Bistrow asked, turning to face Dragon.

Dragon gave him a serious stare, "Out of all the times you've defended me, I've never seen you so quick to have me cop a plea, especially with someone who doesn't know how to keep their end of the bargain." Dragon replied with sarcasm.

"What are you talking about?" Bistrow inquired, placing the papers he had in his hand on the bench.

"Nothing," Dragon answered hanging his head. He had already placed a call to deal with Shane, and wasn't certain how it was going to play out. Either way, he didn't want to draw too much suspicion to himself.

Taking off his glasses, Bistrow gave Dragon a weird look.

"You guys never cease to amaze me; drug dealers and their stupidity. So willing to do the crime, make the money, and spend it like a rock star. In the streets you guys answer to no one, fearless, and most feared. You all execute your own plans, and hold your own court in the street: you are the judge, lawyer, and prosecutor." Bistrow let out a slight laugh, knowing he was about to hit a nerve. "But when you guys get caught, no one ever exercises such bravery, most become cowards and begin to snitch; the same thing they kill fellow dealers for. They look for the easiest way out, or hire some big shot attorney and expect the attorney to work miracles by getting them off, even when the evidence is clear and convincing.

"Are you calling me a snitch?" Dragon asked.

"Technically, you are." Bistrow responded, while putting his glasses back on.

The temper in Dragon's body soared straight to 100 degrees. "You're lucky we're in the courtroom, or else I would put your ass to sleep!" Dragon snarled in the man's face.

Pulling his glasses to the bridge of his nose, he gave Dragon a bored looked; the man had probably heard that a couple times, so Dragon saying it was probably nothing new.

"Watch the words that come from your mouth because it can make a difference in the way your case is being handled."

Dragon sucked his teeth," Whatever."

Footsteps made a clicking sound as they connected with the courthouse tile. One didn't have to lift their head to know it was Shane. The few times Dragon had met with the man, his footsteps were always similar. Shane walked by with an Armani brief case in his hand, wearing a suit that was nothing less than expensive. Dragon stared at the man and wanted to kill him on the spot, but decided against it. That would have been the dumbest move in history. Dragon couldn't help but wonder if the man was a kingpin and just used being an attorney as a cover. To his recollection, ADA's made good money, but not enough to support the kind of clothing and shoes Shane wore.

Walking past both him and his attorney, Shane gave them a nod. Dragon responded with a fake smile. Shane briefly strolled inside the courtroom, then came back out and approached Dragon and Bistrow,

"How you doing man?" He extended his hand for Dragon to shake.

Dragon hesitated at first, but remembering that he didn't want to draw suspicion to himself, he shook his hand.

"I'm good."

He then turned to Bistrow and said, "We need to talk."

Dragon shot his attorney a questioning look which Bistrow ignored.

"We will be back," he stated.

He watched as the two men headed down the hallway, then began heading in the other direction, as if exiting the court-house. Standing in front of the balcony, his eyes scanned below as if he was searching for gold.

The court lobby was empty except for an elderly white lady with full grey hair. The woman was purchasing something from the deli stand. Court officers in their blue uniforms, stood at the entrance talking and lingering, and the metal detector, which usually beeped frequently, was silent.

Dragon's mouth was becoming a little dry, so he thought about getting something to drink from the short Hindu guy working at the deli stand where he had seen the lady earlier. But it was a little too late as the man was preparing to leave. A loud obscenity froze him in his tracks as he was preparing to go down the steps.

"That was not the fucking deal!"

Turning to see where the drama was coming from, Dragon saw his attorney in a rage. Shane had his palms facing up as if he was explaining something. He had no clue as to what was going on, but he had all intentions on finding out. His mind was already made up; he was not going to jail. If he had to grab a gun from one of the court officer's holsters and hold the entire courtroom hostage—so be it. He needed to prove a point; he was going down in history. His cell phone rang, so he took a quick peek, but after seeing it was BabyGirl, he decided to ignore it and continued on his way.

"What's going on?" Dragon approached and asked both men.

Dragon's attorney held down his head. Shane smiled like he had some news he couldn't wait to deliver to Dragon.

"What? What the fuck is going on?" Dragon's voice became even louder as it bounced from wall to wall.

"The DA's plan is to ask the judge to hold you immediately after your trial, so you can start serving your time."

"Why? What grounds do they have for that?"

"I don't know,"

"Can I talk to you for a minute?" Dragon motioned to Shane as he could no longer hold his tongue.

Shane, who was uncertain at first, followed the man to the far right.

"You listen to me, and listen to me good." Dragon said peering into the man's eyes. The fire that he'd tried to hold back was now bursting through every pore. "I don't give a fuck what magic you have to pull, but I'm not going to jail tonight."

Shane chuckled, "Young buck, it ain't about what you

want, it's about what we have to offer you." Shane patted him on the shoulder and was about to walk off.

"Fine, but just be prepared to do jail time too." Dragon responded.

Shane froze in his tracks, "What are you talking about?"

"I know that you told Porsha about me testifying and that I'm about to go into the witness protection program."

"Please, get the hell outta here with that."

"I have proof, Shane," Dragon warned. "Don't act a fool and have me be the reason you lose your license—or worse."

Shane became silent as he looked into the man's face. He turned in the direction of Bistrow, who was sitting on the bench with his legs crossed reading the Law Section of *The New York Times*, the man was oblivious as to what was going on.

"Let me talk to the DA," Shane replied.

Dragon knew Shane was pissed and would kill him if he could. *Who gives a fuck, if the nigga wanna act stupid, then I have every intention to act the same.*

"Yea, you do that," Dragon's anger began to subside, "because I'm not going to jail. I held up my end of the bargain and gave them what they wanted, so they should do the same. I didn't even say bye to my girl, you can't expect me to go in tonight."

Both men walked back over to Bistrow.

"Your girl?" Shane chuckled, "You mean the same one whose ass you busted recently? Since when did she mean so much to you?"

"Fuck you..." Dragon spat and began to walk off. "She means way more to me than Porsha does to you."

Shane became silent, the smile he had on his face was now gone. Dragon knew he was pushing it with that low blow. Dragon's attorney glanced at Shane.

"Cat got your tongue, Shane? Go ahead and tell Bistrow about your sexual escapades, your extra-marital affair with Porsha Hilton, and the fact that you told her I'm a snitch."

Bistrow turned to Shane for an answer.

"Are you even making sense? Why would I leak information to someone I'm trying to bring down?"

"That's a question only you could answer." Dragon replied, throwing the question back in his lap.

"Let's go upstairs," Shane motioned to Dragon's attorney; the heat in the kitchen was beginning to rise, and Shane couldn't handle it. "I'm sure we can reason this out professionally." Both men proceeded to the elevator, Dragon watched as the door closed.

"These motherfucking clowns better come back with something good, or else they will feel the fire from this Dragon."

Needing a bit of fresh air, he headed toward the stairs. When the courtroom lights began to flicker, Dragon stopped to look at the florescent bulb above.

"Have them check the back-up generator." a court officer yelled.

Dragon's eyes were fixated on the bulb when suddenly everything went pitch black.

He could hear the frantic footsteps of confused people running toward him. Reaching for his cell phone, he flipped open the lid to use the light for guidance. He extended his left hand as he felt his way through. This was the perfect opportunity for him to leave. He was closer to freedom than he thought.

"Sir, you gotta go this way," a court officer with a bright flash light spoke. The light almost blinded Dragon.

Dragon followed closely with the other people, placing

himself in the middle so no one would try to haul him away to jail. Just as they were about to exit, the light flicked back on and everyone stopped in their tracks except for Dragon; he was going out the door to join those who had made it out. *Freedom* was the word for the afternoon.

He was about to exit the building when a loud shriek bellowed from the top floor. Dragon turned his head to see what was going on. Curiosity kicked in, but freedom held its ground—*let's go*. Freedom won.

"They're dead," was the next thing he heard. A swarm of court officers raced up the steps, trying to find out who death had taken. Turning on his heels, he raced back up the steps... curiosity had won round two. People gathered around the elevator like freebies were being given out. Dragon used his slender frame and pushed past the people so he could see who it was they were gathered around.

As the scene came into view, Dragon's eyes nearly popped out of his head at the gruesome sight. Blood seeped from Shane's head onto his expensive suit. Bistrow lay not too far from Shane. His chest was pierced open by a bullet.

Blocking out everyone and everything around, Dragon now realized the blackout was no accident. Searching his surroundings, he pulled back, trying to get to the same stairway he'd escaped from earlier. Dragon needed to get away and get away fast, in case someone tried to accuse him of the murders. No telling who saw him and Shane exchange words earlier.

"Get an ambulance now!" he heard a female officer shout into her radio.

"People, you need to back up. This is now a crime scene," another officer spoke.

Dragon moved swiftly toward the courthouse exit, headed

down the building's concrete stairs, and bumped right into a red Audi parked out front. It immediately became clear that the black out and Tony being at the scene were not coincidental.

"Hop in,' Tony demanded.

Dragon hesitated; he was already in too much trouble to risk putting himself in any more.

"You better get in here before you become a suspect," Tony warned.

Dragon opened the door and hopped in. Tony wasted no time and zoomed down Center Street, toward Canal Street.

"What the hell just happened? I know that shit wasn't an accident right there."

Tony continued to drive.

"You not hearing me, what just happened?" Panic was streaking in his voice. "Why would you kill them there? I could have easily been labeled a suspect."

"Well, aren't you?" Tony responded with irony.

"Was it necessary to kill my fuckin' attorney?"

Tony chuckled, "Is this coming from the same Dragon who ran the streets of Harlem? Damn, BabyGirl is slowly turning you into a bitch."

Dragon just sat quietly and watched as people of Asian descent tried to get their hustle on in China Town.

"As a hustler, you should know that rule number one is you cannot leave eye witnesses when you're committing a murder, and two: sometimes killing calls for rash decisions."

"You still didn't have to kill him,"

Tony took his eyes off the road quickly and looked in Dragon's direction for a brief second.

"Who said I killed them, did you see me kill anyone? Besides, what do you care? Shane was about to bring you down, and your attorney, from what I hear, wasn't doing much to stop him."

Dragon became agitated; he saw where things were going. Tony was showing how deadly he could be without leaving a trace of evidence. No other words were exchanged as they sat at the light in silence. Dragon's heart pounded as he wondered if he would be labeled a suspect. He knew Tony wasn't going to defend him, nor admit to killing them. Turning to look at the back seat in the car, he couldn't help but notice a brown case. He wondered what was inside. Sirens heading toward the courthouse could be heard miles away. The light changed to green and Tony drove like mad, with all the evidence about recent events, and Tha Hustle Records sitting in the brown case on the back seat.

Chapter 28

CHASE MANHATTAN BANK: NYC

*P*orsha's heels clicked against the floor with near military precision. She was inches away from Leon.

"Ms. Hilton," Leon, the brown-skinned bank manager greeted after placing the phone on the receiver.

"Hey Leon," she greeted while giving him a hug and a kiss on the cheek. Porsha removed her Chanel shades and glanced around the bank. Customers shifted from side to side as they waited impatiently to be called. Porsha was glad she had a 'connect' and didn't have to join them in waiting.

Two weeks prior to showing up, Porsha placed a call informing Leon that she was coming to close her account. She knew Leon would question her decision, so she made sure she prepared a good response before making the call.

"Would you like any water or coffee while we complete your transaction, Ms. Hilton?" Leon asked.

"No, thank you," she replied. She wanted to get her money and be on her way.

Since she was one of the bank's top clients, Porsha was extended privileges beyond the regular customer. Someone would call her personally when her checks were cleared, daily to inform her of the account balance, and they sent her special customer gifts. Leon, along with the rest of the staff, did every-thing thing they could to ensure that they kept her business. Porsha followed behind as Leon led the way to his office. As soon as they walked through the glass doors, Porsha walked over to the burgundy cushioned chair and sat down. The of-fice was pristine and the wall was covered with Leon's degrees and various certificates and plaques he'd earned. She smiled because she enjoyed being in the presence of people she con-sidered to be in her class.

As Porsha sat back in the chair, a feeling of relief took over. She had given up Tha Hustle Records and was out of the loop. She knew her call to a bank in the Cayman Islands would prove to be a good move. All she had to do was keep the money in a safe place until things died down, and then she would wire her money to the account. Looking down on Leon's desk, she saw a piece of paper with the amount she was withdrawing and the words *'time left'* written on it. She found it kind of odd, but then figured that since she was closing her account, it was probably just procedure.

"We are going to miss doing business with you," Leon spoke while placing her money in the Louis Vuitton bag.

"Aww, me too, you are my favorite person here." Porsha winked.

"Girl, don't have me all teary eyed up in here," Leon's joked, waving his hand in a feminine manner.

As Porsha got up to give him a hug, the program on the 19 inch flat screen TV caught her attention.

"In other news today..." A female voice spoke. "Police are still looking for the suspects who are responsible for the death of District Attorney Rick Shane and Defense attorney Mark Bistrow. Police have no leads and are asking anyone with information to come forward."

Porsha's mind went blank, nothing made sense anymore. *"How the hell is Shane dead?"* was the only thing she could think.

"The world is going to hell in a hand basket when someone can shoot people in the courthouse and get away with it." She said to Leon, with a look of disbelief.

Suddenly, out of nowhere, Porsha felt a startling chill go down her spine and she began to sweat uncontrollably. A sense of danger consumed her. This was a warning, something major was about to happen. She began to panic and started to fidget nervously right where she was standing.

"Are you okay, Ms. Hilton?" Leon questioned as he touched Porsha's shoulder and tried to make eye contact. She tried to speak, but couldn't get the words out. Her breathing became heavy and erratic and her thoughts were scattered. Placing the bag on the desk, Leon inquired, "Do you need a glass of water?"

Giving Leon a menacing stare, she grabbed her bag and proceeded to back away from him.

"Ms. Hilton, what's wrong?"

Judging by the look on her face, one would have thought Leon was the enemy. Walking backward, she stumbled over the chair she sat on earlier. Leon tried to help, but she pushed him away and headed out the door. She pushed and shoved her way out of the bank. All eyes were on her because her strange behavior had made her the center of attention. She thought she might be making a fool of herself, but it didn't matter because in her mind she was saving herself. Problem was, she just didn't know what she was saving herself from.

Porsha held a firm grip on her Vuitton bag as she ran out

the door to her car. Once safely inside, she locked the door and drove off. So busy in thought, she didn't notice the flashing lights behind her.

♥♥♥

"Driver, pull over to the side," the officer demanded over the bullhorn. Her heart pounded harder, her thoughts raced a million miles a second. *What did I do to have the officer chase me? Did they find out Shane and I had a relationship? How would I explain the money in the bag without being tied to Tha Hustle Records?* Whatever it the reason was, she didn't need the bullshit right now. Porsha took a quick look in her rear-view mirror and fixed herself up as best she could while pulling over.

"Good afternoon, Officer," Porsha addressed in a polite manner.

"Ma'am step out of the vehicle," The officer ordered.

"First of all," she started with an attitude. "You need to inform me as to why I'm being pulled over before I'm getting out of this mothafucking car."

"You were driving over the speed limit, bitch, is that good enough for you?" The ruddy NYS trooper replied with his own attitude.

Appalled by his answer, Porsha retaliated, "What the fuck did your cracker ass just call me?" She cocked her head to the side.

"Ma'am step out of the fucking car, we can make this easy or hard – your choice."

His partner, a white female of medium build, stood on the passenger side of the car. Her right hand rested on her gun, which was ready to be drawn at the slightest sign of a threat. Drivers continued to flow with the midday traffic on Hutchinson Parkway; none of them cared enough to be nosey. As the sun beamed down on her Ferrari, Porsha stared boldly into the officer's face,

"Let me have your sergeant's name?"

"Out of the damn car," The female officer ordered, now pointing her gun at Porsha and unlocking the safety.

Not wanting to risk her life, Porsha obliged. She planned on teaching these officers a lesson later on, starting with the bitch who pointed a gun at her.

"You crossed the line, bitch, we shall meet again."

"Turn your ass around." The male officer flung Porsha on the car.

A white Nissan Maxima slowed down to be nosey, but the female officer caught the driver and yelled, "If you don't want to be hauled off to jail tonight, I suggest you keep it moving."

The officer placed Porsha in handcuffs, while holding the gun to her side.

"I sure hope you know your department will be facing a major lawsuit once I'm released."

The officer laughed and pressed the gun further into her side, "Shut up before I pulled the trigger."

Her feet were beginning to hurt as she stood leaning against the car with her legs apart.

"This is a nice position," the officer whispered in her ear, rubbing his limp dick on her ass.

A feeling of disgust engulfed her just at the mere thought of the *fat, nasty, redneck pig* molesting her.

"Found it," the female officer shouted, as she emerged from the red car with the Vuitton bag.

Porsha lowered her head and shook it from side to side; all her dreams and hopes were about to be taken away. How could she have been so careless by not placing the bag in the trunk? Then hit her, this wasn't a routine stop.

"Who the hell sent you?" Porsha questioned.

"You're a smart girl," The officer pulled her off the car and spun her around. "I'm surprised it took you so long to figure it out."

Unzipping the bag, the officers' eyes grew wide in amazement.

"This will be going with us," The female officer motioned with the gun and pointed toward the bag.

"Hell fucking no!" Porsha yelled as she attempted to lunge at the officer even though her hands were still cuffed behind her back. She didn't make it far before she was knocked over by the male officer. The male officer forced her onto the hot asphalt, pressing his dirty shoes between her breasts and soiling her white Dior shirt.

The gun clicked and Porsha winced. She waited for death to steal her soul, but instead, the cop began to rub his gun down the center of her breast. Then he leaned in closer and said,

"Next time we meet, I'm going to rape you."

The female officer paced back and forth as she told whoever she was on the phone with that they had found the money.

"Should we kill her?"

Porsha prayed the answer wouldn't be 'yes.' Her outward appearance showed strength, but inside she was in complete fear.

"Here," the officer gave her the phone. "The person on the phone wants to talk to you."

"Hey baby, thanks for the money," The voice on the other end bragged.

"Tony, Tony Moreno?"

"Ms. Hilton."

"You mothafucker! Wait until I get you—you will never get away with this. You hear me?"

A sarcastic laugh escaped Tony's lips.

"I already have."

"Fuck you, you fucking spic. Fuck you Tony," she wiggled trying to free her hands.

"It's not going to end like this." she shouted.

"Calm your ass down," the male officer warned. His eyes surveyed the area to make sure no one was watching. As soon as he turned back to face her, a wad of spit hit his face.

"Of course this is not the end. I will be meeting with you personally soon, and I want my papers drafted and those bitches names removed from my company. And I expect that to be done in three days."

"Never," she screamed

"Don't push me, Porsha, because I can be a lot worse than a natural disaster."

"It's war, Tony."

"Oh yea, before I go, tell Leon thanks for the tip."

That's when it finally dawned on her, the paper with the time and the amount of money she was withdrawing and Leon hanging up the phone just when she walked in—now it all added up. Leon had put his nose in the wrong person's business and he was going to pay for that mistake.

"It was nice doing business with you," the officer spoke. Porsha couldn't do anything but watch as they drove off with her money and she stood there in handcuffs.

Chapter 29

FEDERAL COURT: MANHATTAN, NYC

$\mathcal{S}$ilence swept through the bright room as everyone sat, resembling mannequins in a museum, and waited for the verdict. It had been two weeks since he'd had that meeting with Porsha and he couldn't wait to see the outcome of the trial so he could make his next move. Tony adjusted in his chair as tension ripped through the courtroom, making it more fit for a Presidential impeachment than a trial. Detective Garfin, Officers Warren and Flynn, and Captain Mahoney all sat together on a long wooden bench.

Tony Moreno sat directly in front of Detective Garfin. Tony tried to maintain his composure as he shifted in his chair, almost wishing he could teleport out of the courtroom to a secure hideout spot, but then again, he was ready to get the trial over with. With such a steady flow of money filtering into the justice system, legally and illegally, he would have thought the chair would have been softer, instead, he felt as though he were sitting on concrete steps.

The stern legal team knew they had Tony right where they wanted him and were convinced he was going down.

With a long, piercing gaze, Tony gave Detective Garfin, the man who'd rather see him executed than to serve life in prison, a deadly stare. Garfin turned his neck each time the brown door swung open, obviously curious to see who else would be in court to play a part in Tony's trial. Wrinkle lines creased his pale forehead.

Tony was guilty without question and he knew Garfin was wondering why the jurors were withholding the one word that would sound like music to his ears *Guilty*.

"I hope you burn in hell," Garfin leaned in and whispered to Moreno so others wouldn't hear. Captain Mahoney saw everything, and couldn't wait to exchange a few words with him.

"Don't count on it," Tony responded with a smile before adding, "The color of the justice system is green." He loosened his tie as warm air blew out of the vent above his head, causing sweat to form on the back of his neck. The temperature outside was cold, but the courtroom was steaming hot. Maybe it was the fact that he was nervously awaiting the verdict, or maybe it was a sign of how things were are going to heat up—if he got off.

Garfin flinched at the sound of Tony's voice, the words from Tony's lips added fuel to an already ignited fire.

Looking straight ahead, Garfin's eyes fixated on the words, 'IN GOD WE TRUST', which were engraved behind the judge's bench. Garfin hoped he could really trust the justice system today.

Without announcement, the jurors entered the courtroom, strolling behind one another like soldiers obeying a command from their lieutenants.

Silence took over the courtroom. Garfin gazed at the jurors as if he were trying to read their minds. A small, bitter smile flashed across his lips.

Tony leaned back in his chair before winking at Garfin. This action alone was an insult and an act of defiance. Garfin clenched his left hand into a fist, the same left hand that had clamped the handcuffs on Tony's wrists.

The judge cleared his throat, breaking the silence. Everyone sat on the edge of their chairs, especially Garfin, waiting for the word "guilty" to flow out of the judge's mouth.

Anticipation showed on everyone's faces as the judge's deep voice uttered, "Foreman, have you reached a verdict?"

"Yes we have, your honor," a slender Caucasian man in his early fifties said. A short, stocky bailiff of Hispanic heritage walked over to the judge and handed him the sheet of paper that held Tony's fate. The judge carefully studied the contents and handed it back to the bailiff. Garfin leaned forward.

Tony grinned as he watched Garfin shift on the edge of the chair as if waiting for the moment to jump up and down to rejoice.

Opening the paper, the Foreman proceeded,

"We the jurors find the defendant, Tony Moreno, on the charge of in the 2nd degree murder—not guilty. On the charge of assault—not guilty. On the charge of money laundering—not guilty.

Garfin's blue eyes widened to the size of golf balls.

A gasp escaped from some of the spectators in the court as Tony Moreno hugged his lawyers and whispered to Garfin, "It's on."

Maribel Moreno sat on the front bench not too far behind her husband wearing a long Gucci trench coat and big oval-shaped Gucci sunglasses. Her hair was tucked to the side in a neat bun, displaying the pink rouge on her smooth, light, unblemished face. She blew her husband a kiss as she stood. To onlookers, they looked like the perfect married couple, but to Tony it was all a facade. She would be dealt with, he already knew about her intended plot to kill him. The shit she'd done with Victor wasn't forgotten either and Tony planned on paying her back for crossing him. Right now he wanted everyone to think they were perfectly happy.

"You bastard," Garfin yelled, leaping up from the bench. "I don't know how I'm gonna bring you down, you son of a bitch, but if I have to spend my whole career doing it, trust me, I will." Garfin raged and pointed his index finger at Tony while his fellow co-workers tried to calm him down.

The faint grin on Tony's lips grew even wider as he said to Captain Mahoney, "Keep your puppy on a leash, he's getting a little too out of control."

To ease the commotion, the other officers escorted Garfin out of the courtroom. Tony trailed behind them; not a single scared bone was in him.

As Tony made his way down the concrete courtroom steps and was several feet from Garfin, he paused to think about the justice system and its fairness. A feeble giggle escaped his mouth. As long as oxygen flowed through Tony's lungs, the justice system would rule in his favor.

The cool breeze swept past Tony as he trudged down the steps. Commuters in traffic tried to navigate their way through the swarm of media who attempted to speak to Tony. Tony chuckled as he watched Garfin struggle to free himself from his escorts. Keeping a watchful eye on them was part of his next plan because he had something in store for them also. He had a mission, one he was surely going to fulfill.

Garfin stopped in his tracks, nearly causing his escorts to stumble. Flynn, Mahoney, and Warren almost lost the grip on his arm. "How are you with decision?" he asked, as he looked up at the gray lady statute that held the balance scale in her hand, and a blindfold over her eyes. Continuing down the steps, the media swarmed him like vultures scavenging a piece of dead meat.

Tony waved and lit up a cigar as Garfin stared at him. It was obvious the man was pissed as hell, but in reality, he wasn't nearly as angry as Tony. Garfin was in for an overdose of pay-back.

A petite reporter with brunette hair, managed to squeeze through the crowd, then held her microphone up to Garfin and asked, "How do you feel, Detective Garfin, knowing that Tony Moreno, the man you have been investigating for months, years... got off?"

Lawyers pushed past them, trying to get inside so they wouldn't be late for their business. Tony, joined at the hip with his wife, inched closer, dying to hear Garfin's response.

Garfin sneered, glanced at Tony, and then looked at the reporter.

"How would you feel if the man who raped your seven-year-old daughter, leaving her on life support grasping for breath got off? If you can relate or imagine how that would feel, then you know how I feel."

The reporter was speechless. Garfin turned, and walked toward his unmarked Impala.

Prison buses, cars, and people passed in slow motion so they could get a glimpse of the event. Someone who was not familiar with the case would have thought a superstar was on trial. Tony and his wife ignored them and headed for their vehicles.

"Tony Moreno! How does the taste of freedom feel?" the same reporter asked. She was one of ABC's top news reporters and everyone knew she was a piranha when it came to making sure her questions were answered.

Removing the cigar from his lips, and releasing Maribel's hand he replied,

"It feels absolutely great." He then drew his wife close to him and gave her a tongue kiss; he wanted it all on camera.

Garfin spun around just to get a glimpse of the circus act Tony was putting on.

Tony waved at Garfin again. "This just goes to show how fair our justice system is, especially with all the police corruption going on these days," he said with a smile and quick wink at Garfin. "These cops having nothing better to do than to oppress successful people and try to frame them."

"Fucking bastard," Garfin yelled as he took a giant step toward Tony, but was restrained by Officer Warren—again.

Tony shifted his attention off the reporter as he heard Flynn mumble, "Leave him, we'll get him soon."

"Good luck trying," Tony responded while the media stood soaking up everything like a Bounty paper towel.

"Believe me," Garfin pulled away from Warren, moving toward Tony and his wife and bringing everything and everyone to a screeching halt.

"The next time we meet, you won't be lucky enough to be standing here a free man talking to the media."

"I'm looking forward to it."

Garfin squinted his eyes with rage. Captain Mahoney moved toward him, but as soon as he made it to the steps, he fell to the ground. A bullet left a hole in his forehead. His eyes were wide open and staring into the clouds.

Flynn, who was standing behind Mahoney, held onto his arm because the bullet had grazed him after it went through Mahoney. Glancing toward the family court building located across the street, Tony watched as the sniper pulled his gun back through the window. It became pandemonium as people began to scatter, duck, and scream in fear.

"Now this is a mothafucking welcome home party," Tony thought. "I'm back and with a vengeance."

Chapter 30

GUTTENBERG, NEW JERSEY

Switching lanes on the George Washington Bridge, Baby-Girl sped through traffic in a rented Trailblazer, hurrying to her destination.

"God damn girl, you'd make a good getaway driver," Fire praised, holding onto the handle above the car window.

She wasn't sure she should take his comment as a compliment, so she simply replied, "Time is of the essence," as she tapped a little harder on the gas. Detective Garfin and the entire 19th precinct had been on her tail, her nightclub had been shut down, and she was recently audited by the IRS. To top it off, Maribel was playing games when it came to handing over the tapes she'd promised.

How the fuck does something that rightfully belongs to me end up giving me such headache? She couldn't quite comprehend. Dragon hadn't followed through with killing Porsha, which meant she would have to do it and then kill him. Something about Dimples didn't sit too well with her either. Plus, she was trying to figure out a way to get the tapes Maribel had.

As the late night traffic flowed smoothly into New Jersey, BabyGirl couldn't help but take a glimpse at her surroundings, taking in the beautiful landscapes.

"Someone is in deep thought," Fire stated, using his left hand to stroke her hair.

Averting her attention to him, she released a smile. Underneath the smile was a girl who was scared—scared of what was ahead.

"What's wrong?"

"I don't know; my whole world seems to be falling apart."

She slowed the car down a bit, matching the mood she was in.

"Well," Fire turned to her, removing his hand from her hair. "Maybe you're taking on more than you can handle and starting to lose sight of your main focus. Have you really asked yourself what is your main goal?"

Silence lingered between them. She never really asked herself that question. Initially, she started out to avenge her father's death and although she took down two of his killers, something else told her there was more to find out."

"I guess I have to figure that one out."

Fire reached out and rubbed her hand as she tapped a little harder on the gas.

"Everything will be alright."

His words were soothing, yet she couldn't forget how life never ceased to show her how wicked it could become.

As the car pulled closer to the Guttenberg, BabyGirl prayed and hoped that her plan wouldn't fall through and that the tapes were where her informant said they were.

Fire squinted his narrow eyes as he struggled to find the address.

"Damn you're worse than the fucking three blind mice" BabyGirl laughed, releasing the tension that consumed her earlier.

"What!" he turned to her," Why don't you try getting your ass over here and have your eyes struggle in this darkness."

Realizing the street did not provide light, BabyGirl remained silent.

"I thought so," he replied.

"You still fucking blind," they both shared a laugh at Fire's expense.

When she pulled up to the building, she didn't have to circle around for a parking space because she found one with ease. As she extended her thick brown legs out of the vehicle, the slit in the front of her yellow button-down dress blew up slightly, exposing her upper thigh. Fire, who had already stepped out of the car, was near the driver's side and caught a glimpse.

"Damn those are some sexy stairways to heaven." Fire said licking his lips.

"Keep your mind focused on the tapes and not on my damn legs, freak," she replied, getting out of the car.

"Damn, can't a brotha give a compliment when it's due? So feisty..."

"Sure, compliments are welcomed, but not when they are followed by nasty thoughts."

Her dress clung to her body, revealing every inch and curve that God had blessed her with. She knew Fire was watching, so she made it her duty to sway her ass from side to side. She tucked her clutch purse under her left arm while holding her Puma bag in the right. Fire, who was lingering behind, ran up, leaned in, and whispered,

"Damn you're sexy."

"I know," Confidence leaped from her lips. "Right now though, you need to fall back so our plan can go through."

Obliging, he moved to the side of the building to conceal himself.

Taking in a deep breath, she opened the glass doors leading

to the lobby of the building. A young lady in her mid-twenties walked by and they gave each other a quick look before heading to their respective destinations.

Soft instrumental music played through speakers in the lobby. It was so soothing, BabyGirl wished she was lying in a tub of bubble bath, sipping some champagne, and listening to the music, rather than undertaking the assignment she was on.

The security guard, who was dressed in a white shirt and a navy blue vest, took his eyes off what he was doing and focused his attention on her.

"Good night, who are you here to see?" the brown-eyed security guard asked.

"I was here to see a friend of mine, but now that you're here, I might as well see you," she leaned over the counter exposing her perky 36C breasts.

The security guard blushed and then he chuckled a bit. He looked around the area to ensure no one had seen what happened - he was in the clear.

"Thanks for the invitation, Miss, but I need to know who you here to see." His proper mannerisms returned.

Walking behind the oval-shaped counter, she bent down to place her bag on the floor. She had purposely decided not to wear any underwear to the excitement. Opening the bag wide, she took out a whip then flipped her dress up, and showed her perfectly shaped ass.

"Spank me, I've been naughty," she purred, taking the handle of the whip and rubbing it between the crack of her ass."

"I need to know a name..." the security guard said, trying to sound firm though his voice was beginning to crack. Baby-Girl knew she had softened him a bit.

"Or else I'll have to call the police."

"Mmmm... handcuffs, I love them" she took a pair out of her bag and dangled them in his face. "You know why you're not gonna call anyone?"

"Why?"`

"Because, I'm going to see Mrs. Moreno and we are lovers."

She moved closer to him and propped her naked ass on his desk, right in front of him.

"Now I suggest you don't call her or the police, and then I will let you in on our little fun," she opened her legs and exposed her shaven pussy. She then dipped her hand into her vagina before taking it out and running her moist finger across the security guard's lips.

The elevator chimed and he quickly told her to get off the desk and hide under the counter. BabyGirl could hear a man and woman talking. She was disgusted by what she had to do, but remembering her life depended on the tapes, she used her hands to fondle the guard's dick through his pants.

"Good night," she heard the couple say.

"Good..." he choked on the words before *night* could follow.

Slowly making her way slowly up from under the counter, she leaned in and whispered,

"I have a little peep show for you." She lifted her dress, pulled out her right breast out of her bra, and proceeded to fondle her pussy. She allowed her moans to escape, though her eyes never left the rack of keys to the different apartments behind him.

"Let's go into the back room so we don't get caught." she suggested.

The gullible security guard agreed. As soon as they got into the room she resumed her seduction. Ten minutes into it, a knock came to the door. With his pants dangling at his knees, he moved from off her, pulled up his pants, and was about to open the door when she knocked him out with a glass bottle. She grabbed the stack of keys on her way past the desk, and then took Fire's hand and raced toward the elevator.

"Damn, your show was off the hook. My friend right here..." he motioned toward his dick. "Is a little jealous from all the attention you gave that punk."

"Don't worry, baby, I will give you an even better show." she replied.

The elevator chimed and the door opened to the 14th floor, her Chloe shoes pressed softly in the navy blue carpet as they approached Maribel's apartment. Putting both their ears to the door, they tried to listen for any movement. Once they were sure no one was home, they both entered the apartment in search of what they set out for. A few minutes into searching, Fire found the safe. BabyGirl turned on the living room television and put it on the channel that monitored the lobby.

"The tapes are in here," Fire yelled out from Tony's bedroom.

Walking in she asked, "How are we going to get them?"

"Relax," Fire held her shoulders. "What we need to do is put our heads together and try to figure out how to open the safe."

When BabyGirl headed back into the living room to see if they had packed anything that would help them open the safe, she noticed that security was starting to move.

"Oh shit, he is getting up, Fire, let's head downstairs."

Walking at a fast pace toward the elevator, BabyGirl pressed the down button. When she stepped off the elevator, the security guard was rubbing the knot on his head and had just picked up the phone to call the police.

"Put the phone down," BabyGirl warned.

"I don't care who you are," he pointed in her direction, "I'm calling the police."

Moving swiftly, Fire brandished his nine millimeter then spoke,

"Put the mothafucking phone down,"

"Don't shoot," the guard begged as he jumped back and dropped the receiver.

"Shut up," Fire ordered. Then he motioned to BabyGirl, "Get the tapes of the escapade between y'all earlier."

"Got it," she shouted from the back.

"I doubt you will be calling the police," Fire whispered while removing the man's driver's license from his wallet. "But in case you do, I will not only come after you, but I will track your family down and slaughter them without mercy."

BabyGirl smiled inwardly; finally she felt someone was protecting her as opposed to her always having to protecting herself.

Heading to the glass door that led out of the building, her killer instinct kicked in. Removing her weapon from her bag, she aimed at the whimpering security guard, and fired one in his torso. Fire, surprised by the sound, almost jumped out of his skin.

"What the hell did you just do?" Fire questioned, still in shock.

Shrugging her shoulders she replied, "He was gonna snitch anyway, so might as well get rid of him now."

Fire stared at her and shook his head. Both BabyGirl and

Fire headed out of the building into the cool night breeze, and eventually to the Trailblazer just like Bonnie and Clyde, or so she thought.

Chapter 31

"*I* can't believe I let Tony to talk me in to this," a frustrated Dragon thought to himself as he sat at the edge of his bed. The blunt he had been pulling on all morning rested between his right index and middle fingers. He buried his face in his left hand as he reflected on his pitiful life. *I wouldn't be in this predicament if I had gotten a hold of that brown briefcase Tony had that day in court...I bet it held all the evidence I needed.*

The 60-inch flat panel television screen that usually held his attention didn't today. He was obviously in a state of depression. He was a half an hour away from having to assist Tony, but the closer it came to the time, the more he wanted to back out. Tony's blackmailing was beginning to get out of control and it was only a matter of time before Tony turned on him.

A loud banging on the front door caused him to put the blunt down in the ashtray instead of at the tip of his mouth.

"What the fuck!" he growled as he got up and headed downstairs to the living room.

Boom...Boom! The door rattled once more.

His slender muscular frame moved over to the front window. He peeked outside before opening the door.

"Shit," he mumbled as he looked around for a means of escape.

The thought of Garfin being at his front door made him nervous. The only time the man visited or popped up on him was when some shit had jumped off and he needed information or when was trying to bring him down. Either way, he knew this was not going to be a pleasant visit.

"Mr. Bentley, open up the door, I know you're in there." He heard Garfin yell through the door.

Dragon didn't respond, he simply leaned against the cream wall trying to figure what the hell was going on.

"Should I yell louder and let your neighbor's know that you're a low life criminal and a fucking snitch?" Garfin continued to taunt.

Shit, you're already yelling my business, so should it even matter? He thought. Dragon was now beginning to question if co-operating with the police was a good move. It's like the more he helped, the more they wanted from him and their demands became more unrealistic.

"Bentley, I'm giving you two minutes before we kick down this door and beat the shit outta you…now open the damn door." Garfin yelled as he continued to pound the door.

Dragon at first wondered how Garfin knew he was there, but it eventually dawned on him that it didn't take a genius to see his BMW was parked in the driveway.

Sighing, Dragon took a peek at his watch; he wanted to see how much time he had left before he had to meet up with Tony. Fueled with rage because the detective constantly invaded his privacy, Dragon swung open the walnut door and shouted,

"What…"

He didn't get a chance to complete his question before Garfin gave him a jab to the face, causing Dragon to fall backwards onto the plush brown carpet.

While Dragon held his face, Garfin stepped in and closed the door behind him. Detective Garfin then leaned over and pointed his silver nine millimeter at Dragon's face and uttered,

"Now fucking what?"

Dragon gave the man a deadly look before saying, "You're not in your mothafucking jurisdiction, so what the hell are you doing at my house?"

"Your house? You don't own shit. The last we checked, it belongs to Natalie Smith. Secondly, I don't need permission to cross jurisdictions to visit your sorry ass. I come after what I want, so don't get it twisted.

"What do you want from me?" Dragon got up off the floor and stood face-to-face with Garfin.

"Be careful how you talk to me, smart ass, I can make your life a living hell, if I'm not doing so already," He chuckled and spit flew out of his mouth when he spoke. Backing out of Dragon's face, his eyes roamed around the living room. Nodding his head, Garfin stated,

"Expensive taste."

With his hand in his pocket and his back resting against the entrance door, Dragon spoke,

"What do you want? I don't have all day."

"Well, for starters, did you know that District Attorney Shane and your lawyer are dead?"

"Yea.

"Well good then, because I plan on charging you with the murders."

"*Ch…ch…charging* me with?" Dragon stuttered, completely shocked.

"You must be joking," Dragon responded, sucking his teeth

and trying not to show his fear.

Taking a seat on the black leather sectional, Garfin continued.

"This is no joke, son; we're planning on charging you with a double homicide."

"You and I both know that's bullshit, so stop wasting my time and get to the real reason why you're here."

Getting up off the sofa, Garfin walked over once again to Dragon's face,

"Is it? I mean, the tapes with your corroborations are gone, and get a load of this, even the courthouse surveillance tapes are gone."

"Yea, ok," Dragon replied in a sarcastic manner.

"Who else would do something like that?"

"You're the police; you tell me."

Stretching out his hand, Garfin pushed Dragon against the wall, pulled the gun from his waist, and used the barrel of the gun to give Dragon a blow to the head.

"Stop playing with me and tell me what you know. We already know you had help."

Dragon was struggling to get free of his grasp.

"I don't know anything about that." Dragon wheezed.

"Let him go," Warren demanded as he stepped into the house and saw what was unfolding. Warren stood at the door in plain clothes, which was unusual since he'd always worn a uniform in the past.

They probably promoted him. Dragon thought to himself.

"You're killing the witness," Warren protested.

Releasing his grip, Garfin stared in Dragon's brown eyes.

"Bring back those tapes or else it's your ass," Garfin warned, before opening the front door and letting himself out with Warren following behind.

Once they pulled off, Dragon sighed and looked at his watch, and then he grabbed his keys and headed out the door.

So caught up with having to meet Tony and by Garfin's unwelcomed visit, Dragon didn't notice BabyGirl parked right across the street watching what had just transpired.

Pulling up a few houses from the Hilton residence, Dragon placed his car in park, shut off his engine, and leaned his head against the white leather headrest. Nervousness consumed his body. To alleviate the feeling, he pulled a pack of cigarettes from his coat pocket, lit one, and allowed clouds of smoke to escape his thick lips. Dragon was not really a cigarette smoker, but with all the stress he was dealing with, he ended up picking up the habit.

His world was crumbling; the relationship between him and BabyGirl was nothing short of rocky, and he knew she could not be trusted. Either he had to get rid of her, or she was going to get rid of him. Somehow, he felt all the wrong that he'd done in the past was coming back in the form of karma. *But what about the fucked up shit that I've been through? Where is my reward?*

Slowly, tears began to stream down his smooth dark face. He used his free hand to cover his face as he cried about how pathetic his life had been.

The lights of an oncoming car creeping up the hill caused Dragon to raise his head. The car drove right past without noticing him, just like most things and people in his life.

Wiping the tears from his face, he put out the cigarette, placed it in the ashtray, and closed his eyes, allowing his mind to drift to his childhood.

"Bitch, get the fuck down," Daquan's little ears overheard someone yell. He had tucked himself in bed earlier, but was having a difficult time falling asleep. His mother was usually nowhere to be found by nightfall; she was either getting high, or sucking someone's dick in order to get high. Dragon wished he had better parents, but with his daddy gone and his mother strung out, he had to be his own role model. He heard a thumping sound like something had fallen to the floor. Being the nosey kid he was, he flew out of his bed to see what was going on. His mother and a man he didn't recognize were lying on the floor side by side, while three men in masks held guns to their heads.

Dragon's first instinct was to not get caught, and he wanted to make sure of that. His eyes continued to roam around as he heard the voice of the tallest of the three men say, "You can run but you can't hide. You thought we wouldn't find you, huh?" The invader asked, now pressing the gun to the man's head.

Dragon's mother started to whimper as she lay face to face with the floor.

"Shut the fuck up, bitch, before I give you something to cry about," Shouted the intruder who held a gun to her head. Dragon remembered how his heart was beating hard and fast, and his mind raced through a million thoughts as he wondered what would happen next.

"Anyone else in the fucking house?" The third man questioned.

Dragon prayed his mother wasn't so high she would tell them her son was in the bedroom. This time, luck was on his side and his mother replied "No one else is here."

The intruders were not convinced so one of the men started to make his way toward Dragon's room. Dragon quickly ran into his closet and dove into the pile of clothes on the floor. Before the drugs took over her life, his mother used to always get on him about cleaning up his closet, but that day he was happy he hadn't. Throwing himself into the pile of clothes, he made sure he was well covered. He could hear footsteps coming toward the room, but he kept still. His closet door flung open, but fortunately the man couldn't hear how hard his heart was beating. The man shuffled through the clothing that was hung up but just as he was about to dig into the pile on the floor, one of the other guys called.

"Manic, come help me tie this one up."

Dragon stood still in his closet and wasn't able to hear anything else until he heard the loud sound of a gun. He prayed his mother hadn't been shot, and her screams confirmed it.

Slowly, he crept back to the door to peek out, but this time, he heard another one of the guys say, "How many times I gotta tell you to shut up? Since you like to scream so much, let me give you something to scream about."

Dragon watched as the man took out his dick, and pushed it into his mother's mouth. Rage filled his body and he wanted to go out there and do something, but he dared not. Instead, he sat there and allowed the tears to fall from his eyes as he asked God why He allowed him to live such a broken life.

Bang…bang…

The sound of someone tapping on his car glass woke him out of his reminiscing.

"Sir," a white lady with blonde hair spoke. "You're blocking my driveway, and I need to get in."

Dragon quickly put the car in reverse, backed up a bit, then placed the car in drive and moved to another spot. Dragon wished the whole ordeal would all just end.

Chapter 32

HILTON'S LAW FIRM: NYC

Porsha looked around her brand new lower Manhattan Office with disappointment. She had plans on furnishing her law firm with the money she'd withdrawn from the bank a week ago, but thanks to Tony and Leon, who was currently lying in the morgue on ice, she didn't have enough money to bring the office to where she wanted it. Immediately after Chin's death, she told herself she would retire from practicing law, but with the latest developments, she retracted that thought and decided to stay the course.

"I can't wait to get my hands on Tony," she fumed as she leaned against the window and looked out. "I'm going to torture him for what he has put me through."

The sounds of car horns and drivers swerving in and out of traffic represented how she felt...*Angry and confused.*

Sauntering from the window, she looked up at the gray clock which stood on the light blue wall. 5 P.M. Porsha was pissed because the interior designer had shown up late, causing her to delay her plans. Then to top it off, the interior designer wanted to charge more than she was worth. Talk about adding insult to injury. She was planning on being on the highway before five so she wouldn't get caught up in traffic on her way to her mother's home.

"Ahhh...I need a drink,' she sighed. She released a frustrated sigh while reaching for the bottle of Hennessey that sat on a second-hand table a neighbor in the building gave her. She missed the mini bar in Tha Hustle Records. Raising the bottle, she poured the last of its contents into a plastic cup before tossing the brown bottle in the garbage bin.

Sitting back on the worn leather chair in a pair of DKNY jeans, she threw her foot up and sipped on the liquor.

She thought about relaxing a while, but time didn't permit it. Deciding to start on her way, she picked up her London Fog luggage and headed for the door. Then it dawned on her that she hadn't called her secretary, Nicole, and she always liked to let her know where she was going.

"Hello?"

"Nicole, just want to go over a couple of things with you before I leave… I'll be returning on Monday. Please take all my messages and inform my clients that I'm away on business. Don't let anyone give you a hard time," Porsha ordered as her mind reflected back to Tony.

"Yes ma'am, enjoy your trip," Nicole said before the call was ended.

Closing the door behind her model-type frame, Porsha stepped outside; only to be hit with an abnormally hot day. Unbuttoning the top two buttons to her soft pink shirt, Porsha couldn't help but think about how hectic things had become lately. She needed to get away from all the stress and a vacation at her parent's home would do just fine.

The streets of lower Manhattan were chaotic. It was the five o' clock rush hour and everyone wanted to get home, especially since the weather man had predicted thunder storms and possible flooding. Like the other drivers, Porsha also wanted to arrive at her destination before the rain came down. She made it to the parking garage with a little hustle, handed the parking attendant her ticket, and in no less than two minutes, she was in her car heading toward the I-87.

Porsha allowed her thoughts to be filled with nothing but the retreat to her parents' home. Porsha couldn't wait to see them, it had been a minute since she last saw them and she wanted to recapture what it was like being around them. If her parents knew how much drama she had gotten herself into since she left them, they would probably faint and her father would surely disinherit her.

She wouldn't have to lie about her profession any longer because she'd finally opened her own law firm and had the documentation to prove it.

"Man, I can't wait to catch up with Juanita," she said as if she had someone in the car with her.

"I miss her cooking," Porsha continued, licking her lips and turning onto the highway.

She hadn't cooked with Juanita in years and she was hoping this vacation would allow her to do so. She also couldn't wait to go fishing with her father. When she was a little girl she hated fishing so much, but now the simple things she took for granted were appreciated a lot more.

The clouds were becoming darker and small rain drops began to pelt against her car window. She pressed her foot down a little more on the gas and her Ferrari raced down the highway swerving in and out of traffic as she tried to beat the weather. As the rain began to fall a little heavier, she smiled to herself as she remembered how Chin used to warn her about speeding in the rain and driving too fast. Despite his thuggish ways, he meant good.

Beeeeeep...Beeeeep! A loud horn honked next to her from a car driven by a middle- aged man. Her daydreaming caused her to veer over into his lane. Porsha looked through her driver side window and stuck up her middle finger at him. She knew she was wrong, but she had to let a bit of arrogance seep through.

"You fucking bitch," the man mouthed back.

"Kiss my ass you dumb fuck," she tried yelling through the glass.

She pulled up a little more and cut the driver off. Her first thought was to keep cutting him off just out of spite, but she decided against it because she didn't want to risk an accident in her expensive Ferrari. Instead, she cracked her window just enough to stick out her hand and extend her middle finger to the driver, and then pulled away from him, leaving him in the dust. Looking back from her rear-view mirror, Porsha smirked and said, "Bitches run this shit!"

Adjusting herself in the black leather seat, she allowed the coolness of the AC to brush against her face. She was beginning to enjoy the feeling when her cell phone rang; looking at the caller I.D., she saw it was her mother.

"Hey Mom,"

"Porsha, where are you? This tardiness is not like you," her mother spoke in a soft yet firm manner.

"I know, I am stuck in traffic," Porsha lied.

"Well, that's why you leave ahead of time, so that these types of things won't happen."

"Yes mother," Porsha answered in an annoyed tone.

"You have your guest here waiting, so hurry. Bye baby."

The phone line went dead before she could respond. Porsha placed the phone back in her bag and wondered about who the mystery guest could be. As far as Porsha was concerned, it didn't matter who they were as long as they didn't interfere with her peace and quiet.

I mean really, what did I ever have to worry about when I was at my parent's house?

Chapter 33

"*I* must apologize for my daughter's tardiness," Mrs. Hilton replied, placing the phone back on its base and flashing Tony a slight smile.

"That's okay, I'm used to it. She always showed up late for our classes." Tony responded.

"Would you like a drink?" the well-shaped brown-skinned woman asked.

"Yes,"

Juanita later brought out a tray with three glasses of Cabernet Sauvignon. It was the bottle of wine Tony had given Mr. Hilton when he arrived at the residence.

"Thanks," Tony took a glass and nodded. "I appreciate it," He added before taking a sip.

"You can call me Juanita," she responded.

"Nice to meet you," He extended his hand.

Placing the tray in one hand, she shook his hand and then turned to head back to the kitchen. Tony couldn't help but admire her shapely physique.

"We didn't raise her that way," Mrs. Hilton emphasized, as if lateness was a crime that should be punished with extreme harshness. "Ever since she got herself entangled with certain groups of people, she has changed."

"What kind of people are we talking about?" Tony asked with a raised eyebrow, "If you don't mind me asking?"

"Let's just say the wrong crowd," her father dipped in, bringing the topic to an end. Mr. Hilton picked up his wine glass and gulped down half its contents.

Tony could tell that money contaminated the couple's every word and thought and was a major part of their lifestyle. Their property was huge; the lawn was well-trimmed, and was watered by a sprinkler that sprayed in every direction. Judging by the design and stature of the structure, the home had to cost them no less than five million.

Porsha is not built for the fast lifestyle, Tony thought. He already knew she was out of her league, but visiting the home of her parents made it even more evident. Tony never planned on taking his plot as far as her parent's home, but Porsha's constant arrogance and refusal to return his empire left him no choice. Now he would have fun not only torturing her, but her parents as well. Tony took another sip of wine and smiled as he thought about how deviously his mind worked.

Thanks to a hacker friend, Tony was able to obtain information on Porsha's parents. Once he had the information, Tony began putting phase two of his plan into effect. He called Porsha's parents, informing them that he was an old friend from NY Law School who hadn't seen her in years because he had relocated to California. He explained that he was in town on business and wanted to surprise Porsha for dinner.

At first, her parents were skeptical and questioned how he had gotten their number. But he explained that while in law school, he and Porsha were best friends and she always told him just in case she changed any of her numbers, he should keep her parents' number because it would never change. Sure enough, her gullible parents bought it, and even made Tony's job easier than expected by inviting him to their home for dinner. It was a deal set in stone.

Tony's thoughts were interrupted by Mrs. Hilton fidgeting in her chair. Her business skirt rode up an inch every time she moved and the matching pumps made her legs look great. The woman was gorgeous, her skin was flawless, and her eyes were as bright as her daughters. Now he saw where Porsha got her looks. Mr. Hilton, who was lurking nearby, looked at his watch every couple of minutes. Tony chuckled at how pathetic they were.

"Oh, Juanita," Mrs. Hilton started as she stood, "You might want to place these in some water." She handed Juanita the flowers Tony brought for her.

Tony could tell the orchids he'd chosen were perfect, they melted her away.

Tony's eyes roamed around the room while he waited for Porsha. Many of Porsha's plaques and awards covered the wall. Tony discovered that she had even graduated Magna Cum Laude.

"No wonder she was able to doctor all that paperwork without a problem." He thought. *"With so much knowledge,"* he continued to ponder, *"Why would she throw it all away and involve herself in this lifestyle?"*

The more he thought about it the easier it became for him to see why Porsha had made the choices she did. Her parents had sheltered her so much that she couldn't wait to taste the excitement of the inner-city streets the first chance she got.

No sooner had those thoughts flooded his mind, the door bell rang. Smiling, he thought to himself, "Let the games begin."

Chapter 34

"You're a dead motherfucker" an angry BabyGirl spat, taking a pointed kitchen knife and throwing it at the poster-sized picture of Dragon that was pasted on the wall of his small studio. Her aim was perfect, the knife landed between his lips.

"How dare he invite the enemy into my home?"

She paced around in circles like she was lost. Not even Jesus himself could have told her something different happened because she'd witnessed him leaving the house with the two detectives. Confusion filled her being and she wasn't able to think clearly. Her body became weak as she couldn't help but to think about her own demise. She'd worked so hard to accomplish what she had, only for it to be jeopardized by some meddling detective, and a coward bitch of a man. Yes, Dragon was nothing but a bitch, because only bitches would do what he'd done.

Holding onto the rail that led into the studio, she sat on the carpeted stairs and placed her head between her hands. She sobbed because she wanted it all to end, but she knew it wasn't going to be that easy. The hole was already too deep and crying wasn't going to help her out of the situation. Five minutes later, she lifted her head. Her eyes were filled with rage, someone, or rather, something else had taken over. Getting up, she made her way to the kitchen to get herself something to drink while contemplating her next move.

"I need to get rid of him," she spoke to herself out loud. "I can't murder him without a motive, especially in my own home." She was slowly beginning to realize that killing Dragon was going to be more difficult than she had thought.

"Shit! If only Porsha had done her job like she'd promised the day we sat in the diner," she whispered to herself. Opening the double-door refrigerator, she pulled out a bottle of water, twisted the cap, and took the clear liquid to the head. Pulling out the stool which was under the island, she sat and continued plotting, but was interrupted by her cell phone. She thought about answering it, but decided against it. The issue at hand required more attention than the person calling. The ringing eventually died out, only to start again and frustrate her. She decided to answer the call and blow off whoever was on the other end so she could get back to her thoughts.

"Hello?" BabyGirl answered in a smug tone.

"Damn, someone must have pissed you off," Fire answered.

"You have no idea," she hissed, before taking another sip of the water.

"Wanna talk about it over dinner?"

As soon as he said the word 'dinner' the plan she was looking for began to form in her head.

"Sure, under one condition." Her feet dangled off the stool.

"What's that?"

"You buy the food and we have dinner at my house."

"What about your husband?"

"What about him?" As she asked, an evil smile crossed her

face.

"He lives there… you forgot?"

"No, I didn't, but we have about three hours to play around before he gets here. Besides, the risk of it all might bring out the animal in me."

The other line became silent. She began to think Fire hung up on her until she heard him sighing.

"Okay, I will be there," he agreed.

"Great, I will see you later, sexy."

With the deal sealed, she ended the phone call before proceeding to dial another familiar number.

"Hey babes."

"Um, hey," Dragon responded in a hesitant voice. She hadn't called him 'babes' in a minute, so she figured he would wonder if she was alright.

"What time do you think you will be home, I miss you?"

"Huh?" Dragon answered, completely lost.

She knew she had fucked up his chain of thought.

"I miss you, I said, but forget it. I see you can't appreciate a woman's kind words."

"Naw, boo, it's just…" He paused for a second to carefully choose his words. "Just that we haven't been like that in a while…"

"Well, I want to try to rekindle that," she convinced him.

"Okay, I will be there in about two hours if things go well."

She thought about asking what he was doing and where he was, but she didn't want to spoil the moment, so she left it alone.

"OK, I will see you when you get home; I have a surprise for you,"

"I love surprises," Dragon laughed.

"Oh baby, this one is to die for," she cooed before hanging up. Placing the phone in her Michael Kors bag, she headed up the stairs to begin her plan.

Chapter 35

CHAPPAQUA, NEW YORK

"It's to die for!" Dragon's raised his brow as he pondered BabyGirl's last statement. Placing the phone back on his hip, he couldn't help but wonder why she was being so loving all of a sudden. They hadn't been like that toward each other for a while, and now she wanted to rekindle the feeling? Dragon found it a little odd. She wanted something, what it was, he couldn't quite place his hands on. Whatever it was she wanted, he planned on finding out, but not before he got some ass. He allowed his mind to drift off to a time when their lovemaking seemed endless, Dragon rubbed his dick at just the thought.

The quietness of Chappaqua surrounded him like a calm volcano before it erupts. His body became restless as the mission he under took by assisting Tony seemed to be taking forever. Boredom was beginning to kick in and an old habit was ready to resurface. He tried to fight the urge, but he was too weak. Reaching in his inner pocket, Dragon pulled out the white powdery stuff, while adjusting himself in the seat. Examining the contents, he sighed as he opened the bag, dipped his fingers in, and tasted it. The product was Grade-A quality. Dragon began to slouch in his seat, but not before taking a quick peek at his surroundings to ensure no one was lurking around. Confirming this, he opened the glove compartment, and removed a piece of glass and a sharp razor blade. Emptying a bit of the product on the glass, he divided it into sections, rolled up a piece of paper, and began snorting line by line.

Blaring headlights startled him and he jumped, dropping the full bag of coke on the car rug in the process. Angered by the fact that his drugs were now tranquilizing the rug, Dragon noticed a red Ferrari, driven by someone who appeared to be Porsha, breeze past him.

"She is always ruining shit," Rage took over, as he banged his fist on the dash board. You're going to pay for this, and everything else you did to me since you took over the label," Dragon promised as he tried to scrape up some of the drugs for later.

The buzz was taking effect and Dragon was beginning to drift into a carefree mood. The concerns and fears he had earlier were now replaced with killer instinct. Images of killing Porsha flashed through his head and gave him a deadly rush. She was going down for not cutting him a piece of the empire, and snitching about his deal with Shane to BabyGirl. At first, Dragon felt bad for Shane, but those feelings were quickly erased when he thought about how crooked Shane was. The way Dragon saw it, if Shane wasn't brought down, he was bound to bring down Dragon deal or no deal. The man got exactly what he deserved. Dragon's only regret was that he hadn't done it himself. However, he'd made a promise that Porsha would be dealt with by him personally.

Darkness was beginning to form and was settling in on Chappaqua's homes and landscapes, just like the coke was beginning to control his body. Removing the piece of steel he had in his waist, Dragon inspected it like a captain of a platoon.

"This should finish it all," an evil grin came across his face.

Once he was finished with Porsha, BabyGirl was next on his list. He knew it was only a matter of time before she killed him, so why not do her first? As he turned on the radio to kill the silence, he kept thinking about how he would bring the great Tony Moreno down. That would be something that required methodical thought because he knew the man was not giving up the empire without a fight. Dragon felt he had just as much a right to the empire as anyone. Afterall, BabyGirl's father had killed his mother. This time he had no time for equality, he wanted it all to himself, even if it meant killing for it.

Chapter 36

"I could have sworn I saw someone sitting in that car," Porsha muttered as she removed her London Fog luggage from the trunk. "Maybe my eyes are playing tricks on me," she rationalized as she closed the trunk and headed toward the front door.

The sprinkler caught Porsha's attention for a brief second.

"My parents are something else, I mean, who waters their lawn late in the evening?" Knowing her parents, she was pretty sure the lawn was watered early that morning as well. "I guess some things never change. Now that's what you call obsessive compulsive disorder." She shook her head as she moved closer to the front steps.

Placing her luggage beside her feet, she took a deep breath, lifted her well-manicured fingers, and rang the bell. Butterflies were beginning to form in her stomach and anxiousness was ready to set in. She had been avoiding her parents for a while because her life wasn't together. Now that she finally had it together, she felt somehow her father would find a way to try and inquire about the gap in her life.

"Damn," she mumbled.

Porsha thought she heard someone unlocking the door,

but she wasn't sure because the door was so thick. She bent to pick up her luggage just as the door opened slowly and her mother's beautiful image appeared. She dropped the bags once more and reached out to her mother. With arms stretched out, her mother pulled her into her warm embrace.

"I am so glad you were able to make it, baby. Your father and I miss you so much," her grip on Porsha was tighter than a person hanging on for dear life. "I miss you and dad too, Ma," She rolled her eyes. She hated when her mother called her baby. No matter how many times she told her mother not to, her mother always insisted that she would always be her baby. Once she was released from her mother's embrace, her father joined in and threw his strong muscular arms around her. As much as her father put on a façade of sternness, underneath he was the most loving person one could ever meet.

"Come in, and close the door," Her mother motioned.

The warmth of home sweet home consumed her. Although she would miss the city a bit, she was glad to be away from the drama, nothing could ruin this perfect moment, *nothing!* She would ensure that. The smell of soul food greeted her nostrils, causing her stomach to rumble a bit. The cornbread and macaroni and cheese made her drool. The scent of sweet yams drew her closer to the kitchen.

"Mother, where is Juanita?" she asked, dropping her bags by the door, she didn't wait for an answer before she headed for the kitchen. Juanita, the family's chef, was making it happen in the kitchen. Juanita had been working for the family since Porsha was ten years old. Although cooking had not even been in Porsha's vocabulary since she left home, she hadn't forgotten all the wonderful recipes Juanita had taught her. Porsha loved and appreciated every minute of her cooking lessons and still thanked Juanita for them. She hoped the weekend would not only allow them to catch up on old times, but to also throw down in the kitchen.

"Juanita," Porsha startled the poor woman as she raced over to give her a hug.

"Chile, don't scare me like that, you almost gave me a heart attack."

Porsha embraced Juanita firmly while telling her how she much missed her so many times she sounded like a broken tape recorder.

"I've missed you too, and I'm so glad you're home. You know we're going to do some cooking this weekend," Juanita held Porsha by the shoulders and looked her in the eyes.

Porsha and Juanita babbled on for a few minutes before Juanita leaned over and said, "Chile, you better go on and greet that fine man waiting in the living room for you.

You know your mama gonna come out here and start talking all kinda mess about how disrespectful you are being to your guest."

"Oh whatever, she can wait. Is he really that fine?" Porsha questioned with a child-like giggle while placing a piece of fruit in her mouth.

"Funny thing is your mother said he didn't even want to reveal who he was, he just told her he was an old friend from law school.

"Well, he is to die for. He's lucky it ain't back in my days, cause I would have sure put it on him." Juanita leaned over and whispered. They both laughed.

"Okay, I trust your judgment, but you know, ain't no one is ever gonna be as fine as my Chin." She leaned back and gave

Juanita that look.

"You and your Chin," Juanita stopped cutting the tomatoes to smile at Porsha. "Fine he was indeed," Juanita joined in agreement.

Porsha always loved Juanita's motherly demeanor, especially when they discussed topics she would never dare go to her parents with. Juanita was a pro. One would have never believed she'd lost her own child to street violence when he was only thirteen years old. The loss had devastated her, but somehow she never allowed it to get her down or make her become bitter. She always said "God knows best," before going off and humming one of her favorite gospel songs. She treated Porsha as if she were her own and she even scolded Porsha like she was her own.

"I got a gift for you, I almost forgot"

"You don't have to…" Juanita insisted.

"Yes, I do," Porsha left the kitchen and headed for the hallway to retrieve the Gucci bag. Walking back into the kitchen, she presented the bag to Juanita.

"Porsha, you need to stop spending your money on gifts." Juanita wiped off her hand in her apron, took the bag from Porsha, and placed it on the island.

"Please, Juanita, open it, it's the least you can do for me. Besides I owe you for everything you have done."

"I loved every minute of it, so you don't have to compensate me with gifts."

"Porsha!" Her mother came in the kitchen. "You're being rude and inconsiderate. You have your friend from law school, someone who hasn't seen in you in God knows how long, waiting."

"I will be out there in a few, Mother. I'm catching up with

Juanita."

"Well, you can catch up with her later. Besides, aren't you here for the entire weekend?" When her mother placed her hands on her hips, Porsha knew she had made her mad.

"Okay."

"Your father is so right, we are definitely going to have to retrain you," her mother mumbled while walking out the kitchen. "I see you picked up some bad habits while living in the city and with that thug Chin." She said his name with disgust.

"I told you," Juanita whispered to Porsha. They both shared another giggle.

"You see the shit I have to put up with? Even in my adult life." she leaned over and spoke.

"Well, you asked for it, I told you to go on out there. We can always catch up later." Juanita kissed her on the check and then turned around to finish preparing the salad for dinner.

Porsha excused herself and headed for the dining room to give her guest a full apology. As she got closer, she still couldn't make out who the person was because they were turned to tbe window that overlooked the back garden. As she stepped down into the living room, the figure adjusted himself, cleared his throat, turned around, and then spoke.

"Well good evening, Ms. Hilton."

Porsha's mouth flew wide open. The mere thought of Tony Moreno standing in her living room was her worst nightmare.

Chapter 37

CHAPPAQUA, NEW YORK

Now that's what Kodak needs to make a moment, Tony thought, referring to the priceless look on Porsha's face.

An uncomfortable silence lingered in the air as Mrs. Hilton, who was expecting a positive reaction, stared at both Tony and Porsha.

"No kisses or running into each other's arms?" Mrs. Hilton inquired in a perky tone.

A worried chuckle escaped Porsha's lips. Tony could tell that a million and one questions were floating in her head.

He was enjoying watching, 'the invincible,' as Chin called her, Porsha Hilton plot her way out of this. For a quick second, he drifted off to the sound of imaginary victory music, until his merry thinking was interrupted by Mr. Hilton clearing his throat.

Mr. Hilton strolled from the window that overlooked the back patio with his hands in his pockets. As he entered the dining room, he had a piercing look in his eyes. The sound of Juanita's sultry voice humming her favorite tune could be heard from the kitchen.

Outstretching his hands, Tony spoke, "Porsha, how good it is to see you again?"

She gave him a deadly glare as she tried her hardest not to attack Tony.

"Maybe your father and I should give you a minute to catch up with your friend," Mrs. Hilton suggested before turning to exit the dining room. She expected Mr. Hilton to follow immediately behind, but he paused to look Tony in the eyes before leaving. Tony chuckled at the man's buffoonery.

Ensuring her parents were out of ear shot, Tony placed his arms around Porsha, leaned in, and whispered, "You fucked with the wrong empire."

"If you don't," Porsha spoke through clenched teeth, her body tensing with each word "get your motherfucking hands off me…"

"You're going to do what?" Tony whispered in a serious tone. In his peripheral vision he could see Mrs. Hilton lurking, so he glanced at her and threw her a smile.

Darkness was beginning to cast its shadow on the home.

"You're a dead man for pulling something like this."

"Ah…" Tony spoke with grace, "Be careful, I don't take threats lightly, especially when they come from someone so heartless and cold-blooded."

"Well, you guys have reacquainted yourselves long enough." Mrs. Hilton said as she pulled out one of the dining table chairs, sat and spread the white linen cloth across her lap.

"Give us another second, Mother," Porsha said courteously, yet firmly.

Her mother sighed, then replied, "Ok."

"Is everything alright?" Mr. Hilton inquired. His heavy baritone voice would bring a chill to anyone, but not Tony, he'd seen it all.

"Yes Dad, everything is fine," Porsha fanned him off, and smiled at him.

Mr. Hilton shook his head and joined his wife at the table.

"This is business, Tony, and my parents are not a part of this."

Juanita, who was exiting the kitchen, passed with a tray of food. Tony paused for a quick second, allowing the soul food aroma to creep into his nostrils before averting his attention back to Porsha.

"Yes, they are. They are considered assets, and once the bank is unable to get their actual money they go after a person's assets." Tony retorted.

"You robbed me of my money, you cut off most of the business connections we had, and you have the audacity to show up here requesting more?" Porsha started. "Just give me one good reason why I shouldn't shoot your ass just on general principle?"

Tony chuckled, "Porsha...Porsha idle threats and no action make this so boring." Tony adjusted his shirt. Shininess from the Glock which was clinging to his waist peaked out.

Porsha squinted her eyes. Tony knew the Glock would send a message that he was not there to play.

"I'll go to the extreme to get what I want, Porsha. I told you I wanted the paperwork drafted to get back my empire prior to me going to trial. I even gave you a second chance by telling you I wanted it back in three days – it's been four days already. Now, do you have the paperwork for my company?"

"Do you have my fucking money?" She shot back. Her boldness was beginning to come out.

"Ha..ha..ha.." he laughed, "you're funny."

"Well, yes or no?" she demanded.

"That's my fucking money…you inherited it off my damn empire," Tony answered.

"So fucking what? My blood and sweat went into that empire too. Don't you think I deserve a cut? Besides, I am no longer the owner of Tha Hustle Records, so why are you even here?" Porsha asked, trying to maintain her composure and keep her voice low.

"Your blood and sweat did not go into shit! The only sweating you did was on your back with Chin. The only bleeding you did was through your pussy, and that's only because you're a bitch. You drafted the paperwork, Porsha; therefore, I'm coming to you, not anyone else."

"Tony, I suggest you leave." She spoke in a nonchalant tone showing him that she wasn't fazed by what he had to say.

"I will create a massacre," Tony warned.

Porsha cringed with rage at the mere thought of someone threatening to kill her parents.

"You won't get away with this," she whispered.

"I'm here, so I already have," Tony replied.

Heading back into the dining room, Tony pulled out Porsha's chair so she could sit. Taking the chair beside Mr. Hilton, he too placed a white cloth across his lap, and then sipped on a glass of champagne.

"Anything we missed, dear?" her mother asked looking at them both.

"No just catching up with Tony on old time things."

Tony laughed to himself thinking, *If only her mother knew.*

"Then let's begin dinner so we can get to know this fine gentleman." Mrs. Hilton said.

Let's see how well you do under pressure, Porsha. You may think you were meant for this, but you weren't built for this.

Chapter 38

NYACK, NEW YORK

BabyGirl's greenish-gray eyes were focused on the two silk robes that lay on the bed. On a normal day, choosing the appropriate robe wouldn't be so difficult, but today wasn't a normal day. Today death was outside her doors waiting to capture its next soul.

"Hmm...I could wear the red, and let it represent the bloody scene that will unfold later or I could wear the black to attend the early funeral."

She picked up the slender champagne glass from the contemporary-style dresser, placed it to her lips and took a sip. The sweet taste slowly took an effect. BET's music videos were playing on her sixty-inch flat screen, but she didn't entertain the sounds; instead she focused her attention on the attire for the evening.

"Red it is," she decided. "I can accessorize with black costume jewelry." She winked at herself in the mirror.

The fast-paced music had slowed down and now Vivian Green's painful voice was bellowing a tune about the ups and downs of a relationship.

"Ah," BabyGirl plopped herself on the queen-size bed after retrieving the champagne glass from the dresser. She took another sip and allowed her body to get in the groove. "I can relate to that one," she lifted her glass in a toasting manner, as if Vivian Green was sitting in front of her. Closing her eyes, her shapely frame rocked to the infectious song.

"That I was being taking for a constant ride, I'm on an emo..." the words didn't finish escaping her lips before her singing was interrupted by the door bell. Looking at the cable box, she realized she had lost track of time.

"Shit" she murmured as she quickly threw the robe on, placed her feet in the bedroom slippers, and raced toward the bedroom door. Hastily making it down the spiral stairway, she kept questioning whether she was forgetting something.

Taking in a deep breath, she placed her hand on the silver doorknob and slowly opened the door. She locked eyes with her visitor, who looked her up and down; she didn't hesitate to do the same.

Captivating her with his sex appeal, she couldn't help but say something. As she opened her mouth to speak, Fire placed his hand on her lips and pulled her close to his well-toned frame. A kiss on the lips was followed by the softest, most sensational kiss along the neck. Closing her eyes tightly, her body unraveled in his sweet embrace. Gracefully they glided inside as he laid her on the reclining part of the sofa. No words were exchanged, only sweet sounds of soft lips working together could be heard. Using his left hand to gently rub her breast, she arched her back closer to his body and a slight moan escaped.

"Hello!" Fire said again, this time waving his hands across her face. "Are you going to let me in?"

She had been so caught up in her fantasy that she failed to acknowledge Fire standing at the door waiting.

"I'm sorry, come on in." BabyGirl responded, embarrassingly snapping out of her daze.

With take-out food still in his hand, Fire stepped in, looked around briefly and asked,

"Where do you want me to put this?"

"In the kitchen," she replied, eyes still focused on his body.

Focus, BabyGirl, her mind told her, though for some reason it wasn't happening. Her body was saying one thing, but her hormones were saying something else.

"So what time are you expecting your man?"

"No time soon," she answered, with a *why are you asking* attitude.

Of course she was lying, but it was all a part of her plan.

"Let's enjoy dinner," she spoke.

"Fine,"

Fire sat at her glass dining table. Moving toward the island, she smiled at the drama she had cooked up,

"This night is going to heat up once the explosion begins." BabyGirl promised as she looked at Fire with a vengeful smile.

Chapter 39

CHAPPAQUA, NEW YORK

Juanita's magnificent voice brought a breath of fresh air to the dining room. As he placed the champagne glass on the table, Tony smiled because each note sounded more beautiful than the one before. Tony didn't know enough about Juanita to even give a damn about her, but something about her brought out the merciful side of him. He felt bad that she had to be caught up in Porsha's mess and wished he could save her, but he knew her loyalty to the Hilton's would only bring him down.

Such a waste of a beautiful voice and body, he thought as his knife pierced through the juicy steak.

The brightness of the overhead chandelier was beginning to affect his vision. Placing the steak knife down, he adjusted in his chair and then resumed cutting his food.

"So how is it at L&M?" Tony questioned, his back pressed further into the walnut-colored chair. He made strong eye contact with Porsha, but she avoided it and continued to chew the piece of meat in her mouth.

Mr. Hilton, who sat adjacent Porsha, wiped his mouth with the white cloth napkin, before looking at his daughter. Tony could tell by the man's expression that he held a great deal of admiration for Porsha.

"Well," Porsha started as she too leaned back and then glanced at everyone for a quick second. "Since you asked, and ruined the surprise, I opened my own law firm."

"What?" Her mother yelled out. She almost spit out all the food she held in her mouth.

"When were you planning on telling us?" Mr. Hilton questioned.

"Today, but the surprise was ruined."

"I'm so proud of you," Mr. Hilton smiled, then threw a quick wink at his daughter.

"Congrats, I think this calls for more champagne," Tony joined.

"Certainly," Mrs. Hilton expressed. "Juanita, could we have another bottle of champagne?"

Tony sat back and let the excitement fill the air, any minute now he was going to change the tone of the dining room. "What made you decide to open up a firm?" Tony continued to probe.

An irritated look came across Porsha's face. He could tell she was beginning to wonder where he was going with the questions, though she continued to play along pretty well.

"Sometimes a person can get too complacent in their comfort zone, so they have to branch out in order to expand."

"Oh really?" sarcasm laced both words. "So what were your co-workers thoughts on such a move?"

Removing the champagne glass from her lips, she answered, "I don't care what my co-workers think because at the end of the day, I'm what matters."

"That's right, baby," Mr. Hilton defended his daughter.

"I'm pretty sure your parents are proud of you."

Taking a sip from his glass and in a smug tone, Mr. Hilton

replied, "We are."

Tony could tell the branch didn't fall too far from the tree. Porsha was just like her dad; deceitful and callous.

"Despite what you said, it must have been a hard decision. L & M is one of the best firms in the country. I have worked with some of the attorney's over there and I must say, they're quite brilliant, especially when it comes to drafting documents. If you don't watch them keenly, they will pull a fast one on you." Tony added as he winked at her.

Clearing his throat, Porsha's father interjected.

"Yes, I must agree that L&M is a good firm; however, this is a cut throat world. Besides we're Hiltons and we take pride in what we do. So if my daughter decided to make a move, then we know she did a lot of thinking on it before she did. She is a smart girl who makes excellent, if not great decisions."

Juanita entered the dining room with a bottle of bubbly in her hand. One could tell she was tired by her posture; however, she continued her servitude with a smile. Turning on her heels, she headed back to the kitchen. Porsha, whose eyes were cast down, couldn't bear to look her father in the face. Tony knew half the decisions she had made were poor ones and would bring disgrace to the family if they were ever revealed.

"Excellent, huh?"

Tony's words caused a curious look to appear across Mr. Hilton's face. Tony could tell he was beginning to work the man's last nerves. Porsha, as smart as she thought she was, decided to divert the attention off of herself and throw it on Tony—a mistake that was about to cost her dearly.

"So Antonio," Porsha began, breaking off a piece of corn-bread. "Tell us about your firm and how it's going? We've been talking about me all this time, but I'm sure my parents would love to hear more about what you do."

"Well, I'm not making big moves like you are" Tony chuckled lightly before wiping his mouth.

"Well, Antonio, not everyone possesses great skills like us Hiltons." Mr. Hilton arrogantly rubbed it in.

"Honey," Mrs. Hilton knocked Mr. Hilton on the shoulder. "Have some respect for our guest."

"Listen sweetheart, you don't have to be making big moves, as long as you're goal-oriented."

"Thanks, but don't be so kind with your modesty; Mr. Hilton is right." Tony assured the woman. Inside, Tony was cringing; he couldn't wait to have Mr. Hilton's life in the palm of his hands.

"And since we are all being frank with one another…"

At this point he'd had enough of the charades, especially after Mr. Hilton's last comment. Getting up, he pushed his chair back and stood.

"I'm not really an attorney," Tony confessed. A look of shock came across both parents' faces.

"I knew something about you wasn't right," Mr. Hilton barked. He was furious.

"However, I was the Co-CEO of a record label until I was shot and my record label was taken from me."

Pressing his fingers on the button on his Nextel walkie-talkie, Tony signaled for Dragon to join him. It was about to go down.

Porsha, who was fine until the words 'shot' escaped Tony's lips; passed out in the chair and fell over onto the hunter green marble floor. Tony knew it was a stunt. The truth was slowly unraveling and a can of worms was about to be opened that a lid could not be put on.

Jumping from her chair, Mrs. Hilton raced over to her daughter's side, leaned down and cried, "Oh God, someone call an ambulance."

Juanita rushed in from out of the kitchen with yellow cleaning gloves still on her hands.

"Relax, relax, she just fainted; get me some smelling salts. She will be fine. Besides, I don't want Porsha to miss out on the juicy story." Tony said, leaning over Porsha. Tony placed the smelling salts he received from Jaunita under Porsha's nose, causing her to spring up straight.

The charades and antics stop here, you made it your business to ruin other people's lives, so I wouldn't want you to miss watching yours crumble. Tony thought to himself.

Helping her around the table, her parents couldn't help but ask if she was alright. Once they got the confirmation that she was fine, the conversation resumed.

"So Antonio, did the authorities ever find the shooter?" Mrs. Hilton inquired.

"No, the shooter is a slippery one."

"Well, I still hope they find him, Antonio." Mrs. Hilton placed some salad on her plate.

"Oh, it's not a him it's her."

A look of bewilderment and shock spread across the family's faces. Each new revelation was proving to be a bit more dramatic than the previous.

"Do you know the shooter?" Mr. Hilton asked.

"Yes," Tony nodded as he took a look in Porsha's direction.

"Then why don't you turn them over to the police?"

Leaning on the table, Tony answered, "Because this has become more personal to me."

"So who is the shooter? That's if you don't mind us asking." Mrs. Hilton asked before placing some salad in her mouth.

"Oh no, I'm glad you did. Go ahead and drink some more champagne because I assure you, things will never be the same after I give you your answer."

"OK, but I do find it quite odd that you would say something like that. I don't see where this would have such an impact on us, of all people.

"So…?" Mr. Hilton gestured while placing the glass on the table and awaiting Tony's answer.

"Porsha Hilton!" Tony said in a voice that sounded more like he was announcing the winner of a game show prize.

"Huh?" Mrs. Hilton leaned back and gave him a queer look.

"Yes, the shooter is Porsha Hilton. You see, she is not as innocent as she has made herself seem. Not only did your little princess sleep with my partner Chin and assure him that she would help to turn the business legit, but all the while she was plotting along with two other bitches to take my record label, or better yet, my drug empire. Go ahead, Porsha, tell them, no need to hide it anymore."

"Excuse me," Mrs. Hilton said, now visibly shaken and frustrated. She threw her linen napkin on the table and pushed back her chair, "I don't know who you think you are, but I want you out of our house." She ordered Tony.

"That won't be happening, I'm here to reclaim my empire and I'm not leaving without it."

"This is absurd, I'm going to call the police," Mr. Hilton raged. He got up only to be greeted with the Glock Tony had placed on his waist earlier.

Juanita, who was close by, attempted to enter into the dining room to see what was going on, but was stopped by Dragon, who entered from the back. He pulled her back then pointed a gun to her head. Dragon then revealed himself to the others; entering the room with Juanita in a choke hold and waving his gun between Mrs. Hilton and Porsha.

"Now we can do this the easy way or the hard way. Porsha, are you going to sign over the documents so I can get my empire, or will I have to create a massacre in here tonight?"

"I can't," the words slipped from her trembling lips.

"And why not?"

"Because I'm no longer the owner of the company."

"Well, I suggest you get the new owners on the phone."

The sound of the gun clicking caused Mrs. Hilton to scream. Mr. Hilton looked on. He was helpless because of the firm grip Tony had on him and the fact that a Glock was pressed against his head.

Chapter 40

"What the hell does she want?" BabyGirl thought when she saw Porsha's number on the caller ID. She didn't answer. Instead, she placed the phone on silent and turned her attention back to Fire.

"You know what's ironic?" Fire asked, lifting the white container holding the rice and piling more on his plate.

"What?" BabyGirl asked, her teeth sinking into the juicy steak.

"Here I am inside your home and I still don't know much about you." He looked into her greenish-gray eyes.

"Why are you here?" She inquired, while throwing him a sexy glance.

"Somehow, I find your mystery intriguing, and a turn on." He put the container back on the counter.

"Hmmm…I guess you enjoy taking exciting risks, huh?"

"What can I say? Maybe we have something in common because here you are, and you know very little about me."

"Well, just like you…," she placed the fork down, "I like mystery. I learned in life that the more you know about a person, the more disappointed you become." She made reference to her past relationships with Dragon and Chin. Her feelings for Fire were slowly kicking in, but a fear of him turning out to be something he was not made her apprehensive.

"Is that so?" Fire smirked as he got up off the stool to get ice from the ice dispenser.

"Yes, have you looked at the divorce rate in this country?"

"Not really; I never was the marrying type." He affirmed.

"Well, I think mystery is best. We all wear a mask every-day; whether it's to work, around our children, or a new lover. I found out that the less you know about a person, the more turned on and curious you will be. It makes the chase worthwhile. Isn't it true in your case?" BabyGirl explained.

"Point taken, but still I want to know more about Baby-Girl."

"What is it you want to know? My motto is, 'I never volunteer information'." She gave him a slight grin.

"Well..." he pulled out the stool to sit. "I guess whatever you feel like revealing," he took a sip of orange juice.

"I'm an average girl who enjoys life to the fullest, something I learned to do after the death of my parents." Her voice became filled with sadness and she cast her eyes toward the ceiling to keep the tears from spilling out.

"Wow, I'm sorry...my condolences."

"Thanks," she sniffled a bit, then spoke, "I thought I could handle this, but... tell me about you while I compose myself."

"Well, I lost my father to the streets" Fire began.

"I'm sorry to hear. How did he die?"

"His business partner gunned him down in the streets of Harlem, took the money, and was fleeing the scene when he got hit by a city bus. People were too afraid to say anything, so he got away with it. Then, to add insult to injury, he turned around and sued the city and claims most of his money was derived from the accident. But that was all bullshit; most of his money came from my father's business."

"I share your grief. My parents died in a similar manner, except they died at the hands of strangers." BabyGirl spoke.

"I remember the incident clearly. It was the day I was on my way to tell him I was accepted into Harvard Law School." Fire stated, holding his head down and sighing. His reflection, one of a grieving soul could be seen through the counter top.

"Law school?" she tilted head, so her eyes could meet with his. "So why are you working with FedEx if you were accepted into law school?"

"I guess I lost motivation," His voice became sullen.

"Well, you need to get back into law school because the amount of money you work for now will never equate to what you could make as a lawyer." BabyGirl interjected.

Fire remained quiet as if he was doing some soul searching.

"I will one day," He got up off the stool and headed over to the kitchen sink where he leaned back and crossed his hands across his chest.

Something about him intrigued her; she wanted to know more.

"Have you ever seen your father's killer again?" she asked.

"No," He said in a dry tone.

She too, got up off the stool and joined him at the counter. Her phone rang once more, but she ignored it.

"Maybe you should answer it; it's probably your husband telling you he's on his way." Fire tried to change the topic.

"No, I will call whoever it is back in a few." BabyGirl insisted, waving the notion off with her free hand. "What about your mother?" she asked attempting to resume the conversation.

Moving from the sink, Fire lifted his hands and placed

them under her cheeks, he kissed her slightly on her lips, "She is fine; now let's enjoy the rest of the evening."

Determined to probe more since Dragon too was vague and she didn't want to repeat the same mistake, she decided to take another approach.

"Maybe you need some assistance to track down the killer. If it wasn't for people's assistance, I wouldn't have known who my parents' killers were and how to bring them to justice."

"Who said I wanted to find them?"

"C'mon, Fire, every child who has lost a parent wants to find the person responsible. Maybe I can assist you."

He laughed and pulled her closer into him, "Have you ever thought about being a detective?"

"Not my style." She laughed back. "So do you need my assistance?"

"Maybe I just feel like some things should remain a mystery."

"Fine." She became quiet…another tactic she learned.

"Does finding my father's killer matter that much to you?"

"Yes."

"Why?"

"Because I went through the same predicament and it ate me alive night and day when I wasn't able to look my parent's killer in the eye." BabyGirl tactfully confessed.

Sighing, he too became quiet. She had hit a nerve.

"I know; I'm just not up to dealing with Tony Moreno right now."

BabyGirl did a double take, "Excuse me, who killed your father?" she asked to make sure she hadn't misheard.

"A man named Tony Moreno."

At that moment, she knew Tony Moreno's days were numbered and his life was slowly coming to an end. She formed the ultimate plan for revenge. The night had turned out far better than she could have ever expected, and it was just getting started.

"Small world."

"Oh, so you know Tony?"

Taking a sip of her drink, she replied, "I know him all too well. What if I bring Tony Moreno to you?"

Fire looked at her with squinted eyes. He was amazed, in disbelief, and curious all at the same time.

"How is that?" he asked hesitantly.

"His children."

Chapter 41

"*D*on't! Even think about it," Tony ordered as he knocked Mr. Hilton upside the head with the butt of the gun. Mr. Hilton was trying to reach for the butter knife that lay on the white linen cloth. Tony picked up the knife and placed it in his back pocket.

"Tony, this is between me and you," Porsha pleaded. "Not my parents".

"Well, that would have been the case until you brought them into it". He walked over to her. "Since you just made this personal, they are considered my assets."

"Are you going to kill us?" Mrs. Hilton asked in a trembling voice.

Tony began to answer her, but his attention was diverted to Juanita.

"*The Lord is my light and my salvation, whom shall I fear. The Lord is the strength of my life, of whom shall I be afraid. When the wicked come up against me to eat my flesh, my enemies and foes they stumble and fell.*" Juanita closed her eyes and prayed Psalm 27.

Dragon though, without an ounce of mercy, pressed the gun further into her side and said "Shut up and don't make me shoot you earlier than your time."

Turning his attention to the Hilton's, Tony spoke, "She has

my empire and money and refuses to give it back."

"If its money you want we can write you a check and settle the matter right here," Mr. Hilton tried to rationalize.

Tony chuckled, "Nope, I'm through with settling." I tried that and your daughter refused.

"Stop being greedy," Porsha began to cry, "You already robbed me on my way back from the bank, don't you have enough already?"

Tony paused for a moment, as if he was in deep thought, "Nah, not even close."

Dragon sat back watching the situation playing out and just laughed to himself.

"Do you believe this shit, Dragon? She stole from me and has the nerve to call me greedy." Tony paused, "Maybe you forgot what you put Dragon through." Tony wanted to spark some fire in Dragon; he could see the flames beginning to blaze through the man's eyes.

"That's a fucking lie. Everything that happened to Dragon, he did to himself." Porsha blurted out. At that very instant and without sympathy, Dragon took the gun and hit her in the head, causing Porsha to fall to the ground.

"Pay me what you owe bitch," he spat on Porsha's body.

"You motherfucker!" Mr. Hilton yelled attempting to free himself from Tony's firm grip and lunge at Dragon. Raising his gun, Dragon fired a shot. Screams could be heard as everyone cried out for their lives. Luckily for Mr. Hilton, the shot missed.

"Keep acting up old man, and I promise next time I won't miss yo' ass." Dragon taunted. By now he was hyped up.

Porsha struggled back to her feet.

"Go ahead tell them, Porsha…tell your parents how you

tricked Chin into signing over his company to you, and then to add insult to injury you attempted to kill us both. The only thing that spared me the same fate as Chin is the fact that I was tipped off by an insider on your team."

Tony let out a sinister laugh.

"Yup, your camp is full of snitches." Dragon added; making sure to avoid eye contact with Tony. No need for explanation, Tony already knew Dragon was one too.

"Thanks to Dimples, I'm standing here alive and prepared to bring you to your own demise." Tony bragged.

"That bitch." Porsha seethed as she spoke through clenched teeth.

"What is he talking about, Porsha?" Her father asked.

Holding down her head, Porsha said, "It's true, except for the fact that I tricked Chin into signing those papers, he signed them voluntarily."

"You tricked him! He would never sign over his company to you. He simply signed them, placing his trust in you, believing that you were making his company legit when you were only making him sign the papers for you to transfer his company in your name." Tony yelled across the table.

"No I didn't," Porsha yelled back before breaking down and crying some more.

"Yes, you did! I mean realistically, how long did you think you would get away with it before I found out? It doesn't take long for a business to be approved." Tony acknowledged.

Mr. Hilton blurted out, "I don't care who you are, but you will no longer hold my family hostage at gunpoint," and attempted to take the gun from Tony. The gun went off hitting Mr. Hilton in the stomach. His body slowly fell to the floor as his wide open eyes settled on Porsha.

"Noooo…" Wailing sounds escaped Porsha's lips, while her mother fell to the floor and began to cry; blaming Porsha as she cradled her near-dead husband in her arms.

"Get out… get out!" she yelled. "I can no longer have you as my daughter."

Juanita attempted to run after Porsha, who was making her way toward the kitchen, but as she ran, Dragon pulled the trigger and shot her in the back. Juanita's body thumped to the ground.

"How many more bodies, Porsha, before I get back my empire?"

"Fuck you, you might as well kill me. I'm not helping you get a damn thing back."

"No problem," Tony pointed the gun in Porsha's direction, but slowly turned it toward her mother. The gun went off, hitting her mother in the head. Mrs. Hilton lay beside a bleeding Mr. Hilton. Tony shot him again to finish him off. Porsha leaped to attack Tony, but Dragon took the knife sitting loosely in Tony's back pocket, which Mr. Hilton attempted to use earlier, and stabbed Porsha in her throat. Her body fell to the ground and blood oozed out onto the floor. Dragon put two follow-up shots into her body.

"This one is for pulling a gun on me that day at Tha Hustle Records and this one is from BabyGirl."

Tony looked on, the cold-blooded murderer in him seeped out.

Chapter 42

Somehow the earlier conversation between Fire and BabyGirl had broken barriers; creating laughter, playful giggles, and flirting between them in the kitchen.

"Let's go into the living room," Fire requested, pulling her closer to him once more.

Their lips began to interlock as they moved from the brightly lit kitchen, to a dimmer atmosphere. Fire didn't hesitate to lay BabyGirl in the softness of the black leather sectional; his body slowly mounting hers. Their foreplay began to intensify as the moments went by, so much that the jiggling of house keys in the door was oblivious to them. A deadly Dragon entered.

"What the fuck?" a fuming Dragon barked, throwing his keys on the side table while slamming the door behind his slender muscular form.

The wrath emerging from Dragon's voice pulled both lovers out of their fantasy world. Dragon attempted to retrieve his gun from its hiding place in the living room, but to his disappointment, it wasn't there, now he wished he had never gotten rid of the gun he'd used to kill Porsha. BabyGirl had already planned the entire set-up. She knew he would reach for it, so she removed the gun earlier that evening. A smirk crossed her lips as she began to revel in how well her plan was going so far.

"Good morning," her voice had a tone of nonchalance in it.

"Good morning?" Dragon repeated with a nasty scowl on his face. "I can't believe this shit," he said with his hand on his forehead. "This bitch has the nerve to tell me good morning when she has a motherfuckin' nigga laying up in my house."

"This is not your house, I paid for it," she reminded him, while reaching her hand in the creases of the sofa.

Dragon didn't allow her last statement to register before he attempted to lunge at her.

"Back the fuck up?" BabyGirl demanded, pointing the gun he was searching for earlier.

"Who the fuck is this nigga?" Dragon said with the rage of a man possessed.

"This is Fire," she replied looking in Fire's direction.

Fire's brown eyes searched her face for answers. She didn't offer any, she was pretty sure her message was clear. This is was a set-up and he had fallen right into it.

"Look out," were the only words that left Fire's lips before pulling BabyGirl over and behind the sofa. Dragon had pulled a knife out of his back pocket and tried to stab BabyGirl.

"You're a whore like your mother," Dragon taunted as she could hear his foot steps moving closer. He laughed an evil sound, one that echoed throughout the house.

"So much for him not being home so soon, huh?" Fire whispered to her while shaking his head.

Taking the gun from her, Fire aimed and fired, hitting Dragon in the leg and causing him to fall to the floor. Without a second thought, BabyGirl raced toward him, jumped on him, and proceeded to pound on his chest and face. Fire, at the same time, stood over Dragon and pointed the gun to his head.

"Go ahead, kill me," Dragon laughed again as blood dripped from the corner of his mouth. "Did you know this was the same position your mother was in when I shot her?"

BabyGirl's body froze, everything spun around her as she tried to make sense of what Dragon had just said.

"What did you just say?" Tears were streaming down her face.

"*I* killed your whore of a mother," he grinned, enjoying the pain he knew she was feeling.

Fire, visibly upset over the blatantly disrespectful revelation, kicked Dragon in his face and side repeatedly before handing the gun back to BabyGirl and giving her a slight nod, signaling for her to finish the job. BabyGirl aimed and fired, splattering brain matter all over the living room floor.

"That's for my mother and Chin's unborn baby," she said and spat on his face.

Dropping the gun beside him, she walked over and picked up the cordless phone, allowing tears to flow out as she dialed 911.

"911, what's your emergency?" the perky operator asked.

"My fiancé tried to kill me, and I shot him in self-defense,"

"Ma'am" what's your address," the operator asked, but BabyGirl didn't respond to anymore questions. The phone fell out of her hand and onto the floor.

♡♡♡

As the sun slowly crept up on Nyack's landscape, swarms of Westchester police officers walked in and out of her home, each gathering every clue they could find. Fire sat by the drive-way, his head hung down. BabyGirl had watched as three different officers questioned him earlier. Dimples stood by BabyGirl, consoling her as she watched the mayhem unfold. Detective Garfin and Warren, who recently became a detective, took notes and pictures. Neighbors in pajamas stood on their well-trimmed lawns, watching in disbelief.

"This is the kind of drama I have been avoiding," she wiped her tears and headed for the door.

"I'm not buying this. I don't know what happened here, but I have all intentions on finding out." Closing his pad, Detective Garfin moved away from the doorway he once blocked, "My gut feeling tells me you killed him intentionally."

Looking up, BabyGirl replied, "Believe what you want Detective, but I don't have time to entertain your nonsense."

"Oh believe me, one day you will."

Moving toward Garfin, she stood face-to-face, "Then prove it, Detective, but right now I have a dead fiancé to mourn. Besides, isn't there a limit to your jurisdiction?"

His blue eyes settled on her greenish-gray ones before he responded, "Nope."

"Let's go, Garfin," Warren signaled.

Fire, finally making his way over, spoke in a solemn tone, "Warn me, instead of surprising me the next time you decide to pull me in some shit—like murder." He turned and headed down the path he'd entered a day before, facing the sunrise as if it was a sort of conviction.

Chapter 43

UNION SQUARE, NYC

The white oversized umbrella outside of the Blue Water Grill restaurant provided shade from the bright sunlight for Tony and Nurse Haywood. It had been two weeks since the death of Porsha Hilton, and Tony had yet to lose a night's sleep over the incident. Tony scanned the menu and every now and then he peeked over to look at Tiffany. They had been quiet throughout the car ride and again sitting there. Tony wondered what was running through her mind.

Clearing her throat, she took up the glass to sip some ice water, and then placed it back down on the table. She folded her arms across her chest and watched the bustling people of NYC passing by.

"I like your hair," Tony broke the ice. The short hair cut she once rocked was replaced with a weave cut in a bob.

"Thanks," Tiffany replied giving Tony a slight smile. "I have something I want to ask," she added.

"Okay," Tony also took a sip of water before giving his full attention to her. The tone in her voice told him she was serious.

"Could you please explain why a man of your stature ends up in such dangerous predicaments?"

He was taken back by her question and thought about it for a few minutes before responding.

"What kind of predicaments?" he hesitantly inquired.

"Bullet wounds, being thrown in a river, and not to mention the gun I found in your closet when I was putting your clothing away." A strand of hair blew in her face and she stopped to place it behind her ears. "You must have been, or still are, involved in some dangerous shit."

Tony stared at her briefly, her face was gorgeous and the sunlight brought out her beauty even more.

Tony chuckled a bit before replying, "And what made you arrive at such a conclusion?"

"Cut the bullshit, Antonio," she banged her hand on the table. The glass rattled in agreement with her. Attitude with a capital "A" was seeping into her voice. "For days, I turned on the news and people affiliated with Tha Hustle Records were turning up dead. I prayed that one of those people wouldn't be you. I called your phone; it went straight to voicemail. I left messages and you didn't return a single call, Antonio. How do you expect me to feel? You expect for me to come here smiling when I haven't heard for you in weeks? Is that what it is, huh?"

"I'm sorry," Tony wholeheartedly conceded. Tony was shocked; he knew she cared, but he never knew she cared so deeply. He got up from the brown wooden chair to proceed to hug her, but she leaned back so that he couldn't.

"Who shot you, Tony, and why? I need to know. Because if I'm going to be a part of your life, I need to know the danger I'm putting myself in."

He knelt in front of her, held her hand, then spoke, "I don't know."

"You don't know who shot you? Cut the bullshit, Antonio," she drew her hands out of his. "I know that you know who shot you. The heated discussion you had with Detective Garfin, the way you talk to your wife…you and I have been close, don't you think it's full time you reveal what's going on?"

Tony was drawn back by her spunk, no one had ever talked to him like that, but for some reason he was allowing her to.

"Listen, if we're going to be around each other, then you need to learn to trust me." Tony argued.

Tony got up, walked back, and sat in his seat. He ran his fingers along the edge of the glass. A serious look crossed his face as he stared at her; one that told her she had overstepped her boundaries. The waitress came by to take their orders.

"We're not ready to order yet, but I would like a strong drink," Tony told the brunette waitress.

"And what would that be?" she inquired. A slight breeze blew by, blowing the pages of her note pad, she flipped it back to the page she was about to write on.

"Give me a glass of Devil Springs on the rocks" Tony requested.

"Anything for you, ma'am?"

"No, I need a sober mind right now."

The waitress turned and headed back inside to place Tony's drink order.

"The last person I trusted laid my business in the hands of strangers who became greedy and conniving. Due to that greed, I wound up empire-less, shot, and placed in the predicament that you see me in."

"Maybe you didn't trust the right people."

"That's the problem, Tiffany, you never know until you have fully invested in that person. My wife is a prefect example of that." He reasoned.

"Here's your drink." The waitress placed the clear liquid on the white tablecloth. The waitress put the drink down and took their order.

"Thanks," Tony responded as his cell vibrated on his hip. Removing his phone, he looked at the number and sighed as he contemplated whether or not to answer. He was already going through enough drama with Tiffany and didn't need Maribel's headache.

"Excuse me," he uttered to Tiffany.

"Uh-hmm," she replied.

"Hello!" Tony answered, holding the phone firmly by his ears. The calm expression he wore earlier was changing and his temper was beginning to flare.

"The...the chi...children have been kidnapped," Maribel struggled to get the words out as uncontrollable sobbing marred most of her voice.

"Maribel!" His heavy Spanish accent kicked in. "Where the hell are my children?"

He had now caught Tiffany's attention and a concerned look crossed her face.

"I don't know," she continued crying.

"Find them, Maribel, because if you don't, it will be your ass," Tony demanded, infuriated beyond imagination.

Reaching in his billfold, he took out a hundred dollars and threw it on the table. He grabbed Tiffany by the hand, "Let's go, we need to find my children." He was not in the mood for explanation. Luckily for her, she read his thoughts.

Entering the car, he turned on the engine and drove like mad through Lower Manhattan. Silence was all that could be heard in the car—and it was deafening.

Chapter 44

KENSICO CEMETERY: VALLAHA, NYC

Sobbing could be heard from onlookers as they watched the body of Porsha Hilton being lowered into the ground. Dimples, who stood beside BabyGirl, was shedding so many tears that every now and then she had to use her white handkerchief to dry her eyes. BabyGirl's black and white pumps stood firmly on the soft green grass. Gray clouds were beginning to form in the otherwise bright sky. Huge trees with branches filled with green leaves swayed as the gentle breeze blew. A minister dressed in full black read a scripture from the Bible.

In the middle of the formal proceedings, BabyGirl's phone rang. Everyone including the minister stopped—all eyes were on her. Embarrassment crossed her face as she apologized and moved away from the funeral and toward the lake that stood in the middle of the cemetery. A brown duck and her duckling glided gracefully along the water, oblivious to what lay beyond the lake.

"Hello,"

"The job has been completed." The deep masculine voice spoke on the other end. "I will pick up the rest of the money at the drop off location. The children are where you requested." The voice reaffirmed.

"Okay," she responded before ending the call.

She thought about placing another call, but she wondered whether it was a good idea. She hadn't heard from Fire since the night Dragon died, despite the numerous messages she left. She wasn't sure if he still wanted to go through with the idea they had discussed that fateful night.

"What does it matter," she spoke to herself. "As long as I gave my final approval on the plan, that's what counts."

She turned to head toward the funeral, but the white Cadillac limousine heading deep into the cemetery caught her attention. Out of curiosity, she wondered why it was white instead of black. She knew she wouldn't get the answer to her question, so she continued walking.

"Make sure your phone is on vibrate this time, you don't want to interrupt the burial process anymore." Dimples whispered with a smile.

BabyGirl smiled back. "I did."

A slender, brown-skinned female, who sort of resembled Porsha, walked up to the grave. A single white rose was in her slender fingers. As she got closer, her body began to tremble and she broke down as she screamed, "I can't watch them lower my sister in the ground." A dark-skinned, tall, bald-headed guy approached her and moved her away, but not before allowing her to throw the rose on top of the white casket.

Tony and Dragon are two cold-blooded motherfuckers. BabyGirl could understand killing Porsha, but she couldn't comprehend murdering the entire family, including the chef. Flashbacks of her own parents' deaths flooded her mind. Tears streamed down her face as she related to the scenario.

"The man is ruthless, Dimples, we have to get rid of him," BabyGirl stated as she turned toward Dimples.

"I agree," Dimples hugged her.

"I refuse to let him make me end up like this," she continued. "Mark my words, what I have in store for Tony will not only stop him in his tracks, but put an end to his shit once and for all."

With a look of surprise, Dimples released BabyGirl, looked into her eyes, and asked, "What's that?"

"It begins with his children." she answered in a cold tone.

What BabyGirl didn't realize was that this scheme might cost her, her life.

Chapter 46

Tony slammed the door of the Red Audi, which caused Nurse Haywood to jump. Tony took giant steps across the parking lot as he headed for the glass doors that led to the lobby of Maribel's building. Checking in his pockets, he realized that he must have left his keys when he stopped by his apartment.

"Shit," he uttered, as he looked to see if anyone was coming.

A middle-aged white security officer stood behind the desk in the lobby, talking away on the phone.

"Why don't you ring the intercom?" Nurse Haywood asked.

Tony didn't answer, he had other plans, which entailed him going upstairs and beating the shit out of Maribel.

Tony's patience was beginning to grow thin and he was about to ring the intercom when two young couple walked toward the door hand-in-hand. Tony smiled as the couple reminded him of back when Maribel and he were young.

"Good afternoon," they spoke.

"Good afternoon to you too," Tony replied.

The door sounded and Tony, along with Nurse Haywood,

entered the lobby behind the couple.

"Excuse me." The security guard now focused his attention on them instead of the telephone conversation.

Tony paid the man no attention as he continued toward the elevator. The couple, who lived on the first floor, entered their apartment.

Emotions of anger, pain, and frustration ran through Tony's body and he couldn't comprehend who would take his children. Putting manhood aside, Tony broke down in tears in the elevator.

"We will find them." Nurse Haywood placed her arms around Tony as she comforted him.

The elevator chimed, and Tony gathered himself. He didn't want to give Maribel the pleasure of seeing him in a weak state. It was bad enough Nurse Haywood had seen him like that.

Tony knocked and waited as Maribel opened the door. The elevator doors opened once more, and the security guard exited.

"Is everything okay, Ms. Moreno?" he asked with his flashlight in one hand and his baton in the other.

"And why wouldn't everything be alright?" Tony replied in a harsh tone, "Who do you think I am?"

Raising her hands, Maribel signaled for Tony to stop. She then answered, "Yes, Gus, this is my so-called husband, Mr. Moreno."

Tony wanted to take her up on that, but decided he would deal with her later. He needed the security guard to be gone.

"Okay," the man replied.

"Go do your flashlight job," Tony taunted.

As soon as the guard was out of earshot, Maribel, with a disgusted look on her face, asked, "What the fuck is *she* doing here?"

Tony paused then looked at her, "Don't asked me any fucking questions," He pushed past her and headed inside the apartment. Haywood followed, making her way to the far right, trying not to get involved.

"What happened to my girls?" his voice rose beyond normal.

"I don't know," Maribel wept.

"What?" Tony's voice shook the apartment.

In a teary voice, Maribel relived the event. "The school bus came to pick them up, but then the school called later on and said that Lissette and Anissa never showed up. I informed the school that was impossible because the school bus came and picked them up. The school then informed me that they would call me back. Five minutes later, the school called and said the bus arrived at the bus stop but the children weren't there. Bu I know I saw them get onto the school bus." Maribel's sobbing became louder.

Tony, whose face was buried in his hands, removed his face and moved toward her.

"Are you fucking stupid?" Tony grabbed her by the neck of her shirt. "Couldn't you tell the difference between the buses?"

"They looked the same," Maribel huddled so Tony wouldn't attack her. "Maybe if you weren't so busy chasing this bitch and paying more attention to your children, then this wouldn't have happened."

"Oh, so now it's my fault," Tony screamed in her face.

"Yes," she replied.

"Maybe if you weren't fucking my cousin Victor then you would have more time to pay attention to our children."

"I don't know what you're talking about," she got up from the light brown velvet sofa.

"Oh, so you thought I wouldn't find out? Don't insult my intelligence, you stupid bitch." Tony's patience was running out.

"And so what if I did?" she threw her hands up in the air. "You were never home anyway." She turned her back to him. "Better yet," she spun around. "He fucked me better than you did, or ever will."

Tony was seething as his bared fists connected with her olive skin. He then grabbed her and threw her on the sofa.

"So he fucked better than me, huh? I got something for your ass." Tony attempted to remove something from his back pocket.

"Let's go," Nurse Haywood demanded.

"No, I have to teach this bitch a lesson, and make an example out of her to all the other bitches. Tony is not the one to play with."

Tony tried to lift her yellow and white skirt. Maribel put up a fight.

"Open your legs." He hit her in the face once more.

"Tony, please stop." she begged as she covered her face to keep from getting another blow.

"Stop, did you tell him to stop?" Tony fought to open her legs. Maribel resisted. "Open your fucking legs," he used his hands to grab her neck and block her airway.

"Please, Tony," she protested as she slowly released her legs, so he would stop choking her.

Tony removed Victor's cold frozen tongue from his pocket and rubbed it against her clit.

"You like it?" he asked.

Maribel tried to push him off her. But Tony held a firm grip on her. She wept as she pleaded.

"I have to get out of here," Nurse Haywood spoke as she ran for the door.

Tony pulled the gun from his waist and spoke, "Get your ass back in the corner," He pointed at her.

Without another word, she went back to where she stood.

The cold tongue, along with him being in control, gave him a sense of power.

"How come I don't get an 'I love you, daddy,' huh? Did he lick it better than I did? Love it, you freak."

He was so consumed by the power he had, that he forgot about his original mission until Nurse Haywood spoke.

"Tony, please, let's go. We have to find your children before someone kills them."

Tony stopped in his tracks as the mere thought of someone hurting his children crossed his mind. He threw the tongue on top of Maribel before calling her a despicable slut. He proceeded to walk to the door, then stopped, turning and speak.

"I will be taking the children and filing for custody."

He didn't even see when Maribel got up; the only thing he heard was, "Over my dead body," and a gunshot. Luckily for Tony, the bullet missed his shoulder and hit the wall. Nurse Haywood screamed as she ducked. Maribel tried to fire another round but the gun jammed.

"That could be arranged" Tony took a giant leap toward her. She attempted to fire once more, but the gun wouldn't shoot. She began to run, but Tony grabbed her by the hair and threw her to the floor.

He proceeded to bang her head against the floor. "You fucking trying to kill me?"

"I should have assisted Porsha and BabyGirl in killing you when I had the chance." Maribel shouted.

"You should have," Tony said. Then he removed his gun and fired a shot in her neck.

Screams once again echoed from Nurse Haywood's lips as a paralyzed Maribel lay hoping for assistance.

"Shut the fuck up before I do you next," Tony warned her. "Let's go find my kids."

Heading out the door, they went down the back stairs in silence, the only interruption was the ringing from his cell.

"Hello!"

Chapter 47

"Hey Daddy," Anissa, Tony's older daughter spoke. Both of his children were clueless about what was taking place. The phone, which was on speaker, allowed Baby-Girl, Dimples, and Fire, who were also in the room, to hear Tony's side of the conversation. The room was silent as they awaited Tony's response.

"Anissa," The heavy Spanish accent rolled off his tongue. "Where are you?" Tony's voice was filled with a mixture of anxiety and caution.

"I am…" BabyGirl grabbed the telephone before Anissa was able to finish the sentence.

"Can I talk to my dad?" Lissette's ponytail bounced as she ran toward the phone.

"Hello…hello" Tony's voice was beginning to rise.

"Hello to you too," BabyGirl replied, while positioning herself on the desk.

"Where are my children, BabyGirl?" Tony asked in a concerned tone.

"At the place you wanted so much,"

"You better not hurt my children," he warned.

As both girls stood beside BabyGirl, Lissette began to cry because she wanted to speak with her father. Turning to Dimples, BabyGirl requested for the children to be taken out of the room and placed somewhere where the conversation couldn't be heard. Ensuring that the children were out of earshot, she answered.

"Now why would I do that?" she folded her hands across her chest. She glanced at Fire, who was behind the desk preparing all the documents Tony had to sign. "I'm not cold blooded like you. You murdered Porsha and her entire family."

"I don't have time for silly games. I'm coming for my children. There better not be a single scratch on them because if there is, I will slice your body piece by piece, and make sure you have a slow death."

"I'm looking forward to it," she let out a slight laugh. Her tone changed like a lizard's skin. "Be here in half an hour because I don't like waiting." She slammed the phone down in Tony's ear.

"I hope our plan works," Fire looked at her.

"Of course it will; Tony's children are his heart." She coldly replied.

Outside, lightning flashed and a crack of thunder followed. The bright sky that shone earlier gave way to darkness. Darkness was slowly caving in as if the unsettled spirits of Tha Hustle Records were roaming or coming back for vengeance.

Dimples became startled by the thunder so she got up and closed the blinds. "This is some scary shit," she mumbled. BabyGirl laughed at her cowardliness. The children, who had been playing peacefully in the other room, ran out screaming in terror, so Fire got up from the desk to cuddle them.

Dimples paced back and forth across the carpet, catching BabyGirl's attention.

"Are you sure this plan is going work? I think we should

just count our losses and give him the company." Dimples reasoned.

"Why?" BabyGirl asked. "Give me one good motherfucking reason why we should give him back the empire. Just in case you forgot, I have rights to this empire. My father's blood was spilled for this empire. So it rightfully belongs to me. I will murder anyone who gets in the way of me keeping it." She said while glaring at Dimples and Fire. BabyGirl walked over to the bar and poured herself a shot of vodka. She took a gulp and slammed the glass on the counter, causing the children to wince. She was beginning to strike fear in everyone.

☒☒☒

Twenty minutes later, the door flung open. Tony and Nurse Haywood entered. Tony's eyes scanned in search of his children.

"Daddy!" Lissette shrieked, attempting to run toward her father; but BabyGirl grabbed her and held her close.

"Not so fast."

"BabyGirl, do not drag my children in this. You don't want to go there." He forewarned.

"I already have," she raised the gun from her waist.

"Please," Tony begged. "Can we take my children out of here? I don't want them to be around this sort of violence."

Nurse Haywood, who stood by Tony, threw Fire a weird look. The look didn't go unnoticed by BabyGirl. Tony, with his hands held out in surrender, spoke.

"Please take my children out of here, and we can settle this."

"No! We can settle this in their presence." She looked at them. A frightened look came across their faces. "Besides, you have already exposed them to the lifestyle."

"Have some compassion as a lady," Nurse Haywood dipped in. "Why would you bring young children into this?"

BabyGirl leaned her head back, raised her eyebrow and uttered, "And who the fuck are you suppose to be?"

"A lady." Nurse Haywood rolled her neck. "Something you're not."

"This heifer got nerve." BabyGirl hissed, looking at both her and Tony.

"Maybe we should let the children go into a different room," Dimples added.

"Whose side are you on?" BabyGirl responded.

Dimples decided to shut up and said nothing else.

"You're going to sign these papers saying that you are giving me total control over the empire."

"Never." he shouted.

BabyGirl placed Anissa on her lap, and then proceeded to gently stroke the child's dark hair. Then she leaned over and kissed Lissette on the forehead. "I know you want them alive. Sign the papers or else," she commanded as the cocking of a gun could be heard.

Chapter 48

THA HUSTLE RECORDS: NYC

*T*ony's blood boiled at the thought of his children being placed in the middle of the situation. His gun was still in the back of his pants, and he was contemplating whether he should use it or not. He didn't want the children to be caught in the middle and get hurt. If only he could give Haywood a signal to reach for the gun in his waistband and shoot, but such a thought was impossible, so he dismissed it. He decided to play the game the best way he knew how. He couldn't help but wonder who the guy was.

"Okay, I will sign the papers," he walked closer. "But please put the gun down around my children."

"Not a problem," BabyGirl said. He knew she had only agreed because the children were still in her possession.

As he held the pen in his hands, he spoke. "You know, Dimples, for someone who had my back since day one and called the police to save me from the cold waters, the least you could have done was tip me off that my children were gonna be kidnapped."

BabyGirl threw an evil glance in Dimples' direction.

"What is he talking about?"

Dimples shrugged her shoulders. "I don't know."

"Don't hide it now," Tony taunted. "The cat is already out of the bag."

Dimples' eyes were cast down, as she couldn't face Baby-Girl.

"I knew you could not be trusted." BabyGirl said to Dimples while picking up her gun to shoot her. Tony, seeing his opportunity, grabbed BabyGirl's arm and they both struggled for the weapon. The gun went off and Lissette's small, slender frame fell. The bullet had pierced through her forehead and lodged in her skull. Tony screamed out in anguish. BabyGirl, who appeared shocked, froze also, she couldn't believe she had shot a child.

"Nooo… my baby!" Tony wailed. Screams echoed as Anissa tried to run out the door. Dimples, who was also close to the door, tried to make her way out, but BabyGirl shot at her. The bullet ripped through Dimples' lower back and hit Anissa in the chest.

Tony felt another sharp pain in his chest as he knew his second daughter was gone. Tony lay on the floor rocking a lifeless Lissette in his arms. He slowly lifted her up and was about to walk over to pick up Anissa when BabyGirl pointed the gun and spoke,

"It's nothing personal to you, just business. But to me it's not only business…it's personal."

BabyGirl didn't get a chance to fire, before Haywood removed her own gun from her boot, and fired. The bullet hit BabyGirl in the chest. She fell back into Fire's arms.

"What did you do?" Fire asked, as he held her. A tear formed in the corner of his eyes.

"Now it's your turn, bitch!" Without mercy Tony raised the gun he had and was ready to shoot, until Nurse Haywood yelled, "Let's leave the cops are on their way."

Tony was hesitant at first because he didn't want to leave his two daughters, but he knew he had unfinished business and he couldn't complete it behind bars. As they headed for the door, Fire shouted.

"I will avenge in the name of King."

Tony spun around and looked. He couldn't believe baby Fire had grown up.

"Let's go," Haywood spoke once more; this time with firmness in her tone. Tony ran out realizing he had just opened another can of worms.

▧▧▧

It was war, DEA Anderson, aka Tiffany Haywood, had just crossed a line that she was going to wish she never did. As he watched the coroners bag each body and police place numbers were bullet shells laid, he threw his badge over his neck, and walked out with his head down. DEA Farrod Jones, aka Fire, knew he would have to show her that once you play with Fire, you will get burned.

Epilogue

WOODLAWN CEMETERY, BRONX NY

Fire placed his shiny shoes outside the limo and made his way over the fresh cut grass toward the white casket. The burial plot was empty except for the men who were putting BabyGirl in the ground. He held a single rose in his hand as he moved closer. He placed his hands on the casket and ran them across its smooth surface.

"Sorry it had to end this way," he apologized as if she could hear. A gentle breeze brushed against his shoulder as if affirming that his apology was heard. The men lowered the casket into the ground as Fire vowed that Tony would pay. He placed the rose he held on top of her casket and fought hard to hold back tears. A black car pulled up behind his limo, a white man with a clean cut came out. He walked up to Fire, tapped him on the shoulder, and began to speak.

"Job well done. I guess I can call the 19th precinct and tell them to close their case" Ramirez spoke; he leaned over and took a look at the casket being lowered into the ground. He'd never had a chance to convict anyone, but the cards played themselves out since everyone except for Tony was dead. Ramirez hoped Tony would be caught wherever he fled.

Tears filled Fire's eyes and he quickly dried them. Turning toward Ramirez, he said, "I hope you're happy that the figures you're producing for your bosses look good, but for fucking once, I wish you would step out of your shell and see how many people got killed, just to bring Moreno and Smith to justice. Two innocent children lost their lives."

Ramirez patted Fire on the back and spoke, "Don't take it personal, it's just business."

Fire wanted to raise his fist and punch him in the head, but how could he punch a fellow worker. Instead, he turned and continued to mourn BabyGirl.

"I expect you and Anderson to be back on the job tomorrow cleaning these streets," said Ramirez.

Fire chuckled to himself because he knew things were about to get ugly between him and his partner of five years. Wherever Tony was, he knew Anderson was with him. He was pretty sure she has fallen in love and she had fallen hard. He was sure he would have to murder her in order to get to Tony, but only time would tell.

Turning toward his limo, Fire said, "If you can't beat them, then join them," he made reference to the reason why he'd got involved in law enforcement in the first place. One thing was certain, he knew his relationship with Anderson would never be the same.

♥♥♥

ST. LUKE'S ROOSEVELT HOSPITAL

The beeps and the lines on the heart monitor flowed at a steady pace. Dimples' lifeless body lay in the bed, and the surgery she'd just undergone was successful. The slugs were removed from her body, but the chances of her surviving were slim. She was able to see and hear, but wasn't able to move. The darkness of the room clouded her, caving her in. Three doctors walked into her room and one asked, "Ms. Crawford, can you turn your head in my direction?" Dimples could hear, but she couldn't respond.

"Once she is well enough, she will need therapy. My guess is she will be paralyzed from the neck down." One doctor determined.

"Dimples wanted to burst into tears at the thought of not being able to move ever again. She listened to every word until the doctors walked out. A flood of tears escaped her eyes. Not long after the doctors walked out, the door opened again and a shadowy figure entered. Leaning over her, she recognized the face—it was Tony Moreno. For a minute she thought he'd given up on her, but his presence assured her that things would be alright. At least she had one person in her camp. Tony placed a kiss on her lips; she couldn't remember the last time, someone had kissed her with such gentleness.

"Thanks for all your help," he said, lifting her hands carefully. He examined the IV in her arm.

"However, your time is up. You see…you could never be a part of my camp; you cannot be trusted, you let greed take over. Your love of money would eventually sell out me and my company. I would rather take your girl BabyGirl than you.

Dimples wanted to get up and knock Tony in his head. She watched as he pulled a needle out of his pocket and she attempted with all her might to reach out for the nurse call button, but she couldn't. Her fate had been sealed.

Pulling back the needle just a bit, Tony injected it into her IV and allowed an air bubble to get in. Dimples' body jerked momentarily and the monitor went dead. Throwing his overcoat over his head, Tony walked out of the hospital ready to face the new world.

There is no fire like passion, there is no shark like hatred, there is no snare like folly, there is no torrent like greed.

-Buddha

**King of Spades:
Deck Reshuffled**
978-0-9795892-1-2
$9.95

Queen of Hearts
978-0-9795892-0-1
$14.95

Lipstick Diaries
0975945394
$14.95

KG PUBLISHING
1159 east. 229th Drive N. suite 10H
BRONX NY 10466
Shipping/handling $ 5.00 plus $1.00 each additional book.

Purchaser Name

Address

City   State   Zip

Total books ordered: